the Fixer

JA 0 4 '17

Games People Play

HELENKAY DIMON

AVONBOOKS

An Imprint of HarperCollinsPublishers

THE FIXER. Copyright © 2017 by HelenKay Dimon. All rights reserved. Printed in the United States of America. No part of this book may be used or reproduced in any manner whatsoever without written permission except in the case of brief quotations embodied in critical articles and reviews. For information, address HarperCollins Publishers, 195 Broadway, New York, NY 10007.

First Avon Books mass market printing: January 2017

ISBN 978-0-06244130-0

17 18 19 20 21 QGM 10 9 8 7 6 5 4 3 2 1

For those who battle the past . . . may you find peace

the
Fixer

CHAPTER 1

Emery's mind kept wandering no matter how hard she tried to concentrate on her skim vanilla latte. She tapped the coffee stirrer against the side of her cup and stared out the large window to the busy Washington, DC, street outside. The sun beat down as the late August humidity trapped passersby in a frizzy-hair, clothing-sticking haze of discomfort.

She enjoyed the air-conditioning of The Beanery. An unfortunate name for the perfect spot. The shop sat right on the edge of Foggy Bottom. Businessmen and students filed in and out, past the wall of bags filled with exotic beans and decorated mugs. The proximity to her house just down the street made the place a convenient stop for quick visits before heading into the office.

At ten o'clock on a Monday she usually sat at her desk. Today she needed room, space to think about the best way to track down the one man she needed to see and couldn't find. Endless computer searches had failed. She'd looked through property records and tried different search engines. Next she'd call in every favor and ask a work contact to check driver's license records. She was *that* desperate.

She didn't hear footsteps or see a shadow until the legs of the chair on the other side of the café table screeched against the tile floor and a man sat down across from her. Strike that, not just a man. Not part of the usual striped-tie, navy-suit business crowd she waded through each day. This one had a lethal look to him. Dark hair with an even darker sense of danger wrapping around him.

He didn't smile or frown while his gaze searched her face. Broad shoulders filled out every inch of the jacket of his expensive black suit. Those bright green eyes matched his tie and provided a shock of color to the whole Tall, Dark and Deadly look he had going on.

He managed to telegraph power without saying a word as a hum of energy pulsed around him. She fought off a shiver and reached for her spoon. Hardly a weapon, but something about this guy made her insides bounce and the blood leave her head, and she had no idea why.

"Excuse me?" She used a tone that let him know just sitting down without asking was not okay. Some women might like the commanding, takeover type of guy who assumed his presence was welcome everywhere. Not her.

"We need to come to an understanding."

The voice, deep and husky with an edge of gravelly heat, skidded across her senses. She felt it as much as she heard it. The tone struck her, held her mesmerized, before the meaning behind the words hit her. "Uh-huh, well, maybe *we* should understand that seat is already taken," she said.

"By?"

"Literally anyone else who wants it." She looked down, making a show of taking the lid off her cup and stirring the few inches of coffee left inside. That struck her as the universal not-interested signal.

She waited for him to grumble or call her a name and scamper off. She had issued a dismissal after all. But his presence loomed and she glanced up again.

"Emery Finn." Her name rolled off his tongue.

That shiver moving through her turned into a full body shake. "Wait, do we know each other?"

"You've been making inquiries."

It was the way he said it as much as what he said. How he sat there without moving. Perfect posture and laser-like focus that stayed on her face, never wavering even as a pretty woman openly gawked at him as she passed by.

The surreal scene had Emery grabbing on to her cup with both hands. "It sounds like you're reading from a really bad screenplay."

"This isn't fiction."

"Uh-huh. You know what it also isn't? Interesting." She waved him off. "Go away."

"You need to stop searching for information." He finally blinked. "No more questions. No more inquiries through back channels at government agencies."

In her line of work she sometimes angered people. Never on purpose, because ticked-off people tended not to open up and share. "I research for a living. If I've somehow upset you or—"

"This is personal, not business."

That sounded . . . not good. Like, time-to-call-the-police not good. "Who are you?"

He continued to stare. He didn't move or threaten her, not directly, but his presence filled the space in front of her. The noise of the café faded into the background. A loud male voice a few tables away flattened to a mumble and the people shuffling by blurred.

"Someone who is trying to help you."

That sounded like something a serial killer might say right before he lured some poor woman into his white van. *Yeah, no thanks.*

She curled her fingers around the spoon just in case. "Maybe you're unclear about the meaning of 'go away,' but I can start screaming and I'm sure someone will explain it to you. Maybe a police officer."

"You're skeptical. Good." He nodded, seemingly not even slightly concerned that she was six seconds from reaching for pepper spray. "But you need to understand the ramifications of all these questions."

She'd heard phrases like that every day in her work life as a researcher for the Jane Doe Network. She searched for the right piece of information to match missing persons to unidentified victims. To bring closure to cold cases and family pain. "I've found that people who say that sort of thing to me have no intention of actually helping me."

"I'm the exception." The corner of his mouth twitched in what seemed to be his version of a smile. "You're being careful right now. That's smart. My only point is that you should continue to do so and heed my advice."

Every word sounded as if it were chosen for maximum impact. No wasted syllables, not even an extra breath. He sat there, stiff and sure with a brooding affect that acted like a warning shot even as something about him reeled her in, had her leaning forward, waiting to hear what he'd say next.

She forced her body to stay still. No fidgeting or spinning her cup. "Tell me what you think I've done that's wrong or dangerous."

"You have been asking questions and taking photographs."

She'd taken exactly two photographs lately. Not for work, for her side project. The one that had haunted her for years and begged for closure. "Both activities, which, if they happened, are legal."

"Wren." He said the word and stopped talking.

Not that he needed to spell it out. The name echoed in her head. It was all she could do not to launch across the table and shake this guy. "Are you him?"

"I'm someone who knows you're searching for Wren."

Because that wasn't an odd answer or anything. If Wren sent someone to find her, stop her, this had turned very personal. She'd been hunting in relative secret. She basically knew the name Wren from a scribble on a piece of paper.

So much for thinking she'd been discreet. She'd called in favors and asked friends to dig quietly. She'd made it clear no one should leave a trail or take unnecessary risks. Either someone had messed up or . . . she didn't even want to think about the "or" part.

She forced her brain to focus. Pushed out the fear and confusion as her mind clicked into gear. This guy had information about Tiffany's disappearance. Emery didn't know what, but something.

The chair creaked as the man sat back. "The point is, you need to stop."

"Yeah, you said a version of that already." Not that she could forget that voice.

His head tilted to the side as if he were examining her and for a second that harsh façade slipped. "What do you hope to accomplish here?"

She held up her cup and shook it. "I'm drinking coffee."

"When you search for a recluse who may or may not exist—"

"He does."

The guy nodded. "Possibly."

"Okay, fine. We can play that game." But she knew the truth. People in power shook their heads and whispered the name Wren. She'd seen it when she talked with the senator who once promised a favor for matching her friend's missing child to a John Doe case four states away. Even the senator backed away at the mention of the guy.

"Do you think if you ask the right question someone is going to hand over Wren's home address?" His hands stayed folded on his lap as he asked the question.

As much as the conversation had her nerves zapping, she needed to keep him talking. Get him to slip up or at least touch the table or something so she could get her resources to check for fingerprints. A desperate hope, but then she dealt daily with desperate hope. "Do you have it? If so, give it to me. This conversation will go a lot faster and you can get back to doing whatever it is you do, which I somehow doubt is legal or particularly nice."

His mouth twitched for the second time. "Why do you want to see Wren?"

Apparently they'd entered the never-ending-questions portion of the conversation. As the minutes passed, she became less interested in participating in his game and more in playing her own. "Tell me your name."

"I'd rather you listen to me." He leaned forward. "You are wading into danger here. There are some people who prefer anonymity. Denying them that brings trouble."

The words shot into her, had her back slamming into her chair. "Are you threatening me?"

"I'm trying to keep you from being hurt." He cleared his throat. "You might awaken a beast you cannot possibly control."

The conversation, this meeting, it all spun in her head. "What does that even mean?"

"I think you know." Without warning, the guy stood up.

"You drop that kind of overly dramatic comment, don't bother telling me who you are or how you know Wren and then storm out?"

"Yes."

She sputtered, trying to think of something brilliant to say after that, but only babble filled her brain.

"And for the record." He actually smiled this time. "I do not storm."

"My word choice offended you?" This guy sure had the whole mysterious thing down. The suit, the stubble . . . that face. But this was a good place to talk. In public with plenty of people *right there* in case she needed to hit him with a chair. "At least get a coffee and sit back down so we can discuss this."

"I already have one." In a few steps he went to the counter and grabbed a to-go cup with the name *Brian* on it that had been sitting there since she picked up her drink more than a half hour ago. Then he was back by her side at the table. "Think about what I said."

She doubted she'd be able to think about anything else. "I don't take orders well."

"Take this one." With a nod he headed for the door.

She scrambled to her feet, grabbing for her purse and swearing when it caught around the back of the chair. She hit the sidewalk a few seconds later, looking up and down, past the groups of people walking and talking. Frustration screamed in her brain as a siren wailed in the distance. Still, nothing. No sign of black-suit guy. He'd disappeared.

CHAPTER 2

You're back." Garrett McGrath handed out that verbal assessment as he walked into the plush office in the nondescript beige building near Capitol Hill. He carried a file and wore his usual ready-for-anything expression. "You didn't have a meeting on your calendar. Where were you?"

From anyone else Wren would ignore the question. Garrett enjoyed the rare ability to say almost anything because in addition to being Wren's second-in-command, they were friends. But that didn't mean Wren felt like providing a long-winded explanation. He nodded in the direction of the empty cup in the middle of his oversized desk. "Getting coffee."

Garrett halted in midstep. "Since when?"

"I drink beverages like normal humans." But seeing the former counterintelligence officer knocked speechless made Wren's unexpected trip outside the office and miles away worth it.

Garrett winced. "You're not really what I'd call normal."

"Meaning?" Wren leaned back in his chair, not sure what he'd hear next.

"I think the comment was pretty self-explanatory."

"Ah." Wren decided not to poke around in that conversation any longer. "Well, it's always nice to have the respect of one's employees."

Garrett once analyzed patterns and devised strategies for the National Geospatial-Intelligence Agency. He could map and plan, command a room while explaining complex ideas in coherent terms. Now he worked for Wren, and Wren found perverse pleasure in watching Garrett lose some of his admirable control.

But Wren had to admit his friend had a point. He usually traveled from home to work, almost always in darkness and never with any fanfare. He lived his life in the shadows, doing the type of work that demanded confidentiality and precision. But after hearing reports about Emery's digging and studying the file he assembled on her, something compelled him to meet her. He couldn't explain it and didn't try.

Garrett's eyes narrowed as he studied the cup. "You don't make coffee runs."

"I needed fresh air." That seemed like something a normal person might do. At least, Wren guessed that might be true. Rather than belabor the point he stared at the file in Garrett's hands. "What do you have for me?"

"You're not going to like it."

"You just described my reaction to most of the work we do here." Owari Enterprises. His baby. The company with nothing more than a name on the door. No advertising, no marketing. He'd opened the doors right after his thirtieth birthday. Now, five years later, it thrived.

His firm's reputation, its ability to get the dirty operations done, spread by word of mouth. The work was demanding, and usually top secret. He knew how to keep his mouth shut and so did the few people who worked in his office and the trusted band of individuals he depended on to do work in the field.

He was a fixer. More to the point, he was *the* fixer. The man powerful people, entire governments, turned to in order to pull off the impossible.

"Ms. Finn is at it again." Garrett walked the rest of the way to the L-shaped desk in the middle of the room and dropped the thick stack of papers on the edge. "She keeps calling Senator Dayton. We need to stop her before someone gets sick of her sneaking around and loses their shit."

"Eloquent, as always."

"How should I have said it? She's on the verge of making a fucking mess." Garrett's smile didn't falter. "Is that better?"

Wren couldn't exactly deny Garrett's claims. Letting Emery go this long on her journey of discovery about his identity may have been a miscalculation. Wren shot down rumors for a living. He evened the playing field. If a pharmaceutical company stumbled onto the formula for a deadly toxin, he made the material disappear with no way to recreate it. If someone in power sold secrets that promised to bring down the government, he extracted those secrets and removed the threat.

He had great leeway to handle cases as he saw fit, but all of that depended on him remaining under the radar. Nothing stopped him. No one intimidated him.

The one time he'd let a woman get close enough to blur his judgment, he learned a harsh lesson and never repeated it.

But there was something about Emery that had his usual common sense misfiring. He'd known about her investigation of him from day one. Been intrigued by the woman staring back at him in the file he collected on her. The shoulder-length brown hair and girl-next-door fresh face, pretty without make-up and sunny as if she'd somehow been lit from within. And those eyes. Big and brown and brimming with life. She was everything he wasn't and he couldn't help but stare.

None of that explained why he'd broken office protocol. He never just ventured out. Rarely engaged in normal everyday activities. His life required privacy and he took his personal protection very seriously.

He also didn't want Emery caught in the crossfire or put in danger. "I'll take care of her. I've already started."

"Just now?"

Wren sensed a verbal trap looming, but walked into it anyway. "This morning, yes."

"Did you threaten her?"

That wasn't his style and Garrett knew that. Never mind Emery had asked the same sort of question. "No."

Garrett's eyebrow lifted. "Were you creepy?"

The conversation had officially crossed over into annoyance. Wren forced his body to relax back into his leather chair. "What kind of question is that?"

"So . . . yes?"

"I'm capable of talking to women, you know." Admittedly, his dating skills had gotten a bit rusty. That's what happened when a guy decided it was easier not to date than to try to come up with fake information about his job, his existence and basically everything about himself.

"If you say so."

For a second Wren wished he were as dangerous as everyone assumed. "I talked with her. It was all very civilized."

Though he had to admit he'd questioned his word choices after he left her. Maybe he came off a bit heavy-handed. Not that she seemed even a little afraid of him. At one point he'd gotten the distinct impression she toyed with the idea of punching him, which he found incredibly hot. Her face, her quick responses, the way she didn't seem even a little intimidated by him . . . so fucking hot.

But since she all but kicked the chair out from under him, maybe his women skills were even rustier than he wanted to believe.

Garrett kept staring. The judgy kind of staring. "Did you use your real name?"

"Do I ever?" He kept up his perfectly crafted image intact, like always. The image where all but a select few thought he was the assistant to some mysterious businessman named Wren. Never mind that he *actually* was Wren. He slept just fine letting people call him Brian Jacobs and view him as someone who answered to the boss. Being able to move around and stoke the whispers only added to his credibility and ability to demand top dollar, so he didn't fight it.

"Well, you screwed up something, my friend." Garrett looked like he was trying to swallow his smile and failing brilliantly at it. "Which I admit is a surprise."

Friend or not, Garrett was enjoying this too much. That made one of them. "Get to your point."

"She made another call to the senator ten minutes ago." Garrett coughed into his hand in what had to be the worst fake cough ever performed. "Probably right after you got coffee this morning."

Wren's temper spiked. The woman refused to listen. He wasn't sure whether to be furious or impressed. People did not ignore his warnings. He'd done her a favor and she'd pushed it aside, as if trying to put him on the defensive.

The hotness thing hit him again. With that attitude, she spiked right off the scale. Pulled his attention in different directions. Off work. On her.

Wren didn't care for the sensation one bit . . . well, maybe a little. "Isn't she enterprising?"

"Maybe her coffee date didn't go well." Garrett cleared his throat. "It appears a creepy man sat down and tried to scare her."

That was just fucking great. "You followed me?"

"Her." Garrett held up his hands. "Hey, you're the one who told me to watch her 'just in case' and all that. It's not my fault that you walked into the middle of my perfect surveillance."

Wren balanced his elbows on the edge of his desk and rubbed his forehead. He tried to close his eyes and think this through, figure out a way to handle the woman without compromising himself. Appealing to her logical side hadn't worked. No question about that.

He looked up at Garrett again. "I thought I could talk some sense into her."

Garrett rested his hands on the back of the chair in front of him. "And how did that go exactly?"

"Clearly not well." That would teach him to try to reason problems through rather than just make a plan and implement it from a distance.

Not in the mood for Garrett's joking, Wren picked up the file and opened the cover. Paged through the newest round of photos of Emery. She looked confident and in control. That was nothing compared to the real-life version. The version that seemed to be kicking his ass.

"Did you tell her where you work or use your usual alias? In other words, did you lose your mind and give her enough information to trace you back here?" Garrett asked.

Wren decided to ignore the amusement in Garrett's voice. As if this was his first day in covert operations. "Don't be ridiculous."

"Right. I'm the one acting strange today." Garrett's smile faded and a serious thread tinged his tone. "She really is trouble."

No way could Wren deny that. "No kidding."

"Not someone you should be rushing off to meet for coffee."

"Agreed." And that wasn't what happened, but Wren didn't feel as if he had the moral high ground to fight that battle right now. Not when all he could think about was going back and finding her.

"Should I try to talk with her?"

"I'll handle her." He created this mess by letting who she was, with her do-good job and quiet life, get to him. By not shutting down her digging right at the start. For the way her face floated through his mind when he closed his eyes and sometimes when they were open.

Garrett frowned. "When you say handle . . . ?"

"I'm not sure yet." That wasn't a lie. No subterfuge there. Wren had tried the easy way and she'd barely waited until he left her side before calling on her political contacts again. She was the not-easy-to-back-down type, which he feared he was just figuring out might be *his* type.

Garrett hummed. "This is a first."

"She's innocent." Wren continued to page through the new information in the file, which consisted mostly of her movements and more photos. Both interested him far too much. "We need to tread carefully."

"Okay."

Wren's head popped up and he pinned Garrett with a glare. "Don't."

Garrett held out his arms. "I'm just standing here."

"Some people are smart enough to be afraid of me." The people who knew his name, which constituted a small circle. Most people had never heard of him, which was exactly how he wanted it. That way he could strike without warning then retreat into the shadows.

"Not me." Garrett shrugged. "Sorry."

"When did that happen? I just want to know so I don't repeat the mistake with the person I pick to replace you."

Garrett laughed. "You didn't hire me to be a 'yes' man and you're not going to fire me if we disagree. You told me that when you gave me the job."

"A decision I regret at the moment." Which was not the case at all. Wren relied on Garrett far more than he ever intended to, but he'd gotten used to having someone to discuss strategy with and had liked Garrett from the moment they met. That was a big statement since he didn't take the time to like many people.

"You'll remember from my reports on her that Ms. Finn goes to that coffee shop almost every weekday." Garrett stood up straight again as he pointed out lines in the report. "Though it might be better if you ignore that fact."

Wren almost hated to ask. "Why?"

"Because if you get any creepier she'll never sleep with you."

"That's not going to happen." Wren wasn't completely sure which part he was responding to.

"Right." Garrett shot him a nice-try grin. "When you meet her for coffee tomorrow will you bring back one for me?"

CHAPTER 3

This guy needed to be taught a lesson.

As if she couldn't see him sitting out there in his fancy car, right across the street. Whatever Wren paid this enforcer or minion, or whatever he was, it was too much. He seemed to suck at subterfuge. Really, she spotted him out there without pulling back her curtain or getting binoculars.

The guy from the coffee shop. The runner. He dropped his mysterious, nonsense comments then took off. And now it looked like he'd followed her home, or worse, he'd figured out where she lived without her help and stationed himself in front of her apartment building.

The jackass.

Emery debated calling the police or a male friend—someone who could go out there with her while she yelled at him. She knew better to go out alone . . . mostly. But for some reason when she thought of this guy she didn't get hit with a punch of fear. She lived in the city. She knew that sensation. The itchiness at the base of her neck that made her pick up her pace while walking home from the metro on dark nights.

She'd long ago developed the skill of looking forward while scanning her surroundings and not moving her head. Positioning her keys just right for a strike in her hand, if needed. Ignoring the catcalls. Planning her schedule so that she minimized risk. She hated that she had to take precautions, but life had taught her a harsh lesson about how easy it is for a young woman to disappear. The faces staring back at her in the missing-persons databases she searched all day long just highlighted that horror.

But she refused to be a victim. If Wren wanted to talk to her then he could crawl out from whatever rock he hid under. Sending his sidekick to bully her, or whatever that was supposed to be back in the coffeehouse, was not the answer. Not him. Sure, this guy threw her off. Made her restless and urged her to fight back, but he didn't scare her. She should find him creepy, because it sure seemed like that was the impression he was aiming for, but there was something else. So, she wanted him gone.

Grabbing her phone and the bat she kept near the door, she headed for the hallway. Snuck down the corridor to the emergency staircase at the back instead of to the apartment building's entrance. There was no need to make this easy on him. If he wanted to skulk around, fine. But she refused to pretend he wasn't out there.

She'd give him one chance to leave. Her next move was a 9–1–1 call.

Her sneakers thudded against the steps. She turned and slipped into the laundry room and kept going. Pressed her key fob against the security pad and opened the door at the far end. Then it was a quick walk to the emergency exit a few feet away. The not-so-obvious exit.

She skipped running through the alley because no way was that happening. She insisted on using well-lit paths only. A jog around the building next to hers took her to the end of the block. From there she ducked as she sprinted across the street and slipped between two cars.

It was all a bit covert and dramatic for her taste. She preferred a quieter, practical existence. One that didn't include racing around with a bat, but she refused to hide. He needed to see her coming. She had a point to make and would use the weapon to do that, if needed.

She slid along the side of his sedan. Black, of course. It had an expensive, foreboding feel, just like him. For whatever reason he hadn't parked in a dark corner. Nope. He idled right there in a prime parking space, which had to be a violation of city parking etiquette. Taking up space *just because* did not go over well with her neighbors.

Streetlights lit her path and bathed the area around her in a sharp yellow glow. Fine with her. The more light, the better.

After a quick nod to the couple standing at the building entrance across from hers, some of her anxiety eased. Witnesses . . . perfect. With the slight twinge of worry gone, the adrenaline coursing through her ticked up. She was pretty sure she could lift his car if she had to right now.

She stopped on the driver's side and tapped the end

of the bat against the window. The guy didn't even jump. Hell, he looked close to smiling.

He reached down and the door started to open. She slammed her foot against it and shoved with all her might. Did not lower the bat as the door clicked shut again.

He wasn't smiling now.

"Open the window." She shouted the order more from the energy pounding through her than any worry about being heard.

Cars traveled down the street. The couple watched from twenty feet away, fully engaged now. Emery blocked it all and focused on her would-be stalker.

The window lowered as his eyebrow rose. "Yes?"

"I called the police."

His gaze dipped to her bat then back to her face again. "I don't think so."

Okay, no. Still . . . "You're awfully sure of yourself."

The cocky bastard didn't show any surprise. Didn't appear to wet his pants, which was a shame. She'd kind of hoped for that reaction when she brought the bat.

"If you'd called, the dispatcher would have told you to wait inside and definitely not confront me." His hands rested at the bottom of the steering wheel, well within view and not moving. "While I think you're impulsive, you're also clearly smart."

That's it. He spouted off police jargon then stopped after another nonsense sentence. "This is your last warning."

He closed one eye and peeked up at her. "About what exactly?"

She decided to ignore that. Opted to look up and down the side of the car instead. "I bet it's expensive to replace the glass on this thing."

"Okay, tell me this. What law am I breaking?"

She refused to babble or back down. "You're stalking me."

She actually didn't know what he was doing. Probably protecting his boss's interests and checking her out for some sort of security file. Whatever it was, she didn't like it. Didn't appreciate the way it made her feel as the action robbed her of both control and privacy.

One of his hands lifted before settling back on the wheel again. "I'm sitting in a car on a street in the city I live in."

So smooth. She fought the temptation to smash his side mirror. "Look, if you want to do this dance, we will."

This time he frowned. "Excuse me?"

"You follow me. I'll follow you." She liked the idea as soon as it left her mouth.

"You think you're going to—"

"Exactly." She'd bet he'd hate that, which made her warm to the idea even more. "Eventually, you'll lead me back to Wren, so let's go."

His frown hadn't eased. "Do you even have a car?"

"Is that the point?" It kind of was a big downside to her follow-him plan.

"I think you're a little confused about what's happening here."

"You're watching me for him." She felt more secure with every sentence. This guy—Brian or whatever was written on his coffee cup—didn't make any move to hurt her. She could see inside his car and didn't spot a weapon. He'd even toned down his threats. So far. "I get it. I asked around about Mr. Mysterious and it ticked him off."

"This is fascinating."

Man, some of the stuff he said made her want to punch him. "You know what?"

That almost-smile came roaring back. "I'm sure you're about to tell me."

"I don't care if he's pissed." She tapped the end of the bat into her palm. Not hard enough to sting, but with enough oomph to make a noise. "He should stop hiding behind you and come out and talk to me."

"You think he's a coward?" The guy choked on the last word.

Sure, why not? "That's right."

"If he is as dangerous as you say then—"

"I called him mysterious." Everyone else called Wren dangerous. She was desperately trying to ignore that point as well as the honking from the guy who pulled up next to her and clearly wanted this parking space. She finally motioned for him to move on. When she looked back to this Brian guy all traces of amusement had disappeared from his face.

"Men who stay out of the spotlight do so for a reason," he said in a deeper, more serious voice.

"You have a tendency to talk in boring riddles." She glared at him. "It's annoying."

"Then let me try this—" His fingers tightened on the wheel. "Back off."

Not quite what she expected, but okay. "I'm the one with the bat."

"I'm not even going to comment on how little that matters to me."

She remembered his weight and height advantage and shot a quick glance in the couple's direction nearby. Still there. That renewed her confidence a bit. "You're at my house."

He lifted both hands. "I'm sitting in a car."

"Say that again and I'm slamming this bat against the hood of your car."

He dropped his hands and the heel of one hit the wheel with a thud. "That would not be wise."

She stopped just before delivering an eye roll. "Talk like a normal person."

"Don't. Do. It."

Well, that was clearer. An edge moved into his voice. Turned out he was human after all. So was she. "Don't tempt me."

"I was just about to say the same thing to you."

The tone . . . something sounded different right then. She let the bat rest in her palm. "What?"

He reached down and turned on the car. "We'll see each other soon."

She didn't hate that idea. She hated that she didn't hate it. "I'm thinking you're not listening to me."

"The feeling is mutual." He hit the gas but the car was in park, so the engine just revved.

"Is that supposed to impress me?"

"I'm listening to you. Following your instructions."

He leaned closer to her. "*That* is the impressive part here. You just don't know it yet."

"I don't get you."

"You will." He motioned for her to back up and then he guided the car out of the space. Closed the window as he drove away.

"You go, sweetie!"

At the sound of the female voice, Emery tore her gaze away from the car's taillights and glanced at the couple who had silently been watching over her. They were cheering her on. She raised the bat in salute. "Damn straight."

She was halfway across the street before she realized the car Wren's man drove didn't have a license plate. That had to be a bad sign.

WREN DROVE AROUND the corner and put the car in park. He waited, half expecting Emery to run after him swinging that bat. When she didn't he was almost disappointed.

The fact she'd spotted him at all was damned impressive. Sure, he hadn't been hiding. If he had, she never would have seen him. He'd been doing the hide-in-plain-sight thing for so long that he'd gotten damned good at it. Most people didn't take in the details. They went home after work, closed their doors and shut out everything on the other side of the door. She hadn't, and that made his evening more interesting. Potentially problematic, but very interesting.

He took out his cell and checked the tracer. The dot

appeared a second later. The car he needed was only a few feet away. No one had come running to his rescue, which was exactly how he wanted it. He hired people who knew when to move in and when to hold back.

He turned the car off and shut the door. The lock chirped as he hit the button on his key chain. His gaze stayed on her window as he ventured back onto her street and stopped at the first car. Opening the back door, he slipped inside.

"You okay, sir?" the driver asked.

Wren understood his employee's concern, but appreciated his discretion even more. He'd refused to ask Garrett for mission details. Him knowing about the coffee stop was bad enough, so Wren relied on the case file for the surveillance details. That's where he got the tracer number and knew the stakeout information. He did own the damn business after all.

"She didn't actually take a swing at me." But she'd wanted to. She made that clear. The heat. The way energy pulsed off her.

Damn, he wanted her. Like strip-her-naked-and-touch-each-other-all-over wanted her. He had to believe she'd be great in bed. She'd tell him what she needed and how to please her. Not be shy.

Fucking hell.

The driver shifted in his seat. "How did she know you were out here?"

"She's careful. Smart." So sexy. "Keep that in mind as you follow her. She'll be on alert."

"Yes, sir." Both men up front answered at the same time.

"Do you have the plates?"

The driver handed the license plate over the seat. "Here."

"While you're watching, figure out how she got out of the building without using the front door. If she snuck out once, she'll do it again." She was exactly the type to make simple surveillance difficult.

The men glanced at each other before looking at him again. "You want us to keep following her?"

"Until Garrett tells you to stop." Wren let a few minutes of quiet drag on between his words. "She is your top priority, and I want to know where she is at all times."

"Yes, sir." The driver cleared his throat. "Will you be out here again tomorrow?"

He sure as hell hoped not. He *had* to possess more control than that. "You should assume I'm watching."

"Right."

Thinking he made his point, he opened the door. Then he hesitated. There was one more thing. "You can leave this episode out of the report."

The driver had the nerve to smile. "The part with the bat?"

"I see that in a report and you're both fired."

CHAPTER 4

Emery's hand cramped from the hold she had on the strap of her shoulder bag. She'd slept all of an hour last night thanks to that idiot hanging around on her street.

By the time she got back to her apartment and looked out the window after their altercation, not hiding her interest that time, his car was long gone. She'd half expected him to circle around the block and come back, but she didn't see any sign of that. God knew she looked. Looked and kept looking. Peeked out the window every twenty minutes or so for hours. Listened for strange sounds and jumped at every creak and rumble of noise. Just sat there on the chair in her small family room area, staring and waiting.

The guy owed her one night's sleep.

She should have used the bat when she had the chance.

But today was a new day and she needed to erase his face from her mind. Put him out of her head. Forget him.

For some reason that seemed easy to say, but every few minutes she'd replay their conversations and hear his voice. In between the threats and cryptic comments lurked something else. An easy banter. A back and forth that challenged her. The fact she found that sexy made her think she needed to go back to the therapist.

There was probably a book or two or a thousand out there about women who felt a connection with the wrong men. Like, totally wrong. After she hunted down Senator Dayton, she'd get online and buy those books. But right now, she needed to talk with the senator.

The receptionist in her office upstairs talked about her being in a committee meeting. Before that, the excuse had something to do with her visiting with a constituent's business. All likely valid excuses, but to Emery they were still just excuses. She needed some information about this mysterious Wren and now. If the senator happened to know something about this Brian character then that was fine, too.

Emery walked down the hall of the Russell Senate Office Building. Her heels clicked against the marble as she dodged Hill staffers rushing by and tourists huddled around maps. When she finally reached the elevator two men hovered behind her talking about what it would take to get a certain senator to sign on as a cosponsor to a bill.

On any other day she'd find the talk interesting. Today she needed to concentrate. She'd prepared her arguments and had some documents with her. If the senator needed to be convinced to help then Emery would launch into speech. She would have done all of that over the phone, but it was harder to ignore someone in person, or at least she hoped that was true.

The elevator bell chimed and the doors opened. Excitement built inside her. She was ready to negotiate and convince. But the churning in her stomach suggested something bigger was happening. She just wished she knew what it was.

WREN CONGRATULATED HIMSELF for not getting coffee the next morning. True, he debated "just stopping in" and abandoned the idea. The refusal to give Garrett the satisfaction was enough to kill the idea.

Not that he'd moved on from the Emery Finn problem. Just the opposite. Even now he stood in the middle of Senator Sheila Dayton's plush blue office, waiting for her to return from a committee meeting so they could discuss Emery. Most senate office visitors had to wait in the welcome area outside her door. Not him. Not ever.

Being alone in the room allowed him to wander. He glanced at the diplomas from Princeton and Howard. The family photographs that showed off two smiling boys who towered above her even in their early teens. Not an easy feat since Wren was six feet two and the senator was only a few inches shorter than he was.

He dragged a finger along the spines of the books lined up on the bookcase. As he reached the end of the wall unit he looked at the window behind the senator's desk and the flags standing on each side, one for the US and the other for Maryland, the state she'd represented for almost three years.

He wasn't much of a pomp and circumstance kind of guy. Some people hid behind big concepts like patriotism but didn't actually do anything. That's one of the reasons he'd supported Senator Dayton from the beginning. She didn't just deliver lip service. She was strong, smart and practical, a winning combination in his mind.

When a nasty faction tried to derail her career because she had the nerve to be female and black and seek power, he'd stepped in. She'd rewarded him both with a sizable check in payment for his services and by being the leader she'd promised the voters she would be. Now, for some reason, she'd been dragged into the middle of the Emery Finn controversy, and he needed to know why.

Just as he rounded the front of her desk and picked up her nameplate, the door opened. The senator stood there with stacks of folders in her arms and a flurry of activity behind her as staffers tried to get her attention. She traded the paperwork for two coffee mugs then closed the door behind her, leaving the chaos outside.

"Stop fondling my office supplies." Amusement played in her voice as she walked through her office never breaking stride.

He set the nameplate down. "Yes, ma'am."

She dropped one of the mugs on the desk in front of him and carried the other with her as she walked around to slide into her oversized chair. "This is always the point in the greeting when I try to figure out what name I'm supposed to use. Brian, Wren . . . or did you come up with a new one this week? I always saw you as a Matthew."

The senator knew his identity. His history . . . or the

pieces he reluctantly shared. She was one of the few people who made it into his inner circle. Their relationship started out as business, but it turned into a tenuous friendship. She helped to open doors for him by recommending his company when powerful people needed discreet assistance.

She also played another role in his life. He stumbled with human interaction. She and Garrett were the people he asked when he had to litmus test a problem. He was able to be more informal with them. Admittedly, his informal equaled most people's starchy, but he was different with the two of them.

As his business exploded over the last few years, she was the one who suggested the conceit about him pretending to be Wren's right-hand man rather than Wren. The ruse allowed him some space to maneuver when he did need to meet directly with clients. It also afforded him the privacy he craved, all while preserving the idea of the mysterious Mr. Wren.

She understood him. She talked tough and didn't think twice about trying to push him around if she wanted him to do something. He admired that about her. The only thing he didn't like was her unknown link to the Emery situation.

"It's probably safest to go with Brian," he said.

Her lip twitched. "Do you think the office is bugged?"

"Do you honestly think it isn't?" That amounted to a lost opportunity, as far as he was concerned.

"Never change." She settled back in her chair. "So, I hear you've been busy."

She was a force of nature. Not one to waste time, which he'd always appreciated. "I could say the same about you, Senator."

"Since when do you call me anything but Sheila?" She gestured for him to take the seat on the opposite side of the desk.

"When I sense I'm about to get a lecture." Which almost made him want to stay on his feet. He sat anyway. Picked up the mug but didn't take a drink. Not yet. Not until he knew which one of them would take the lead in the conversation.

She leaned forward with her elbows balanced on her desk. "How long have we known each other?"

Her, then. "I have to tell you, Sheila. No good conversation ever started with those words."

"Very true."

Interesting. "Just how bad is this lecture going to be?"

She folded her hands together. Looked every inch of the tough mother of promising lacrosse players. "You freaked out Emery Finn on your first meeting."

So that was it. "I said hello."

"Apparently you had a threatening tone."

He'd heard that his entire adult life. If talking tough scared people, so be it. "I really only have one tone."

"Then you repeated the mistake by going to her house and scaring her again."

Oh, come on. "That woman is not afraid of me."

Sheila frowned. "That was reckless and it's not like you to be reckless."

"I haven't been reckless in years." And that was the

truth. When he was younger his entire personality consisted of impulse and bad judgment. Not any longer.

"Yet you told her to back off."

"Maybe she misunderstood my intent."

"We both know you can be . . ." Sheila closed one eye and looked as if she were weighing her words. "A bit dark."

He'd been called far worse. "That's not exactly a secret."

"Intense."

He picked up the mug and cradled it in one hand. "Again, I'm not denying the description."

He'd wanted Emery to get the point. Sounded as if maybe she had. Now she could move on . . . though he had to admit the idea of her giving up and running away hit him wrong.

He'd enjoyed sparring with her, which likely made him an even bigger dick than people assumed. Still, she hadn't backed down or panicked like the few people who met him face-to-face tended to do. On more than one occasion he'd sent grown men—fierce and powerful businesspeople—scurrying. She'd fought back and he'd found that more than a little hot.

Sheila tapped her fingertips on the side of her mug. "She said your name was Brian. I'm surprised you gave her that much."

"I can explain that."

"Uh-huh."

"She knows that first name only." He gave in and took a long sip of the strong black coffee. "But how exactly did you know it was me she met with and who went to her street? I clearly didn't tell her who I really am."

"She described you, but really the whole 'listen to me and obey' speech you gave her is classic you."

"I thought I was . . ." He debated saying "friendly" and immediately abandoned the idea. "Clear."

"Of course you did." Sheila sighed as she leaned against the back of her chair. "You led her to believe awful things would happen if she didn't stop looking for you."

He had to admit that might have happened. "Too much?"

"Definitely." Sheila smiled. "I got the sense you acted just this side of unhinged."

Again, probably fair. "That seems like a strong way of saying it."

Her eyebrow lifted. "But accurate?"

"Garrett didn't seem impressed with my choice to confront her either." Wren brushed a stray string off his pants. "Everyone's a critic these days."

"Garrett was with you when you met Emery?"

Wren knew where this was going and refused to balk. He wasn't the type. He held the eye contact, silently daring Sheila to go too far. "No."

"Ah, there's your other mistake." The senator nodded. "Always take him with you."

"That sounds tedious." Not wrong, just exhausting. On the rare occasion he strayed from his usual pattern he should be able to do it without four armed guards and his second-in-command in tow. Should but probably couldn't.

"Since when do you venture out of the office during the day to tell people to leave you alone, or stalk a woman to her home?"

There was that word again. "Stalk, really? That's the word we're using?"

She nodded. "Yes, it is."

Wren took another sip, this time almost draining the small mug. "Granted, in hindsight my choices as to Emery seem like a miscalculation."

"You are the king of understatement today."

He actually thought of himself as straightforward, but why argue? "Which is one of the reasons you like me."

Some of the amusement left her face. "That and the fact you made it possible for me to be elected."

"I don't like blackmailers." The memories shuffled in his head. The men who tracked down those old photos didn't care that she'd been a freshman in college when they were taken or that the photographer had been a vengeful asshole of a former boyfriend. They just wanted her out of the race and were willing to ruin and embarrass her to do it. Wren hated men who shit all over women. "Your opponent was also an idiot. I don't live in Maryland, but I have a low tolerance for people who wave the Constitution around without actually reading it."

"Unfortunately, that's not an odd occurrence on Capitol Hill." She set down her mug. "So, to business. I know why I wanted to see you, but why did you insist on seeing me?"

With the mindless chatter out of the way, Wren dove in. "Why is Emery Finn looking for me?"

"Maybe it's your sparkling personality?"

Part of him actually wished an attraction to him was the answer. "Here I thought she was just nosy. Dangerously so."

"You're using that threatening tone right now. In my office." Sheila pointed at him. "Knock it off."

"Some people are afraid of me."

"Those people don't know you. They're actually afraid of some shadowy figure who hides behind a curtain." When he just sat there she smiled at him. "Do you not get the movie reference?"

"What movie reference?"

"I see." She rocked a bit in her big chair. "We—meaning you—need to deal with the Emery issue."

"I'm trying, but I need more information about her angle."

Sheila's smile widened. "It's convenient you came in, then."

She seemed far too amused all of a sudden. "Excuse me?"

"I think we should ask her."

That sounded simple enough, but no. "I tried."

"I meant in a normal way, preferably without scaring the hell out of her. Maybe with a smart, eloquent third party present." Then Sheila sat there, not moving and looking far too pleased with herself.

Wren saw the trap. A friendly one, but still, he'd been maneuvered. Sheila seemed determined to deal with this Emery situation and drag him out into the light. His preference was to ignore all of this until Emery went away . . . or it had been until he met her and an unexpected bit of interest sparked.

"What did you do?" He set his mug down nice and slow, careful not to crack it from the force of his grip on the handle.

"You're not the only one who insisted on seeing me today." The senator's words jumbled together as she spoke faster than usual. "She keeps contacting me."

There was more to the story. He read people for a living, and she was not immune to his skills. "Sheila."

"I know. I'm sorry." She held up her hand. "You can say no, but keep in mind I do have constituent work to do. I can't referee forever this strange relationship you two have brewing."

He stood up. "Right."

"Huh." Sheila played with the handle of her mug. "I didn't think you'd pick running."

Blow landed. Sheila didn't dance around. She went right to the ego shot. He would have done the same thing. He was just not used to being on the receiving end of the offensive maneuver.

"She's here now?" he asked, knowing the answer.

"Right outside. Should I send her away?" Sheila's finger hovered over the intercom button on her phone.

He could leave out the side door and through the room where the staffers sat. She was giving him the out and any other time he would have taken it, but Emery's dogged pursuit had him intrigued. He admired the determination. The idea she hadn't given up or heeded his warning should have pissed him off. He seemed to have the exact opposite reaction.

"No." This one time he would break his rules and

give in to his curiosity. He really didn't have an explanation for the change other than he sensed Emery wouldn't stop even if it meant walking through the halls of the Capitol shouting his name. His gut also told him it was time for this showdown, and he rarely ignored his gut.

The senator reached for the intercom, giving him every chance to call this off. When he didn't say anything, she hit the button. "Show Emery in."

"Good." He didn't realize he said the word until it echoed through the room.

"This is your last chance to duck out."

He sat back in the chair again. "I'm not exactly the type to go into hiding."

"I'm familiar with your private life, but I'll ignore that comment anyway."

He was too busy staring at the door to respond. "I'm going to regret this."

"True, but it will make my life less difficult." She moved the mug around on her desk.

There it was. The small show of concern. The senator didn't give much away, but sometimes her voice would rise or she'd move around too much. The fact she wasn't as sure that this was a good idea as she was saying shifted control back to him. "I'm also going to remember this moment the next time you come asking for a favor."

"That's the great thing about you. You won't." Her fingers traced the inside of the mug's handle. "See, I know you and the only thing bigger than your badass reputation is your sense of loyalty."

He wasn't sure if that was a good thing or not. "You're pushing the boundaries."

"How do you think I got where I am today?"

Hard work, discipline. Brains. "As you just pointed out, I helped you."

"Very true. Now, let me help resolve this situation."

CHAPTER 5

The door opened a fraction and Sheila motioned with her hand. "Emery, please come in."

Emery took two steps and her gaze flew to him. She stopped. "You."

"Me." Tension chocked the room. The awareness hit him with the force of a brutal punch. Something about her called to him. She wore gray dress pants and a silky-looking blouse, but her cheeks flushed and her eyes flashed with fire.

"This is the guy." She pointed at him as she moved closer.

"The creepy one?" Sheila asked.

"Okay." He'd just about reached his limit on that view. "Maybe we could use the word *mysterious*?"

"Okay, Brian," Emery snapped back in a sarcastic tone. "Is that even your real name?"

Never mind that he had a reason to use the fake name and that *she* was the one stalking *him*. "Since I only plan to be here for a few minutes, you should use your time wisely and ask only the questions you really need to ask."

She stood there, hovering by his chair with her hands

balled into fists at her sides. "I see the menacing thing you do is still in place."

"You're down to four minutes." He had no idea if any time had passed, but he glanced down at his watch to make his point.

Her shoulders fell as her mouth dropped open. "Who are you?"

Wrong question. "Let's do it this way. Why do you want to talk to Wren?"

Emery looked at the senator, who nodded and gestured for Emery to take the seat next to him. "Go ahead."

Emery hesitated on both. "I'm just supposed to trust him?"

Sheila nodded. "Yes."

That level of unconditional trust made Wren happier than he wanted to admit. "See?"

When no one said anything else, Emery dragged the chair another foot away from his and sat down. "Fine." She kept her attention on the senator. "I believe he knows something about Tiffany Younger."

"Who?" He actually had no clue who that was. He searched his memory for any recollection and came up empty. Since he rarely forgot a name or a number, that meant she'd been hunting for the wrong man the entire time. He felt a kick of regret at the thought.

"Tiffany is my cousin."

He still had no idea what that had to do with him. "Okay."

Emery's eyebrow lifted. "She's missing."

Now she had his attention again. He knew a lot about this subject. Too much. "From the DC area?"

Emery nodded. "It happened thirteen years ago."

The timing didn't make sense, but at least it explained why the case wasn't on his radar. "And you're talking about it now?"

"She's still missing."

"Fair enough." That drive for answers, the need for completion, he totally understood that. The not knowing didn't ease with time. It compounded. The doubts lingered. The sense of security never came back. But none of that explained what this had to do with him. "You think Wren has some connection to this woman?"

She finally looked at him. Hit him full-on with those big eyes and that haunted expression. "I think he abducted her."

The air punched out of him. *"What?"*

She waved her hand in front of her face as if trying to wave the words away. "You heard me."

"You're confused." She also was dead fucking wrong.

"Your boss is involved or he knows who took Tiffany. Either way, he is not innocent in this." Emery crossed her arms in front of her. "Sorry to spring that hard truth on you, but there it is."

The accusation sat there. Wren weighed her words and tried to figure out how she could have gotten this information so wrong. He knew all about her job. She poured through missing-persons files all day long. She directed experts on age progression work on missing children who would now be teens. Honorable work. Difficult work.

Scrolling through the mounds of intel Garrett had collected took a toll. Wren remembered every photo even though he tried not to focus too long on any. He'd forced his mind to remain still and not slip into old memories as he waded through the information because he knew all too well about the grief behind all those posters and pleas to find missing loved ones.

The idea of him being a perpetrator was as big a misfire as Emery could have made. If she only knew . . . but she couldn't.

He didn't rush to defend himself, though the temptation hovered right there. His heartbeat kicked up and the revving started inside him. "Where did you get Wren's name and how are you tying it to something that happened years ago?"

"Tiffany's father kept files. Boxes and boxes of information he'd collected on the abduction." Emery's white-knuckle grip on the armrests of the chair eased as she looked back and forth between him and the senator. "When he died, I got them."

"*Got* them?" Wren doubted they just fell into her car. She shook her head. "That's not important."

"I sense it is, but go on." Every bit he learned about her proved just how resourceful she was. How dedicated. If she weren't throwing around wild and baseless accusations he might have taken a minute to be impressed. Instead, he waited for more intel.

"There is a notation about this Wren and I've searched

everything. It took me forever to figure out it was a person." She leaned forward as she talked. With every word she became more passionate, more intense, as if she were desperate to win them over. "I don't know if Wren is a first name or a last name, but I'll figure it out unless you want to save me some time and just tell me."

Wren knew she was headed in the wrong direction, so he poked around in what could be the right one. "When did he die?"

"Gavin Younger? Last year."

A wall. Wren hated those. Now for the tougher question. "And Tiffany is—"

"She's never been seen again. There are no other leads."

He could see Emery swallow. He rarely let emotion lead him, but in that moment her frustration hit him in a rush. Her need to find answers almost pulsed off her. "I'm sorry, Emery."

She shifted in her chair. "If that's true, point me toward Wren."

"You have a bigger problem than identity."

She gave him one of those men-are-so-stupid sighs. "Do you ever just talk like a normal person?"

The senator shrugged at him. "Hey, it's a fair question."

Since he had no idea what they were talking about, he kept going. Focused on Emery and willed her to listen. "I fear your basic information is incorrect."

Emery's eyes narrowed. "Which part?"

At least she was listening. He took that as a good sign. "All of it."

Emery looked at the senator. "How is this helping?"

"Brian knows Wren better than anyone else."

Emery's gaze flipped back and forth between the senator and Wren. "Your name is really Brian."

Sheila nodded. "Brian Jacobs."

He felt like he was riding a runaway train. In another second or two the thing would careen and crash. He could feel it coming. Sense the trouble closing in, but not for the reason Emery or Sheila might think. No, they were heading for disaster because he hovered on the brink of doing something really fucking dumb. Something he never did.

"But he's not Wren. He can't know what his boss was doing years ago." Emery's arms tightened around her middle. "Wren does pay his salary after all."

"I'm going to let Brian answer that one," Sheila said, then looked at Wren.

If he didn't end this soon the tension building in the room would suffocate them. There was an obvious, easy way to handle this. An answer he could give about knowing Wren for a long time. About background checks and other garbage that should throw Emery off. But it wouldn't work for long. She was not one to be sidetracked.

He'd met people like her before. All of them in a business context and all insisting they could only deal directly with Wren on a deal. In the role of Brian, he pushed back. He should do that here. Of course. That's what made sense. That's what would preserve his image and the ruse and . . . what had Sheila called it? The curtain.

But he wasn't a man who let his life be limited by what he *should* do.

"Wren has never heard of Tiffany Younger." He said the words with a bit more bite in his voice than he intended.

Emery frowned at him. "And you know this because . . . ?"

It was time to lie or go all in. "I do."

She frowned. "But how?"

"I'm him."

CHAPTER 6

Emery jumped up from the chair. With that news it was a wonder she didn't leap right out the window. All she could do was stare at the man who sat there as if he hadn't just spilled one of the biggest secrets in the DC metro area.

The senator whistled. "I did not see that coming."

Brian or Wren or whatever his name was just shook his head. "Me either."

"What is this?" She couldn't form a more coherent sentence, so she went with that one.

He had the nerve to hold his hand up, as if he were trying to soothe her. "Settle down."

That tone, all smooth and cool, called out to her to punch him. She couldn't figure out if he meant to be condescending or that was just his natural state. To be fair, she couldn't figure out a lot of things because she could barely think.

She'd memorized those files. She saw the word *Wren* written in her uncle's heavy scrawl almost every time she closed her eyes. And now . . . this.

"Don't tell me to . . ." She couldn't even finish the sentence over the frantic heartbeat thundering in her chest. She glanced at the one person in the room who might explain all of this. "Senator?"

"It's okay." The senator shot her a pained expression. A mix of sympathy and a wince. "Emery, you don't need to panic."

"You just told me his name was Brian." She searched her mind for the last name the senator dropped, but her brain cells refused to function. She hoped to kick it out later because she'd need it when she searched. And she would be doing a search.

The senator shrugged. "It usually is."

"Emery," he said with a booming voice. "I am Wren. Not many people know that, and we'll have a serious discussion about discretion and the importance of you keeping this secret, but I assure you that's my name."

Her brain clicked into action again. "And I'm supposed to believe you."

"I promise you it's fine," the senator said.

"How can you say that?" Emery felt the exact opposite of fine. Her pulse raced and the room started spinning. She had to focus on the senator's face to keep from grabbing on to the edge of the desk or falling down.

"I've known him for years." Some of the stiffness left the senator's shoulders. "And there are guards everywhere in this place. He wouldn't touch you, but even if he wanted to he can't."

"Thanks for the vote of confidence," he said.

"You're Wren." Emery held on to the back of the chair she just abandoned. Dug her fingers into the leather. Willed her brain to catch up with the discussion so she wouldn't feel as if she were trapped in a maze.

"Yes." That's it. No explanation. Nothing.

"You are actually him." She needed to repeat it to make it sink in.

His eyebrow lifted. "Still, yes."

"I'm supposed to believe some mysterious guy whose name scares the crap out of everyone in power in this town just walked into a coffee shop and had a chat with me yesterday." But a part of her had to admit it made sense. He'd studied her, assessed every word. She wrote the whole strange scene off as something he was ordered to do and report back to the *real* Wren. Now she knew better.

The senator's chair creaked as she leaned back. "We're all confused about that part of the story."

He nodded as he sat down in the chair next to her. "Out of character, I agree."

"I assure you, Emery. This is him," the senator said, talking right over him.

Emery had so many questions. The basic ones and the ones guaranteed to get a reaction. She'd been thinking about him, building a picture in her mind. He didn't fit her image at all. She'd expected an older man. Someone she would look at and be able to tell if he hurt Tiffany. Not a logical assumption, of course, but she had to believe the evilness would ooze out of someone who grabbed a teen girl right off the sidewalk in broad daylight.

Instead of getting clarity, she got young and objectively hot in a brooding, possibly dangerous way. Not her type at all and certainly not someone she could read. That left her exactly where she started when she walked into the room fifteen minutes ago. But she could ask questions. The senator's presence might actually convince this guy to answer a few.

"Is Wren a last name or a first name?" When her hands started to cramp from her tight grip on the chair, Emery eased her fingers open. She didn't let go because she needed something to do with her fingers. It was either hug the chair or wrap them around his throat. Both options sounded good to her right now.

He shook his head. "Not important."

Her palms slid off the chair. "How can you—"

"Listen to me." He shifted, not far, but enough for the room to close in a bit. "I don't know this Tiffany and I can promise you that I've never kidnapped anyone . . . well, not a young girl and not in the way you suggest."

The spinning in her head morphed into a wild swing. She was two seconds from throwing up. "What kind of answer is that?"

"An honest one."

"Which is stranger that you can imagine." The senator's voice sounded more stern this time. "Emery, please sit down."

"I trusted you." Emery tried to keep the pleading out of her voice but a thin thread slipped in.

"Yes, and I arranged a meeting between you and Wren, just as you asked."

Emery hated to admit that was true.

"Right." Wren shot the senator an undecipherable look. "And we'll discuss that decision later."

Despite the energy pinging around the room, the

senator seemed to find a reason to smile. "You two have something in common."

Emery bit back a snort. "Hardly."

"What could that possibly be?" he asked at the same time.

"You are the one who matched my friend's missing son to a John Doe." She pointed first at Emery then to him. "Wren is the one who found his murderer."

Emery remembered every fact of the case. A college freshman killed by a fellow student after a bar fight gone terribly wrong. The kid drove for miles, probably days, to hide it. A horrible situation, but one where she connected the dots that led the police in one state to identify the body of what was thought to be a young homeless man found in another.

Nothing about the case pointed to a man named Wren or a millionaire with a thing for black suits. Still, hearing he played a role made her skeptical of all of it. "Are you sure he didn't do it?"

"Is there anyone you don't think I've killed?" His tone barely changed after being accused of a vicious crime.

The lightness touched off her temper. Sent it spiking. "Maybe. I can't rule you out since I don't know you."

"She has you there," the senator said.

Emery pulled the chair back and sat down facing him. "Are you supposed to be some sort of private investigator?"

He frowned. "Definitely not."

Before she could fire off another question, the senator stepped in. "He fixes things."

That didn't explain anything. Emery started to wonder if everyone was talking in code. "Like clogged sinks?"

"More like he makes the problems of companies and government, and sometimes private citizens, go away," the senator said.

Emery looked at Wren. For whatever reason, he was letting the senator do most of the talking. That had to be on purpose and he must have a reason because he struck her as a guy who insisted on being in control.

She wanted him to start talking. "That's an actual job?"

He nodded. "A very lucrative one, yes."

Of course it was. He practically dripped of money. "That explains the fancy suit."

He glanced down at his lap. "It's black."

The same color as the one he wore yesterday. Today's tie was a slightly different shade and had a pattern. She guessed the suit was the second of fifty identical ones he had hanging in his closet. This guy just looked like the type to color code his clothes and line them up with an inch between each hanger.

For some reason that thought made her even more cranky. "It probably cost more than my car."

He didn't break eye contact. "I guess that depends on what you drive."

The senator cleared her voice. She also rolled her eyes. "That's not helpful."

Something in her tone or comment must have spurred him on because he started talking without being prompted. "Thirteen years ago I was in graduate school."

"Where?"

He shook his head. "Nowhere near here."

She wanted to yell, "Gotcha!" but settled for a self-satisfied smirk. "I didn't say where Tiffany disappeared from."

"Touché." For a second a smile edged the corner of his mouth, but it quickly disappeared. "Still, you have the wrong man, Ms. Finn."

"Because you say so?"

He stood up. Without warning or any fanfare he pushed his chair closer to the desk and rebuttoned his suit jacket. "We've met, as you wanted, so you can now stop digging for information on me and move on."

There is no way he could think those answers satisfied her. "You are an arrogant ass."

"Not the first time I've heard that." He glanced over at the senator. "Thanks for the lovely meeting."

As he pivoted to leave, Emery shot up and stood in front of him. Didn't touch him, but stepped right into his path, daring him to push past her. Heat rolled off his body and smacked into her. This close she could see the whiskers on his chin. Even fought the urge to run a finger over them.

She should hate him, be scared of him—something. He stood for everything she hated. He used his power to push people around. He'd basically threatened her. Forget the whole stupidly handsome thing, that dark, mysterious quality that had her wanting to know more. It wasn't as if he'd ever even been nice to her. She'd been searching and he had the answers and he hid. She shouldn't be short of breath. Shouldn't have this cloud of confusion muddling her brain.

"Well?" He looked down as if waiting to see what she planned to do.

Good question. She'd only thought this far. "You can't leave."

"Watch me." He stepped around her.

She shifted in front of him a second time. "Wren . . ."

She grabbed on to the sleeve of his jacket and he immediately stopped. When her hand dropped again, he nodded and left. Walked right to the door without even bothering to look back.

EMERY JUST STOOD there, stuck to the spot. Her legs refused to move and the air whistled in her lungs. It took all of her energy to think through the conversation she just had. A noise broke through. It took another few seconds for her to realize the senator was talking to her. Emery spun around to face her.

"Emery, please sit down."

She couldn't do anything but stand there. "He just got up and left."

"I know." She smiled. "It's sort of his go-to move for exiting a room."

Emery couldn't process the last five minutes. "Him, as in Brian or Wren or whatever we're calling him."

"He's Wren. He goes by Brian Jacobs so that people don't know he's actually Wren. It's a shield of sorts." The senator cleared her throat. "Very few people know who he really is. I've seen him badgered by the best and never admit he's Wren."

"But he told me." Which didn't make sense. Like, not at all.

"Interesting, isn't it?"

Emery didn't know what that meant or why the senator kept biting back a smile. She felt anything but amused and happy. "I have been searching for him for . . . longer than I want to admit. I didn't know if he was a 'him' and not an 'it' for months. He answers a few questions with vague responses and takes off."

"I know Wren. He is not the man you're looking for." The sincerity was right there in the senator's voice, in the softening around her eyes that signaled concern.

"Then explain to me who he really is, and I'm not talking about the name. I mean the man."

"That is not my story to tell." The senator shrugged. "But it appears he wants to share with you, so who knows what you'll be able to find out."

Emery ignored the strange vibration under the senator's words. "His name was in the file."

She wanted to believe that the senator was telling the truth, but if she was that meant the lead had gone nowhere. Emery didn't have another string to pull.

She'd been searching her entire adult life. She took the job she did as a way to help Tiffany. After seeing all those faces and being plowed under by all that pain, the job had become more than a vow she intended to honor, but she'd made that promise to find answers.

The senator shook her head. "I can't explain that. I really don't know why that would be."

That gave Emery hope, but not really. Not real hope. The idea of squaring off with a guy like Wren—not old and ready to admit to his sins, but someone young and totally wrong—left her shaking. "Then he can tell me."

"You need to be careful. Maybe heed his warning to back off." When Emery started to argue, the senator held up a hand and talked louder. "And, of course, as I say that, I remember what you do for a living and realize you have no intention of letting this drop, do you?"

"No." After a lifetime of guilt she could not just let it go. Tiffany deserved more. She could be out there. Emery knew only a shocking case of good luck had spared her and doomed Tiffany. Even now, after all those years and all that therapy, Emery had trouble living with that.

The senator hummed. "This will certainly be interesting to watch."

That's not the word Emery would pick. "You could help me."

"I just did."

Emery tried to appreciate that. She understood the senator had probably taken risks and called in favors to get Wren there. But the not-being-able-to-keep-him-there thing was a big hole in the plan. "He walked out on me without providing one bit of usable information."

The senator leaned forward with both arms resting on her desk. "Do you honestly think a man like that is just going to forget the accusations you made against him and go away?"

"I didn't actually accuse him . . ." Emery saw the senator's eyes widen and rushed to keep from veering too far off the truth path. "Okay, I did."

"He's not someone who's accustomed to having his integrity challenged."

Yeah, she'd picked up on that. "I don't really care."

"You are one of the few people he's agreed to meet."

Not that she understood why. He'd cornered her in the coffee shop then showed up in this office. Neither seemed in character or made much sense. Maybe he liked games and this was all some big joke to him.

Emery hung on to that explanation. That one made it easy to see him as the enemy and hold her edge. With him as the jerk, possibly a dangerous one. She could forget the high cheekbones and athletic build. Ignore the near-perfect face.

"He's powerful. I get that." Possibly even more powerful than she expected. "But you have to agree he can be a little much."

The senator smiled. "You have no idea."

The senator actually *liked* the guy. That fact hit Emery out of nowhere. The senator didn't tolerate Wren or fear him. This wasn't about her office or him being a donor. No, on some level Emery knew their bond ran deeper. She'd found something redeeming in him and *that* caught Emery's interest. "Fill me in."

"I'll leave it to him."

Emery didn't love that possibility. If he kept showing up while she drank her coffee she'd need to switch to decaf. "That sounds ominous."

"When Wren wants to know more, and he will, he'll find you." The senator managed to make that sound like a good thing.

Emery wasn't convinced. "I'm not sure being near him is all that safe or smart."

"He's harmless, or he will be to you." The senator

sat back in her chair again. "Besides that, I like the idea of him having to work for it."

Once again the conversation looped around and Emery totally got lost. Much more of this and her headache might become permanent. "For what exactly?"

"Anything."

CHAPTER 7

Emery dropped her duffel bag on the floor beside her desk chair. Next came the purse. She threw that, nearly knocking over one of the walls of her cubicle. Apparently she was a bit more tense than she thought. So much for the theory that the walk from the metro would help clear her mind.

Her chair spun when she sat down. She had to grab on to the edge of the desk to keep from twirling. She was not in a twirling mood.

She toed off her sneakers and leaned over to dig through her bag. One jerk and the zipper got stuck in the material. She tugged and the tracks went crooked. She couldn't get the teeth to come loose.

"That's just freaking great." She let the bag fall back to the floor with a thud and stared down at her socks. Another win for office decorum.

Phones rang on the main line. She glanced at the little lights and saw three people on hold. Looked like the usual busy day at the Jane Doe Network.

Before Emery could play phone backup, Caroline Montgomery stepped into the small space, all tall and sure and in charge. "You seem to be in a good mood."

She'd joined the organization in her early thirties and now ran it ten years later. She functioned as listener, mentor and head ass-kicker, depending on what Emery needed at that moment. But mostly, she was a friend. Smart and committed with two kids and a partner at home. Emery coveted her long auburn hair and . . . well, everything. Caroline had the whole balanced-life, good-person combination down.

By comparison, Emery felt like an unmade bed. Today she blamed Brian or Wren—or whatever he was calling himself—for the messy sensation. "This day basically sucks."

After a quick glance at her watch, Caroline frowned. "It's not even lunchtime."

God, was it even that late? "Exactly."

"I guess I don't need to ask how the meeting with the senator went." Caroline stepped around the cubicle wall and leaned against the edge of Emery's desk. "Did she even agree to see you?"

Caroline had money connections and worked them hard. She raised the cash and filed the paperwork that brought in the funding and kept the lights on. As her assistant and one of only five paid staffers, Emery ran the hundred volunteers and kept the workload afloat. One of the benefits was that she enjoyed a good relationship with Senator Dayton, but today it had flipped sideways on her at some point.

Now to explain that to Caroline.

Emery flopped back in her chair. "Oh, she invited me in."

"That sounds . . . stop shaking your head and tell

me what happened." Caroline sounded open and eager to hear the details, but she crossed her arms in front of her. Not a good sign.

"She had a guest." Emery still hadn't dislodged her stomach from her throat from the surprise of walking in and seeing *him* in the office. "The guy I told you about from the coffee place yesterday."

Caroline's eyes widened. "The creepy one with the hot outer wrapping."

The words screeched across Emery's brain. "Who said hot?"

Okay, he was. Objectively. She could admit that much. She'd never gone for the moody type. And the whole careful-word-choice thing? So annoying. But the perfect-body, perfect-face combo did have some merit. Not that she remembered saying any of that to Caroline.

"Uh, you did." Caroline smiled. "You danced around it a bit, but I could decipher the code words."

"I'm going to pretend that never happened." Emery needed to focus on the other side. The not-hot side. "Creepy is more accurate. He actually showed up on my street last night."

Caroline dropped her arms. "What?"

"No, it was fine." She put up a hand to stop Caroline when she headed for the phone. "I threatened him with a bat."

When Emery didn't say anything else, Caroline sighed. "Okay, we'll come back to that. So, this Wren sent his minion to a meeting with you and the senator." She shrugged. "That sounds like progress. Sort of."

It also sounded like her very smart boss was not understanding what really happened. Emery tried again. "Wren."

Caroline froze. "What?"

Now she was getting it. "The creepy guy is Wren."

Caroline's frown only deepened. "Wait . . ."

"No minion. The guy with the coffee was actually Wren. He identified himself and the senator confirmed it. I think they're friends, but who the hell knows." They could be anything to each other, and Emery did not want to study that line of thought too much.

Some of the color left Caroline's face. "What did you say to him?"

"I asked him about Tiffany." Like she'd been waiting to do forever. Not that it helped. Emery knew she'd replay every word, fixating on how she could have handled the interview better and learned more. The desperate worry she'd blown it churned in her gut. At this rate she'd never be able to eat again.

All of the brightness drained from Caroline's face, leaving her looking drawn, almost pained. "You asked the man you described as having a dangerous vibe if he kidnapped your cousin right off the street and never returned her?"

Now Emery understood the look. The senator might have been there for the initial talk, but she wouldn't always be there. That left a lot of wiggle room for Wren to do something very bad. Emery didn't think he would. It was just a feeling, one with no basis in reality because she knew absolutely nothing about him other than his love for black business suits and sentences with too many words, and both of those struck her as over the top.

Maybe she trusted the senator's instincts. Emery couldn't really explain it, but part of her did worry that this is how men like Wren got what they wanted. They won women over. Unlucky for him, she possessed more than the usual amount of distrust when it came to strangers insisting they were safe. "I was more subtle than that."

"Are you sure?"

Emery pretended Caroline didn't look horrified and two seconds away from calling 9–1–1. "He said he didn't do it and left," Emery explained.

Silence descended in the cubicle. Phones rang in the office. The sounds of conversation floated around and people laughed over by the kitchenette. But in that cubicle for those few seconds everything stopped.

After some rapid blinking Caroline spoke again. "There had to be more than that."

"I talk with law enforcement people all day. Have conversations with people who have lost loved ones. When it came to this guy I got three questions out, he blew off two of them and walked out." Thinking back Emery wasn't even sure she got to ask three full questions. She certainly didn't get much in the way of answers.

"Was he angry?"

Emery swiveled her chair back and forth and searched for the right way to describe it. The words didn't come. Probably because Wren was sort of hard to decipher. You kind of had to experience him to believe it. "I don't even know how to tell."

"But you have somewhere to start, right?" Someone called out to Caroline, but she shook her head and kept her focus on Emery. "Now we have a name and we know the senator has some background intel. You can investigate from there."

"As if what I've said isn't weird enough, try this: no."

"What are you answering?"

Emery couldn't blame her boss for the confusion. She guessed she wore the same sort of pinched look, wrinkled brown expression in the senator's office. "We have a name—Brian Jacobs."

"Who is that?"

Good freaking question. "Wren."

Caroline shook her head. It looked like she was trying to figure out what was happening. "You lost me. Again."

That made two of them. "That's the name Wren uses. And on the subject of Wren, I don't know his name."

Caroline sputtered a few times before getting any words out. "I don't—"

"It could be a first name or a last name. I have no clue."

"I wish I knew what question to ask next."

"Now you know how it feels to have a conversation with Wren. It's like wading through peanut butter." That didn't really nail it, but Emery didn't have anything else. She feared she'd spend a good part of the evening thinking about Wren and trying to come up with another description.

Some of the color rushed back into Caroline's face. "Interesting metaphor."

"You didn't see him. You didn't try to understand his sentences."

When another person called out Caroline's name, she held up a finger and nodded. "Someone clearly wants to talk to me, but I'm intrigued with your visit. I want to know more."

"He's probably a kidnapper and a killer." Emery could almost imagine him sitting in his house alone, tapping his fingers together as he plotted his next crime.

"Right, you don't believe that." Caroline stood up. "Doesn't matter. Figure it out."

Not exactly the *you can't do this . . . be careful* response Emery expected. "What?"

"This is what you do for other people. Do it here. Call the detective who was on the case. Talk to your dad and to . . ." Caroline drifted off for a second. "What's with that look?"

Emery hadn't even tried to hide the wince. "I forgot I have dinner with Dad tonight."

"You sound thrilled."

Her father tended to lapse into full-on professor mode every Monday night, just as she arrived. He talked philosophy and got all haughty. He reiterated how much he despised her job and her reluctance to get a master's degree.

He didn't exactly hide that she was a complete embarrassment to him. Emery hated to think how he described her when he got together with his professor friends. She bet he frowned a lot. "He hates it when I talk about Tiffany."

Caroline snorted. "Tough shit."

Yeah, that's what Emery thought, too. He never seemed to care that Tiffany was his niece, the daughter of his wife's baby sister. He saw Tiffany as an extension of her mother and he hated Aunt Louise. Thought she drank too much, liked to party too much, wasn't serious enough. Certainly wasn't good enough for his best friend, Gavin, and only brought his wife down when the sisters got together.

And she couldn't defend herself. Could no longer fight for Tiffany. Aunt Louise had died years ago. Ran her car into a tree and never woke up. Uncle Gavin had already lost a daughter and had to make the call to take his wife off life support. But they were over long before that. Emery remembered watching as time and pain ate away at both their souls. Turned them inside out and ripped them apart.

After Tiffany disappeared, Uncle Gavin stopped defending his wife. He no longer talked about her being funny and sweet. Emery suspected the mix of guilt and her father's negative comments wore on Uncle Gavin.

Some said alcohol killed Aunt Louise. Others blamed Uncle Gavin's indifference and the cold that moved between them and froze them both from the inside out. Still others thought she never recovered after losing Tiffany. She became an empty shell, shuffling around the house and circling the phone as if *the call* could come at any moment.

Emery believed her aunt died because she gave up. Uncle Gavin ran around, pushing the police and putting up posters. Aunt Louise withered. With both of them gone, that left her as the sole person to speak for, to fight for, her cousin. The idea of Tiffany being out there, needing help and for someone to storm in, had haunted Emery's sleep for years.

With time, some memories had faded but she fought to hold onto mental snapshots, small pieces of her days with her free-spirited cousin and best friend. The hikes, the bike rides, the visits to the water park they loved. The debates they'd have over which movie star was cuter, and which one they'd marry. Stupid girl stuff that would double them over in laughter or have them communicating in code or sneaking behind their parents' backs.

That sneaking had cost Tiffany everything.

Emery had tried to engage her dad about what he remembered since they'd lived a few doors apart for almost three decades. Right there on the tree-lined street in Bethesda, just three blocks from where Tiffany disappeared forever. He insisted there was nothing left to tell.

But Caroline supported her. Encouraged the investigation, and that made Emery's life so much easier. "Your tough love is why I love it here."

Caroline winked at her. "And your refusal to be bullied and pushed around is why I hired you."

"I also volunteered as free labor while I went to college and then begged you to give me any position around here, no matter how low the pay." She started by changing the printer's toner cartridges and emptying trash cans.

The memory almost made Emery laugh. She'd been so eager, so happy to be close to the people who might find Tiffany one day, or at least be able to explain what happened. She carried that same hope today even after meeting Wren.

"Oh, I hired you for your willingness to work for pennies." Caroline's smile came back. "That, too."

"I feel anxious and jumpy. Like I'm right on the edge of finding that one piece that will open this case up." Emery said it because she knew Caroline would understand. The office found answers for so many families. That rush as the information started to fall into place never went away.

Caroline held up a hand. "You know I have to warn you—"

"Not to get too excited or wound up in the emotion of the hunt," Emery said, finishing the sentence. "Follow the facts."

"Do I say that a lot? If so, I'm brilliant." This time when the person manning the phones called out Caroline's name she responded. "I'll be there in a second."

"Thanks for letting me work on this." Emery meant that. Not many jobs would let her pursue a lifelong vow.

"Our job is to bring them all home. The ones we know and the ones we don't." She winked. "Keep digging."

Emery planned to do just that.

WREN EYED UP the folders spread across his dining room table. He wasn't one to entertain, so it was about time the room saw some action. Figured it was in the form of work and not actual food.

He picked up the takeout Chinese container and

jabbed a shrimp with his fork. Mrs. Hayes would yell at him tomorrow. She came in most weekdays, straightened up, cleaned, organized even though nothing was ever out of order and made him dinner. Tonight he'd ignored whatever was on the plate and bribed Garrett into ordering at the office. Only Garrett, who was extremely well paid, would insist on a free dinner before he'd make a phone call and order.

Most days Wren wouldn't have cared about getting home, but tonight something drove him. A strange sensation nagged at him ever since he left the senator's office. He worked until after eight in the office, earlier than his usual workday end, then headed out because he wanted to close the door, block all distractions and dig into his new side project.

Tiffany Younger. She literally vanished off a Maryland sidewalk at age thirteen.

Tiffany was Emery's cousin. Wren happened to know exactly what happened when a relative disappeared. How everything changed. How you never felt settled again.

He hated that Emery lived with that sensation every day.

He had Garrett throw together as much intel as he could find. Wren depended on his unauthorized back door access into the police department's computer system to help with the rest. In this case he planned to search systems for both the Metropolitan Police Department, DC's police force, and the police in Montgomery County, Maryland, where Tiffany lived. Sometimes his MPD contacts could provide an assist, but he didn't know enough to ask the right questions yet.

Tomorrow he would gather more intel and keep gathering until he found whatever piece would make the entire case click together in his head. That's how it worked for him. He studied and assessed, blocked out everything else and focused on the details.

Not that he or his office handled cold criminal cases on a regular basis, because he made sure that did not happen. He stayed away from work that hit on such a personal level. The FBI and police could handle those matters.

But it was more than that. The facts and emotions involved in missing-persons cases struck too close to the life that almost killed him years before. He could still hear the sirens and remember the police detectives' questions. All that confusion. The betrayal.

That mixed-up kid was a long way from his current life. Even now he sat in his four-story town house on Embassy Row, on the stretch of Massachusetts Avenue in DC known as Millionaires Row. The property next door used to be the Georgian Embassy.

The existence of so many international powerbrokers and politicians meant the neighborhood remained under constant guard. The security presence never eased. He appreciated the safety, but he did crave more quiet, less street congestion.

But he could relax on this side of the house, away from the fray. He leaned back in his chair and stared out the floor-to-ceiling windows that looked out into the small garden behind his house. An elaborate gate and strategically planted trees afforded him some privacy, but from this position on the second floor he could look straight across and see lights on in windows on other properties. He kind of hated that.

He shuffled the folders and brought one in particular back to the stack. The one not about Tiffany. This one contained the surveillance reports on Emery. He opened the cover and flipped through the pages. Saw photo after photo, all culled from public records and Garrett's surveillance. They spelled out part of her history even as they failed to capture the life that burst into the room whenever she stepped inside.

"What really happened that night? What has you so obsessed all these years later?" He asked the questions in his quiet house, not expecting any real answers. The police had failed to find any for more than a decade. While he believed in the concept of *fresh eyes* and all that, he didn't expect to solve anything.

What he really needed to know was how his name got bound up in this tragedy. He had enough of a troubled past to handle on his own and didn't need to take on someone else's.

The report blurred into a black ink streak on the page. Rubbing his eyes didn't help. He flipped back to the photos—Emery then and now.

He'd gotten sucked in. None of that would have happened if he'd ignored her attempts to contact him and stayed the hell out of that coffee shop. Now he was exposed. Now he had to do something.

He could tolerate being thought of as dangerous and

domineering, even lethal. He couldn't tolerate the idea of being viewed as someone who would kidnap and hurt a woman. He refused to let anyone, whether they knew about his past or not, saddle him with "the apple doesn't fall far from the tree" tag.

One thing was clear. His dealings with Emery Finn were far from over.

CHAPTER 8

"D ad?" Emery entered the front door of the brick split-level house she grew up in. Despite living there for eighteen years, she always felt like she should knock. It wasn't as if she considered this her home. She hadn't for years. If she were being honest she'd have to admit she never really felt welcome.

Before she took one step out of the entry, she took off her shoes. That qualified as the household's number one rule. There were others. So many others. No eating in the bedrooms. No being in the kitchen after dinner was over, except to get water. No fumbling with the curtains to the big picture window in the living room at the front of the house. As soon as she'd conquered what she thought was the entire list, he'd come up with new ones. The man did like order.

He also liked women. An impressive series of girl-friends and wives had moved through the place over the years. Her mother had been dead for less than seven months when the first woman showed up with her suitcase. One bag with all her stuff, that was all her father had allowed.

Emery had almost no memory of that woman. She

was probably very nice, just like the rest of them, but being a young girl barely out of second grade Emery hadn't taken the idea of a new woman in the house particularly well. Her father threatened her with boarding school. She never went, but he blamed her for that breakup and the many that followed anyway.

The two stepmothers didn't stick around long. They came in one after the other, and knowing her father they probably overlapped in some way. He was clear he found fidelity to be an outdated notion. With each new partner, the woman's age dropped. The last one—Marilee—moved out about a month ago and had been exactly one year younger than Emery, almost to the day.

But that wasn't her issue with her father. Emery long ago stopped judging or even attempting to understand the revolving door on her father's bedroom. The women were of a type—blond, young and very pretty. Most tried to be friends with her. One or two tried to be more.

To his credit, he somehow managed to win over really charming women. Emery just didn't know what they ever saw in him because they deserved better. Every one of them.

Her father wasn't a nice man. Smart and highly respected, yes. Loving and warm—absolutely not. He was the demanding scholarly type. His expectation for Emery was that she'd model her life after his.

No thank you.

His requirements were very clear and drummed into her from an early age. Nothing that required her to beg for money or perform. Law was out because he found the career path beneath a member of the Finn family. He didn't think she had the aptitude for medicine, and he was right. Nothing silly. Certainly nothing in the fine arts. When she tried out for the school play as a junior his head nearly shot off.

No, her charge was to find an appropriate academic field and excel. She did the opposite. Not much of a book learner and totally disinterested in the idea of pursuing the years of study needed to earn a PhD, Emery disappointed him. But then, that was nothing new. She'd had a lifetime of practice. She'd always worn the wrong clothes. Had the wrong friends. Had the nerve to act like a teenager.

And he focused much of his anger back then at Tiffany. He'd hated that she didn't always listen when he told her to do something and how she frequently talked back. She acted like a normal teen in most ways, a little rebellious and maybe a bit more mouthy. She wasn't impressed with him, and he couldn't comprehend that.

She also had the nerve to be spontaneous and look just like her mom, the sister-in-law he despised. Little did he know Tiffany smoked and liked to sneak out of the house at night and head to the park to sit on the swings. Those things would have driven him to fury.

Maybe if he had eased up back then things would have ended differently. Emery winced at the thought as she hung her bag on the hook over the shelf that now held her shoes. She knew the logic was flawed and the accusation unfair, but that night years ago she'd been delayed in sneaking out to meet Tiffany because her dad had made her sit in his study and memorize an epic poem by Ezra Pound. Complete torture, in general, and almost the end of the world for a twelve-year-old. It was punishment for some mundane household failure and it meant she was not outside as planned when Tiffany disappeared.

She should probably be grateful that she wasn't there when *it* happened. Instead, she blamed him for keeping her from possibly saving Tiffany that night.

She heard footsteps then he rounded the wall of the kitchen and looked at her. Studied her navy pantsuit with his usual look of disgust. "You're late."

"And hello to you, Dad." She didn't hug him because that never felt right. She settled for going up on tiptoe and kissing his check. Since he was well over six feet and not the type to lean down and make the process easier it took some stretching on her part. She backed away as soon as the task was over. "What are we having?"

"Roast chicken." He delivered the answer then walked back into the galley-style kitchen, clearly intending for her to follow.

She did, not only because it was her daughterly duty, but because she loved food. The scent of garlic and rosemary filled the small space. In addition to having waiting lists for his class and articles published in journals, her father was an excellent cook. She had no idea what it was about his teaching style that had students lining up to hear him speak. Him lecturing qualified as her nightmare.

But she did know where the cooking skills came

from. He took several classes, along with wine tasting seminars, because he hated not being an expert in all things culinary when he thought it paired well with his philosophical pursuits. Emery really didn't get the logic of that either.

She leaned her back against the counter and watched him search for the proper utensil to lift the potatoes and carrots out of the roast pan. "Smells good."

He shot her a quick glance. "Do not sit on the counter."

As if she'd lose her mind and commit such a heinous household offense. "I'm resting."

He frowned at her before going back to scooping. "You're perfectly capable of standing up straight."

"Right." She sighed as she turned around and opened the cabinet door. Setting the table seemed innocent enough, so she got the dishes down and started that. "How's everything at school?"

"The university is as challenging as always."

She stifled a groan. Not facing him at that moment helped. Also allowed her to perform the perfect eye roll. Apparently it was going to be one of those nights. She decided if the mood stayed here at the just-above-squirming level she may as well plunge ahead and make it turn the energy toxic.

"May I ask you something?" She folded the napkins, careful to line up the edges and smooth the crease in a perfect line.

"Of course." He started to carve the chicken. "I am always open to a robust discussion."

He made her head hurt. "When Uncle Gavin died—"

"No." The cabinet rattled from the force of him

slamming the carving utensils against the counter. "Stop this."

She spun around to face him. Took in the fury holding every muscle in his body tense and the jutting chin. He'd gone from his usual level of disappointment to enraged in less than a minute. "I didn't ask anything yet."

For a second he just stared at her. He held so still that the kitchen fell into obedient silence. "I see where this is going and we will not talk about Tiffany. This is our weekly family dinner, not an invitation to open issues long settled."

Settled? Her hands shook from the force of the anger surging through her. She had to put down the plates to keep them from clanking together. "She's still missing."

"I am aware of that, Emery."

"Then what's the problem?"

A nerve twitched in his cheek, likely from the way she phrased the question. Possibly from the fact she dared to ask one at all.

"It's been thirteen years. You need to deal with the reality that she is not coming back." He went back to carving the chicken. Gone was the smooth slide of the knife. His movements were jerky now. "Your job, this incessant need to pick at old wounds, it is all so unhealthy."

She had nothing to grab on to or hold . . . or throw. She reached behind her and wrapped her fingers around the top of the chair. "It's about closure. She deserves to have a real ending."

"She has one."

The cruelty of that statement shot through Emery. "Tiffany is your niece."

"This holds you back." He pointed at her with the knife. When a piece of chicken skin fell off the edge and onto the floor, he glared at it before glaring at her again. "You are unable to move on and find a career that suits you so long as you are searching after useless clues."

Adrenaline pumped through her. All the words, all the arguments, lodged in her throat in a rush to come out. She had to fight the urge to pick up the chair and throw it. "I would hope someone—anyone—would look for me if I just vanished."

He reached down and wiped up the floor. "You wouldn't do that."

She knew where he was headed with this. She'd heard this speech so many times that the idea of a replay had her ready to jump out the sliding glass door by the head of the table. First, he would refer to Tiffany's smart mouth and how he'd always thought she'd run into trouble. Then he'd move on to his theory about her running away. Truth was, part of him blamed Tiffany and what he viewed as her out-of-control personality for being taken, and Emery had never been able to forgive him for that.

"She did not run away." She would have made contact and there had never been any attempts. She'd never been seen anywhere and Emery knew from the detective who once worked the case that her social security number was never used again.

"That is your theory, but there is not one scrap of evidence that suggests otherwise."

"And there's not one bit that supports your theory of her running off with someone." Emery knew all about Tiffany's crushes and the boy she kissed the week before she disappeared. They'd talked about everything, and nothing pointed to her running off without a word. Not one thing.

Her father sighed as he picked up the platter of partially cut chicken and brought it over to the table. "She was a troubled girl. I know you don't want to believe that, but Gavin and I talked about her issues. He was concerned about her growing behavioral issues and wanted her to go to boarding school. Louise fought it, but it would have happened."

"That's not true."

The platter hit the table with a thud. "You've recreated this image of her to make her some sort of a saint, but that is not reality."

Emery refused to move out of his way as she pivoted to take her seat. Sure, it was childish, but food was the last thing on her mind at the moment. "She didn't deserve to die."

He turned away from her. Glanced at her as he walked back to the counter and picked up the side dishes. "I didn't say she did."

She stepped in front of him again because he needed to stop moving around and just talk to her. "Did Uncle Gavin believe she ran away? Because he never said that. He fought for her, looked for her, until the end."

Her father reached around her and set the platters down before taking his seat at the head of the table. "Gavin was obsessed just as you're obsessed. His came from guilt. I'm not sure where yours comes from, but the obsession must stop."

"That's not fair." The word grated across her nerves. Others had used it. Tyler, the friend who grew up with them. The same boy who had professed undying love for Tiffany and kissed her right before she vanished. The detective. Caroline never said it, no one at work did, but Emery wondered if they thought it, too.

"I buried my best friend and I will not bury my only child." Her dad pulled out the chair with a bit too much strength and the legs left the floor. He lowered it to the hardwood again without scraping against the floor. "End of story."

She knew he actually believed that would stop the conversation. Because he said so. But this was not his classroom and she was no longer twelve and afraid of his temper. "What do you think is going to happen to me?"

"It's already happened. It's starting to look as if this is not a passing interest. That you're never going to move on." He leaned back in his chair as if daring her to deny it. "You live in the past. Even now you're bringing this subject up over dinner."

"We need to talk about her. We need to have answers." She did. Down to her soul. The guilt. The not knowing. Waking up every day thinking Tiffany could be one of those poor women chained to a bed somewhere in some sick bastard's basement, unable to get out.

The horrible possibilities ate at Emery. Stole her sense of security. Some days it warped her until she feared she was losing her mind. The desperate searching for an age-progressed version of Tiffany's face in the files at work never ended. Without finding her—without knowing the truth—it never would.

"We need to eat dinner." He picked up the serving dish with the chicken and slid a portion to his plate.

She kept her fingers locked on the back of the chair. "Dad."

"I am done with this topic." He didn't even look up as he snapped his napkin open and laid it across his lap. "Sit."

The quiet thundered in her ears, broken only by the sound of the clinking of his silverware. She glanced around at the familiar space, the all-white kitchen and crisp navy drapes outlining the door to the back patio. The house should bring her comfort, but being here only made her long to get out again.

And she could. She wasn't a kid anymore. The hold her dad had on her snapped a long time ago.

She pushed back from the chair. "No thanks."

He put down his fork. "What do you think you're doing?"

"I'm not hungry." Her stomach had turned over and flipped inside out. The idea of food made her want to hurl.

"Don't be juvenile." He gestured toward her usual chair. "Sit down and eat."

"That's the great thing about being almost twenty-five, Dad. I decide when I eat."

All emotion left his face. He treated her to a blank stare. "I expect better of you."

"Yeah, well. Chalk it up as one more disappointment." She had a hard time catching her breath. She wanted to scream and cry and swear. None of those would move him and that would only make her emotions explode even more. "That's what I do, right?"

"I am not going to engage in this ridiculous debate." With that he picked up his fork and started eating carrots.

She just couldn't think of anything related to finding Tiffany as ridiculous. "Enjoy your dinner."

CHAPTER 9

Wren waited two whole days before going back to the coffee shop. Not exactly a cause for congratulations. He spent the time doing what he needed to do—work—and gathering all the intel he could on Tiffany. The latter took him down a hole that he had some difficulty crawling out of.

He hated unanswered questions. He didn't have to guess what it felt like to live with uncertainty because he knew all too well. Not many people could claim an expertise in living with the open-ended loss of someone close. It was a pretty shitty club to join and the membership was purely involuntary and unending. The fact Emery shared that secret knowledge and dealt with that level of unrelenting pain just sucked.

That's why he was in the coffee shop, standing at the back of the line while his driver waited a few doors down. He tried to blend in, which he knew was not his forte. He was not a head-down, stare-at-his-shoes type, but he worked those unused skills now. The last time he made eye contact in this particular store he wound up admitting at least part of his name to a stranger. The same stranger he hoped to see here again today, but if she stuck to her usual schedule she wouldn't come in for another twenty minutes.

As soon as he finished the thought he felt a presence looming next to him. His head shot up and he looked right into Emery's big brown eyes. He beat back the need to blink. She'd snuck up on him, which was not something that happened . . . ever.

She held out her hand. "Here."

He looked at the white cup with the name *Brian* scrawled on the side and tried to figure out the chances she planned on poisoning him. "What is it?"

She shook it at him. "Black coffee. You seem like a nothing-fancy, no-sugar kind of guy."

Right on the first try. Not bad for a woman he'd met all of three times.

He took the coffee and followed her to the small bistro table in the back. Took the seat by the wall. She didn't seem nervous or upset, and he had no idea what to make of that.

"I feel like you're trying to tell me something," he said.

"If I want to tell you something, I will." She looked two seconds away from rolling her eyes.

"Fair enough."

She also looked a bit too sexy for his peace of mind in her khaki-colored pantsuit with a pink shirt. Something about the shade lit up her face. The bounce in her walk, the hair around her shoulders, the smirk when she got the drop on him and handed over the coffee. She appealed to him in a raw want-to-abandon-his-responsibilities-and-fuck-her kind of way, which was just about the last thing he needed.

She sat there and toyed with her cup. Spun it around between her palms as she watched him. "Why are you here?"

He thought about coming up with an excuse but abandoned the idea. Emery didn't strike him as the type to buy nonsense talk. "I realized that the last few times we met I may have acted a little—"

"Arrogant. Annoying. Dickish."

She seemed to have those descriptions ready to go. He preferred to use one of his own. "Bossy."

"Wow, that wasn't even in my top ten, even though it fits." She shifted her chair to the right when someone pushed past her on the way to the bathroom. "I like my list better."

He didn't doubt that. "I'm not normally one who goes back and rethinks his actions."

"Are you one who apologizes?"

She sounded serious, so he gave her an honest answer. "Hardly."

"I figured." She leaned in with her elbows on the table. "So, tell me the truth. Did the senator make you come find me?"

"It's interesting you think anyone can *make* me do anything." No one had ever accused him of that before.

"I thought maybe the two of you were . . ." She waved a hand in the air.

He had no clue what that meant. "Yes?"

"You know."

"I actually don't. Finish the sentence." He pushed his cup to the side and leaned on his edge of the table. The move put them within easier whispering distance, though neither of them had lowered their voices all that much. He just sensed it was coming.

Then there was the part where he could smell her. Not sugary or like vanilla. This was something more sultry. A light touch of a floral scent, but with a bit of musk. It filled his head.

"I thought you might be together," Emery said.

He wasn't clear how he felt about the comment. It seemed to suggest he lacked fidelity, or the senator did. "I'm not sure her husband would approve of that."

"Hey, I don't care what consenting adults do in their private time. I'm not judging." This time she held up both hands in what looked like some sort of disingenuous mock surrender. "In fact, if you were together in that way she might have some sway over you and get you to actually answer one of my questions."

He was intrigued by how her mind worked. She made connections and looked for angles. Good skills, but this time her instincts or whatever was guiding her had misfired. He liked and respected the senator. He met her in the first place through her equally successful law partner husband.

Wren had received work from both of them and continued to cultivate both contacts. He did not fool around with married women and he couldn't really see the senator cheating. "No."

Another bathroom goer bumped into the side of her chair. This time she picked it up and moved it until she sat almost next to him, only a few feet away. "You're going to need to be more specific with that answer. We seem to have several comments flying around. What are you answering?"

"No, I'm not with the senator in any way except having worked with her." He moved both of their coffee cups out of spilling range. "And no, she did not send me."

"You just happened to be in this coffee shop again today."

"I came to find you." Which seemed obvious to him since he already told her that.

"But not apologize."

Emery could keep trying, but he had no intention of saying he was sorry. He wasn't. "I fear we're spinning in circles."

She stared at him. "The way you talk is endlessly fascinating. Annoying as hell, but also fascinating."

He had no idea how to respond to that, so he skipped ahead to his point. If he didn't finish this soon, his driver and probably Garrett would come storming in to find him. "I wanted to make sure you understood the facts."

"Which are?"

"I didn't know your cousin. I certainly didn't kidnap her and I don't know who did. I wasn't anywhere near the DC area when she was taken."

The main points, all of which pointed to him as being innocent, which he was. He lived back and forth between Michigan and Massachusetts at the time. He'd never even heard Tiffany's name until Emery gave it to him.

She tapped her fingernails against the tabletop. "Why was your name in Gavin Younger's file?"

The clicking echoed in his brain. "You mean your uncle. This is a family matter for you."

"I see you've been busy digging around in my personal business. How charming."

He couldn't exactly deny it, so he didn't try. "I have no idea why he had my name but, and here's my actual reason for talking to you today, I intend to find out."

"How?" She kept drumming. *Click. Click. Click.*

"It's what I do."

"I'm still unclear on the category of what it is you do as an actual job."

He glanced at her fingers, hoping she'd get the point and stop. Somehow the sound rose above the murmur of conversation in the packed shop. He didn't even know how that was possible. "I fix things."

"Ah, yes. You're all about the fixing." She sat back in her seat and put her hand on the back of his chair, right by his shoulder. "But answer one question."

The sudden closeness had his mind racing to other topics. "Possibly."

Then she shifted again and now their legs touched. She just kept moving. It was as if energy kept pinging around inside of her, pushing her to stay in motion. It was driving him crazy. Not annoyed crazy. No, not that at all. A different kind of crazy . . . the kind that came with bad decision making.

"You're hysterical," she said.

"I can assure you no one has ever said that before."

Her hair brushed against her cheek as she tucked

one leg under the other. "Why should I believe anything you say about Tiffany?"

"You don't have any reason to." It took all of his control not to put a hand on her leg and hold her there. He could sit still for hours while concentrating on a task. She couldn't seem to go without fidgeting for ten seconds.

She frowned at him, which seemed to be becoming a habit. "Yeah, I know. That was my point."

"Yet, I think you do know, at least on some level, that I'm telling the truth."

"You keep forgetting I don't know you at all." Her head tilted and her hair slid over her shoulder.

For a second he couldn't remember what they were talking about then it came winging back to him. "We need to make a deal."

"That sounds like a terrible thing for me to do."

"You don't even know the terms." That mouth and those full lips. Jesus, he couldn't see anything else.

His usual self-control abandoned him. She sat about a foot away from him now, maybe less, and he'd gone into an uncharacteristic tailspin. Instead of following along and holding his ground, his mind wandered. Something about her threw off his concentration. He didn't like the strange power she seemed to have over him, especially after such a short time.

Without thinking he took a sip of the coffee. The bitter liquid hit the back of his throat, reviving him. This is why he loved caffeine.

He tried to regain the upper hand, to the extent he ever possessed it. "I will track down the answer as to why my name was in the file and provide proof that I was not in the area when—"

"Proof I can corroborate. I'm not taking your word for it."

He had never met a woman who made his eye twitch and had him thinking about kissing at the same time. "Speaking of charming."

"Would you just believe anything I said?"

"Maybe." He hated to admit that answer wasn't a lie.

She clearly didn't agree because she snorted. "Oh, please."

A strange haze fell over him. It blocked the noise of the café and the constant shuffling of people around them. "In return for the intel, plus the corroboration, you will stop asking around about me. That's a dangerous game."

"You mean for you."

"No, Emery, for you. You are not the only person who wants to know more about me. If you give any indication that you actually do, you could walk into trouble."

She made a face. "This secrecy thing is a tad overdramatic, don't you think?"

That sobered him. He had the bodyguards to prove it. "No."

"It is when you combine it with the black suit . . ." She studied his jacket. "Do you own, like, twenty of them?"

He fought the urge to follow her gaze and look down. "We're discussing my fashion choices?"

She shrugged. "Just making an observation, but yes.

Fine. I'll agree to your deal, but I won't stop investigating you until I'm satisfied you're telling the truth and not involved."

It didn't take a master negotiator to see the trap. This is what he did for a living. He knew how to bait and what to give up. He didn't see that she was budging on much at all. "How are those good terms for me? I don't win anything."

"You poor thing."

Her sarcasm nearly knocked him over. "You clearly don't belong to the 'a male ego is a fragile thing' way of thinking."

"I don't care if it is or not. You'll have to get someone else to stroke yours."

The word vibrated through him. She knew what she was doing. She had to. "Interesting."

She reached for her cup and held it in a tight grip in front of her. "Frankly, I have a feeling you'll be fine if you don't get your way just this once."

He couldn't argue with that. She made a good case, and really, she'd poked at his curiosity until he couldn't stop thinking about her or her cousin. And he should leave it at that. Make the deal, go away and check in later. But *should* was a strange word . . .

He reached into his pocket and slipped out the small card he'd placed there in the car ride over. "Here."

She looked at the block lettering then turned it over. Then did it again. "What's this?"

"My phone number."

She flipped the card around. "It's actually just a number. No name."

"Yes."

"Weird." She dropped it on the table as if it were on fire. "Look, I get that you're hot and all. Not to me, of course, but how someone who never actually heard you speak could find you to be—"

"What are you talking about?" He almost preferred the fidgeting to the babbling.

"I was trying to coddle that fragile ego of yours, but truth is I'm not interested."

It took him a second for his brain to catch up. He smiled, not because of what she said but because the thought of the card being about something else even popped into her mind. *Very interesting.* "It's for you to contact me if you get any more information."

Her face actually fell. "Oh."

"It's private. Only I answer it." Only a handful of people shared that access. Most had a work number or another cell number he used for cases with particular clients and his employees. This one truly belonged to a very small circle.

She turned the card around and studied it. Ran her fingers over the numbers. "You know I could do a reverse search on this and find out everything about you."

"No, you couldn't." She continued to underestimate him, which was an odd sensation. No one else did that. Of course, few others ever stood up to him and he couldn't think of anyone other than Garrett who would have the nerve to track him down.

She shrugged. "I have resources."

He knew anything he said would sound condescending, so he kept as close to the facts as possible. "They aren't better than mine. I guarantee it."

"Huh." She turned over the card, looked at every angle one last time, before pocketing it.

He had no idea what point she was trying to make. "Which means what?"

"Deal."

"Good." But he wasn't sure it was. She'd gotten what she wanted and letting that happen could prove difficult going forward.

She tilted her head to the side again. "So, do I still call you Brian or are you going to tell me your full name?"

He decided that was his signal to leave. He should have dropped the card and walked out five minutes ago, but something about her made him want to linger . . . and that was enough to make him get up now.

He took the coffee with him. No reason to waste that. "I'll be in touch."

She nodded. "I'll count on that."

LATER THAT AFTERNOON Garrett walked into Wren's office without bothering to knock. He carried three thick folders and a computer tablet. "Tell me who Tiffany Younger is again."

Wren kept working. "Emery Finn's cousin who went missing years ago."

Garrett set his armload on the desk in front of Wren. "Oh, that clears it right up."

There was no need to put off this conversation. This was the sort of thing Garrett would poke and question until he had the specifics.

Wren sat forward and opened the top file. "Emery thinks I'm involved."

"Yeah, you told me that yesterday." Garrett put his hand on the folder, slapping it closed before Wren could read a word. "You're not. Game over. Walk away and be done with her, right?"

"Does Ms. Finn strike you as someone who will just take my word and scurry off?"

A growl rumbled in Garrett's throat. "Oh, shit."

This did not sound good. "What?"

"You're more than just intrigued by her. There's something else going on here."

Three nights of research made that one hard to deny. "Of course. This woman, Tiffany, is missing, presumed dead."

"No." Garrett made a dramatic groaning sound. "I meant about Emery."

Wren refused to discuss her. It was bad enough he kept imagining her naked and wondering what her hands might feel like as she touched him. That he thought about her last night when he should have been catching a few hours of sleep. That comments she made would come back to him and make him smile.

Her face kept floating through his mind. That impressive body. The way she looked on the verge of rolling her eyes every time he opened his mouth.

Not that he had any intention of divulging how intrigued he was by any of that. "I'm doing this as a favor."

Garrett stared at him. "To whom?"

Good question. "The senator."

"Try again."

"Is it too late in the day to fire you?"

"You usually threaten to fake fire me around noon. You're late today." Garrett folded his arms across his chest. "Of course, you might not remember that since you were out on a coffee date again this morning."

That fucking surveillance made having some privacy impossible. Wren toyed with the idea of canceling it. If Emery didn't seem like the type who could walk right into trouble while digging around for clues and throwing his name around, he might have. "That was nothing."

"What about your visit to her house?"

He should have known Garrett would find that out no matter what he threatened. "I have the sudden urge to fire people."

"Not going to happen."

Rather than debate employee relations or his interest in her, which he continued to hope was nonexistent or an aberration or a momentary confusion, Wren focused on the bigger issue. "I want to clear my name."

"You haven't been implicated. Part of your name was written on a piece of paper on some random guy's notepad. How is this even an issue worth discussing?"

Wren couldn't figure out if that looked bad for him or not. Didn't really matter. He was all for stoking a dangerous reputation and letting that benefit him at work, but he couldn't tolerate this. Other sins he accepted without question, but not this one. "The missing girl's father. Not a random guy."

"Okay, look." Garrett dropped his arms. Sighed. Even shifted his weight around.

Whatever he was about to say made Wren nervous, and he did not get nervous. "Just spit it out."

"We've known each other for a long time," Garrett continued. "Tell me this is not about—"

"You'd be wise to stop right there." Whatever connections might exist between his mother and Emery's missing friend in terms of understanding the toll that sort of devastation takes, Wren refused to think his interest in one was a result of living with the other. He'd walked out of therapy years ago and never went back. He didn't need an informal version of it now.

"You have a soft spot for missing women."

That was a safe topic. Wren could keep it off a personal level. "We all should."

Garrett swore under his breath. "Don't try to make me sound like an ass. You know what I'm saying."

From anyone else . . . actually, that couldn't come from anyone else. No one else in the building knew about his real identity or his mother or the father he never talked about. "This isn't about my mother."

Garrett didn't move. "Are you sure?"

"Did you get a psychology degree when I wasn't looking?"

"You have to admit there are parallels here."

He actually didn't. "Not any I'm willing to discuss."

Silence screamed through the room.

After a few seconds, Garrett nodded. "So, we're going to open a case on Tiffany Younger. Got it."

With that emotional trap avoided, Wren pushed on. He needed to stay technical and distanced. He could do that if he thought of Tiffany as a case and not a person.

Never mind the fact he could compartmentalize like that made him a shit.

"You're to operate as if the case is ours even though, in fact, there is no case," Wren explained.

"Didn't I just say that? You know, right before you tried to fire me."

Wren could hear the amusement in Garrett's voice. The building tension evaporated and they returned to their usual back and forth. "What's the point of owning a company that deals in information if I can't use it on a personal matter?"

"Huh. That almost sounds logical. I hate that."

"Only you would hate logic."

"Wait." Garrett glanced at the ceiling. "I'm thinking of a way around agreeing with you."

"While you're doing that, get started." Wren reached out and grabbed the files, stacking them on his lap.

"You having coffee again tomorrow?"

Wren refused to look up and see Garrett's annoying grin. Hearing it in his voice was bad enough. "You have your own office. Work in there."

"This is going to backfire, you know."

That time Wren glanced up. "I won't let it."

"We'll see."

CHAPTER 10

Emery worked later than planned that Friday. The early summer light had faded, so now she walked from the metro to her Foggy Bottom apartment in the dark.

Not a big deal. The area hopped with activity. People poured in and out of nearby restaurants and bars. She spied a line of red brake lights as cars backed up at the intersections. The drunken revelry was still a few hours away, but from the sound of the yelling and cheering coming from the line of bars and restaurants around the block, it sounded as if a few people got an early start.

The last two turns put her in a more residential section. Multistory town houses divided into multiple residences. In the spring the trees budded and framed the street in a flurry of pink. Tonight it was just sticky hot and not very pleasant.

In part because of the air-conditioning, she did love her place. It had been listed as a junior one bedroom on the street level of an older red brick building, which was code for an oversized studio with a partial wall separating off the actual bed. Apparently once the landlord tagged it with the whole "junior" thing she got to charge more. Emery thought that sucked, but she didn't get that much of a say. Plus, the apartment had the benefit of being familiar. She'd moved in during her final year at George Washington University.

Her sneakers hit against the pavement as she walked at a steady clip. Between Wren and her father, she'd wrestled with anxiety from the time she got up to the time she went to bed. She hoped the fresh air would clear her head, but there wasn't even a touch of a breeze. She'd be sweating through her silk shirt by the time she got to her door.

The original plan was to leave the office a bit early, grab dinner and settle down with a mindless movie, preferably one without family drama. But her dad had called several times to complain about her leaving their dinner earlier in the week. He insisted on seeing her again, but she claimed to have a work issue. Guilt then compelled her to actually hang around the office until everyone else had gone and she'd blown past her scheduled leave time.

Wren hadn't contacted her since yesterday's coffee shop meeting. But after he just showed up there she half expected to see him pop up everywhere. She wished she hated that idea more than she did. She wished she hated it at all.

She blamed the handsome face and that whole broody, mysterious thing he had going on. That type never appealed to her before and she wanted to believe it still didn't, but she kept thinking about him. Not in a he's-dangerous sort of way. No, this was in an I-wonder-if-he-kisses-as-good-as-he-looks sort of way.

Damn him for being in her head.

She thought about the whole private number thing, how she acted like she wasn't interested despite the fact her heart had swooped a stupid loop-de-loop in her chest when he handed it over. Even now the note with his number sat in the drawer right next to her bed. She'd added it to her cell contact list under a fake name. Clearly he had her as paranoid as he was, but she'd kept the note. She had no idea why and refused to believe it was because she wanted some sort of connection with him.

Really, damn him.

Just thinking about the men hanging around her life right now made her exhausted. She hit the last corner and had to drag her body to keep moving. Whistling helped. So did focusing on the . . . *whoa*.

She stopped three houses before her own because Wren stood there, right on the sidewalk in his usual dark suit. For a second she worried just thinking about him had conjured him up.

He stared.

She stared back.

Then she noticed the activity behind him. A police car and another dark sedan with its lights on parked right out front of her building. An officer moved around in the main doorway by the mailboxes, talking to one of her neighbors. Part of Emery wanted to run to Wren and demand an explanation. The rest of her wanted to stay put until she woke up from whatever hottie-induced dream she was in at the moment.

Her choice didn't end up mattering all that much because Wren walked toward her. Using long strides, he ate up the distance between them and stopped in front of her.

She said the first thing that popped into her head. "What are you doing here?"

"Someone tried to break into your apartment."

"How can that . . ." Her world tilted.

In a flash, he was there with a hand on her arm. "Emery?"

His face came back into focus. A wave of shock hit next. She'd never been robbed. The building had security and an alarm system, which she knew were only as effective as long as the people in the building didn't do something silly, like let a complete stranger walk right in. That had happened in the building across the street last year.

He snapped his fingers. "Emery?"

"Don't do that." The sound brought her winging back to the here and now. "It's annoying."

"You sure sound fine." He dropped his hand. "The color rushed out of your face for a second, but it's coming back along with that tone."

She thought about pushing past him but wasn't willing to give him the easy out. "What tone?"

"The one where you sound like you're barely tolerating my existence."

"Okay, that's about right." Then the reality of the moment hit her with full force. "You're at my house again."

He nodded. "Yes."

Of course he thought that explained everything.

Standing there in his usual black suit, but this time with a blue tie. He was really changing it up. "I thought we talked about this."

"You threatened me with a bat. I ignored it."

"You're being over-the-top creepy again." Just when she thought he'd pulled back from the edge and eased into human territory, this sort of thing happened. Not that she knew what was really happening, but she sure planned to find out. "Did you break into my house?"

He had the nerve to frown at her. "Does that strike you as my style?"

"No, you'd slip through the air-conditioning vent or something." Though she had to admit for a shadowy figure who insisted no one know his name or be able to find him, he seemed to spend a lot of time in public. Near her. On her street.

This time he sighed at her. "Your imagination is a bit out of control."

She was about to demand a real explanation when a familiar face came into view. He walked right up behind Wren and stopped beside him. "Detective Cryer?"

Rick Cryer, the Maryland police officer from Tiffany's case. Here in DC, at her house. This felt like the oddest walk down memory lane ever. Worse, Emery had no idea what was going on, and she hated that. Being vulnerable, not having any control, having to depend on others . . . not her thing.

He smiled as he held out a hand to her. "Retired detective, and please call me Rick."

She shook his hand as her gaze went from him to Wren and back again. "What are you doing here?"

The detective hitched a thumb in Wren's general direction. "He called me."

She was two seconds away from needing to sit down. She wasn't the fainting type and had no intention of starting that nonsense now, but with Wren just popping up in her life, knowing the people she knew, some of her blood left her brain. She couldn't concentrate long enough and hard enough to put the pieces together in her head.

She inhaled nice and deep and tried to keep her voice from rising to the screaming-for-her-life range. "Okay, someone explain."

Rick gestured behind him. "His people—"

"Okay, wait." Already he'd lost her.

Wren turned to the detective. "She's more difficult than usual this evening. I blame the shock of the police cars."

"Stop talking." She actually put a hand on Wren's chest. She meant to shove him out of the way, but she stayed there . . . touching him. Go figure. She looked at Rick, the detective she'd known for years and always trusted. "Do you know Wren?"

Rick shook his head. "Not in person, but I do know Brian."

"You mean this guy." She gestured toward Wren.

The detective threw her a funny look, too, as if her question didn't make much sense. "Of course."

She refused to believe she was the confused one. "Don't say it like that."

His eyes narrowed. "I don't understand."

"So, you know Brian, here, and his boss, Wren." She

waited for the detective to nod. "Is Wren a first name or a last name?"

"Let's stay focused." Wren put his hand over hers while he talked to the detective. "Is anything missing inside?"

She tried to ignore the warmth and how much bigger his palm was than hers. And forget about the energy surging through her. That meant nothing. She would make sure it meant nothing.

"We'll need her to look around, but it looks pretty clean," Rick said.

She let her hand slide down Wren's chest toward his stomach, just for a second and only a few inches. Enough to feel the firmness and send her mind scrambling again.

She shook her head to push out the wild thoughts and the images that formed right behind them. Added in a bit of throat clearing as she backed up a step. "There actually was a break-in?"

"Brian said Wren's people saw the lights on inside and some movement, noted you weren't home and called me. I called the police." The detective listed off the events as if the words cleared up anything.

Wren's people? "None of this makes sense."

The blue light from the police car snapped off and the neighbors wandering around on the street started to head back to the front of their own buildings. The dark sedan didn't move, and she was pretty sure she saw two guys sitting in it.

Wren touched her arm, right by the elbow. "Maybe you should do a walk-through?"

She pulled away. The whole touching thing was not going to make the next few minutes run any smoother. "All of a sudden you know all the police lingo and hang out with detectives?"

"Wren helped us with an internal department issue a few years back. Sent Brian to work with us," Rick explained.

That seemed too convenient for her taste. "I'm sure he did."

"Maybe we should check inside?" Wren ended the comment by throwing her the look a teacher might give a naughty student. Not the sexy, grown-up-play way. No, the actual you're-going-to-regret-this way.

Then there was the use of the word *we*. She ignored that, figuring there was no way to keep Wren out of her house at this point. Knowing him, he'd already been through and cataloged everything.

"I guess saying no would be futile." She whispered the comment under her breath to Wren as soon as someone called the detective away.

Wren stared down at her. "You need to ask yourself if you feel better with me by your side or watching from a distance."

That was easy—neither. "You're being creepy again."

"I fear that will be a reoccurring theme in our relationship."

A few days ago that sort of statement might have sounded ominous. Now the way he talked started sounding normal to her. Except for one glaring thing. "Relationship?"

"Believe it or not." He dipped his head as he lowered his voice. "I've seen more of you over the last few days than almost any other person I know."

She couldn't tell from his deep voice if he thought that was a good thing or a bad thing. It did confirm his "loner" personality in her mind. It fit with everything else she knew about him, which was not all that much. But the guy gave off a vibe and she was still trying to find the right word to describe it. Moody, maybe?

"You know that fact speaks to your weirdness, right?" she asked.

He exhaled. "At least around you I'll never have to worry about my ego going out of control."

"You strike me as the type who needs to be reined in."

"Are you planning on reining me in, Emery?" He sounded amused by the thought.

She was too busy trying to ignore the sexual overtone. She knew she should end that. Give a good "that's never going to happen" lecture and cut off any possibility of him getting the wrong idea.

Yeah, she didn't feel like doing any of those things. "I don't know yet."

This time he let out a short humming noise. "I'm eager to see what you decide."

That made two of them.

CHAPTER 11

Rather than really answer, Emery started moving. She walked down the sidewalk and up the stairs with Wren at her side. She didn't need her keys, but couldn't seem to let go of them. They jangled in her hand. She heard the noise in the background as her gaze scanned over every inch of the place. Soft yellow walls lined with photographs from the summer she spent traveling through Europe on a budget postgraduation. Her coffee mug still sitting on the kitchen counter. The calendar on the fridge.

It all looked to be in order. She turned to tell Wren and ran right into his chest.

He put his hands on her arms to steady her then dropped them just as fast. "You're still jumpy."

She was ten seconds away from leaping out of her skin. "Do you blame me?"

"It wasn't an accusation."

For some reason a lot of what he said sounded that way. She didn't feel like fighting over something stupid, so she let that drop. She had bigger issues.

After a quick check to make sure no one was listening, she asked the question kicking around her brain. "The detective doesn't know you're Wren."

"Almost no one does."

She wasn't sure what to say to that . . . or about the severe frown he shot her. "Except me."

"Trust me, you knowing surprises me as much as it surprises you." He exhaled. "And I'd like to keep the circle small on who knows that detail."

It kind of figured he thought of his real name as a detail. "Agreed."

His eyes widened. "Really?"

Now that was insulting. He acted like she couldn't keep a secret or that she'd blackmail him with the information. Well, she might claim to do that just to poke at him, but she'd never actually divulge his secret. He went by a top-secret name and she figured he had a reason for that. Probably had something to do with being difficult and eccentric, but she'd still hold the confidence because it meant something that he'd shared with her. What, she wasn't quite sure.

"Don't touch anything." She mostly meant the boxes stacked up next to her love seat. She knew he had to have noticed. The fact they said *Tiffany Younger* on the sides in thick black ink was a giveaway.

His gaze never left her face. "This isn't my first crime scene."

"Who says that sort of thing?" When she first met him she'd thought the way he put sentences together carried a message, telling her to be wary. Now she wondered if he truly believed normal people talked that way. "You do that on purpose, right?"

He frowned. "What?"

"You make a statement like that so that I'll wonder

if you're a criminal or law enforcement of some type. You want to keep me guessing."

Rick walked up behind Wren. "You think he's a criminal?"

She had no idea what to think at this point. She just kept shaking the keys in her hand. "Is he?"

"Of course not." The detective stared at her closed fist. "Didn't Gavin introduce you two?"

Her hand stopped moving for a second and her stomach dropped. "What?"

"Explain what you mean by that," Wren said at the same time.

"Before he died . . . well, he was understandably a mess," Rick said. "Can't blame him. Tiffany's case has haunted me for years. Imagine what it does to a father." He shook his head. "Anyway, his drinking kept getting worse, destroying his body faster than the cancer could at some points."

"You gave him Wren's name." Wren didn't sound too happy about that piece of information.

Rick must have picked up on the tone because he held up a hand in a placating gesture. "I mentioned that I knew a guy who might be able to help."

"Who could do what, exactly?" It struck her that for a guy who supposedly lived in the shadows a lot of people sure seemed to seek him out. Fake name or not, she'd bet he hated that.

"Fix things." The detective looked from her to Wren. "Look, I'm not sure if Wren takes on cases like this, and I know I should have asked first. I just wanted to give the guy something."

"It's fine." Without breaking eye contact with Rick, Wren put his hand over hers and the annoying jingling stopped. "It also explains why the name Wren was in that file."

She slipped her hand out from under his and shoved the keys in her pocket. "Like so much else with you, it feels convenient."

Wren gave the detective a man-to-man look. "She thinks Wren is dangerous and that, by extension, so am I."

Rick shrugged. "That's probably fair."

Anxious to break the tension rumbling around inside her, Emery started walking. She pivoted around the police officer standing in the middle of her family room and kept going. At the far end of the room she turned the corner and looked into the small alcove that housed her bed. Covers thrown over the pillows, which passed as her way of making the bed. Some clothes stacked on the windowsill. Nothing weird, which was a relief.

She heard the click of footsteps against her hardwood floor a beat too late. She swung around, but Wren was already there, staring at the partial wall directly across from her bed.

"Well, damn. That's impressive." He had his hands on his hips and his focus centered on her private work.

Her gaze followed his. She didn't really need to study anything. She knew every inch of the handmade mosaic. The photos of Tiffany. The newspaper clippings. Her notes. She'd taped it all up there. Stared at it every night before she went to bed. Never let the case move even an inch out of her mind.

Rick traced his fingers over the lines of handwritten notes before facing her again. "You promised me you would stop doing this and leave the investigating to the police."

"You retired." She'd trusted him to see it through. He cared, followed the case until he suffered a heart attack and had to back down. Even now he tracked clues, but it wasn't enough. Too much time had passed without any new leads.

"This isn't your job. It's not really Wren's or his company's either, but I would feel better with his people, led by Brian, digging around than with you doing it."

Wren dropped his hands to his sides. "I agree and we'll take care of it."

"Do you need to talk to Wren first?" the detective asked.

Wren nodded. "We're good."

She tried to take in the concern in their voices and the looks of horror on their faces. Their worry moved through the room and wrapped around her. She expected the reaction from one of them, but not both.

She looked at Wren. Really looked, trying to read him. "You're stepping in?"

"Believe it or not, the idea of someone snatching young women off the street is pretty disturbing to me."

She had no idea what to say to that. What he said sounded decent and genuine, but she couldn't shake the fear that letting go of any part of her personal quest meant letting go of Tiffany.

All those memories of racing home from school only to pick up the phone and talk to Tiffany again.

The back and forth to each other's houses. Them playing while their parents sat around the family room and did whatever grown-ups did back then. Talking about boys and what a loser their biology teacher was. When she closed her eyes and concentrated, Emery could still hear her cousin's voice. Faint but there. She couldn't remember much about her mother other than her face and how quiet she was. How she could blend into the background and never contradicted her father. But Tiffany's memory lingered.

"Is anything missing in here?" Rick asked.

Emery shook her head and answered without really thinking. "Not that I can tell. I can go through the boxes and make sure it's all there."

Not that it would matter. She'd committed most of the Tiffany files to memory. Tiny details, big items. What people said. She was the foremost expert on Tiffany, something Emery never wanted to be.

He let out a frustrated huffing sound. "It's odd since we saw the surveillance video. Someone was in there and ran when Wren's people flushed them out."

The words clicked together in Emery's head. "Video?"

The detective talked right over her. "Do you have somewhere to stay tonight?"

Wren picked that moment to shift. He stopped staring at her wall and put his back to it. "She can stay with me."

"No." She almost screamed the answer because it struck her as a terrible idea. Her common sense tended to fizzle with him around. There, in the small apartment—yeah, terrible idea. "I'm fine."

"My money is on Brian to win this debate."

She refused to take that bet. "Wait—"

"The police are going to want to talk to you. I'll see if I can cut down on some of that, but you both have my number." Rick shook Wren's hand then looked at her. "Be safe, Emery."

She continued to stare at Wren. It was just the two of them . . . in her bedroom.

"What?" he asked.

"You need to tell him." She knew he liked secrecy, but she didn't. The idea of living that way made her head spin.

He didn't pretend to misunderstand. "Why?"

"I get you have this need for anonymity, but he's a retired detective." She sighed. "If you're going to work on this case you'll be talking to him. I'll be talking with him. When we're all together I could slip up."

"Is that a warning?" Wren kept on staring and his voice stayed flat.

This wasn't about winning or scoring points. "I'm really just being practical."

After a few seconds he nodded. "If the need arises, I'll fill him in."

The importance of his words hit her head-on. "That's a big deal to you, right? Conceding that?"

"The biggest."

She didn't know what to say to that so she jumped to the other topic on her mind. "You've been to crime scenes. You know the detectives."

"Yes." He drew out the word until it lasted for three syllables.

"You have people watching me and there's apparently a tape, which we're going to talk about at some point." She tried to put it all together in her mind and make the idea of this stranger swooping in make sense. "Now you're going to step up and work the case, fix it all somehow."

Police continued to walk around the family room area just on the other side of the wall. She could hear Rick's voice and someone else's as they talked. Every light was on in the apartment and every nerve in her body kept pinging, but all she could see was the man in front of her. The one who confused her when they first met and continued to confuse her, but in a very different way now.

"Do you still think I'm a killer?" he asked.

She didn't. She hadn't since she talked to the senator. Something about the way people in power knew Wren and talked about him with admiration rather than fear had her opinion morphing. But that didn't mean she understood him. Trouble was, she was starting to *want* to. "I can't get a handle on what you are."

"Someone who wants to help you."

"When people say that, I get nervous." A lot of well-meaning people had messed up cases she'd worked on. They got the facts wrong or came up with wild theories. She waded through all of that noise at work. She hated that the cycle now repeated in her private life.

"Isn't giving people closure, assisting them through this process, what you do for a living?"

It was as if he read her mind, which was truly annoying. The one defense she had against this guy was to lock him out of her thoughts. That and fake outrage, but it was getting harder to hold on to that. "Don't be logical."

"Sorry." He smiled as he moved in closer. "Are you really okay? Seeing the police cars had to be a shock."

"I will be once I know why you have me under surveillance. No bat this time. Just a simple question." It really wasn't an accusation. More of a curiosity, which was so unlike her. She came out fighting. With him, she relished the verbal battle but couldn't seem to maintain her outrage.

"Because you were trying to find me and I didn't know why. It started out for my protection." He took another step, closed the gap between them. "Now it's for yours."

They stood at the end of her bed, in the small space between the mattress and the wall. She should guide them back into the family room. Keep them well away from this part of the apartment.

She moved in closer. "Stop it. I'm not kidding."

"What are you referring to exactly?"

That was a great question. "Whatever is happening here. The bold way you burst into my life."

"Actually, you tracked me down."

They stood just inches apart. Without thinking she rested her hand against his chest again, loving the stretch of his muscles under her palm just as much this time. "Don't change the subject."

He slipped his hand over hers and slowly massaged her skin with his thumb. A gentle back and forth that had her mesmerized as she looked up into those green eyes.

"I would point out that if not for my men, the person who broke in here still could have been in your place when you got home." His voice dipped lower. "I can't tolerate that."

She tried to gasp in more air, to get her lungs to function, but she felt winded and a little dizzy. "Don't try to scare me either."

"I'm trying to get you to be practical. Speaking of that, I can put you in a hotel."

She leaned in until her lips hovered over his. "I can put me in a hotel."

He lifted his other hand and tucked her hair behind her ear. Let his palm skim over the side of her head. "It wasn't a comment on your financial stability."

She struggled to keep up with the conversation while her heartbeat galloped in her chest. "Yeah, I know." Her breaths came out in pants now. "I really just want to be in my own house."

"Then my people aren't moving."

"I . . ." This close the brightness of his eyes stunned her. The shade came close to that of newly mowed grass in summer. So clear. So unblinking. "Okay."

His eyebrows lifted. "I expected a fight on that."

She couldn't raise any anger. Her thoughts were jumbled. Trying to process it all at once with so little space to think—Wren having her followed, someone in her house, her whole life getting turned upside down— sucked the life out of her. "I want to say it's because I'm not a martyr and not stupid, but I fear the real answer is that I'm too exhausted to go to battle with you."

"That's almost disappointing." His fingertips skimmed over her shoulder.

The whole touching-her-but-not-enough thing started a revving deep in her stomach. Not that she wanted him to stop. Chalk it up to adrenaline, emotional upheaval or too much caffeine. Something inside her kept changing the more time she spent with him.

But she wasn't a pushover, and he needed to know that. "At some point we are going to have a long discussion about boundaries."

"That's more like the answer I expect from you." He gave her arm a squeeze. "But must we?"

He was right *there*. All compelling and tall and kissable.

Yeah, that couldn't happen. She backed up as she inhaled nice and deep. Tried to force the smart, defense-oriented part of her brain to click into action. "I'm sure tonight was some weird fluke thing. Mistaken identity or whatever."

"The lock wasn't broken."

Her insides froze. "Your point?"

"I was just making a comment." He straightened his tie. "Now I'll go."

A change came over him. She watched it happen but couldn't really say what shifted. He didn't get taller, because that just seemed silly, but he suddenly took up more space.

The low mumble of talking from the other room filtered back to her. The thought of being alone, even if his men watched . . . she'd never sleep. "Do you . . ."

"Yes?"

"You know."

He shook his head. "Actually, no. I don't."

Just once he could make a conversation easy instead of hard. "You're going to make me ask."

"Mind reading is not one of my skills." But he knew. That hint of a smile suggested he did. "In addition to that, I've been accused of being controlling, along with other things. I'm not going to presume anything."

She shifted her weight from foot to foot. She wanted to kick the cycle where she saw him, her insides started dancing and then the fidgeting began. She dealt in high stress situations all day and never shifted around like a nervous teen. Not until him.

"I never ask anyone for anything. That's sort of my thing." He had her babbling. She bit down on her bottom lip to stop.

"Understood."

She was hoping for more of a response than that. "I don't really want to now."

His smile grew a little bit wider. "But you're going to have to say the words. I don't want any confusion. You've already used the word *creepy* at least once tonight."

"With good reason."

"Emery, ask."

"Fine." He could get her whipped around and ticked off faster than anyone else she knew. "Would you stay and help me direct the police traffic in and out of here?"

"Of course." He nodded. "I'll stay until you're comfortable enough for me to leave. But my guards stay no matter what."

Relief whooshed through her. But he got his role here all wrong. He didn't make her feel comfortable. The exact opposite. She got all tingly and her brain went haywire. But when he said he'd keep her safe it felt like a vow. One she could count on.

"You still scare me a little." She didn't know why she admitted that, but it was absolutely true.

There was no mistaking his smile now. "The feeling is mutual."

CHAPTER 12

Wren was pretty sure when he looked back on the last hour he would want to kick his ass. Getting called out into the open by his men to deal with a fizzled break-in was one thing. He talked with an old acquaintance and handled the police on Emery's behalf. Now, alone with her in the apartment, he stood by the refrigerator as if this were a regular occurrence and any of this was normal for him to do.

He craved routine. He enjoyed going home at night, in the darkness. The last few nights he'd poured over every last scrap of intel he could find on Tiffany's case. Rick Cryer was clear about one thing—they'd had potential suspects and no real evidence to charge any of them. Tiffany's own father had been in the spotlight for a long time, but the detective thought he was clean.

Not that the case was the thing on Wren's mind right now. No, the woman standing in the middle of her family room, looking around with a glazed expression on her face, took that prize.

She'd showered and changed into something she called lounge pants. Not really a concept he was familiar with, but he recognized sweatpants, and the navy bottoms looked close . . . except for the formfitting part. He'd hoped she'd walk out wearing bulky over-sized clothing. No such luck. Even now she tugged at the bottom of her white V-neck T-shirt.

But he wasn't a fucking animal. She'd been through a lot tonight and, well, for thirteen years. She needed a break and not for him to make an ill-timed pass. "Feel better?"

She spun around and stared at her hands as she turned them over. "It's weird, right? Nothing is missing and nothing happened, yet I can't stop shaking."

"Nothing?" It appeared they had very different definitions of that word.

She shrugged. "You know what I mean."

"There's nothing weird about being scared." Though he doubted she let herself go there very often.

His quick conversation with the detective suggested Emery had spent her entire adult life digging around in the investigation about Tiffany. She'd ticked off one of the detectives on the case when he insisted the runaway angle was more likely than the kidnap angle and she exploded.

She dropped her arms to her sides and stopped moving around. "You get scared a lot, do you?"

She'd made it clear more than once that she thought he was a robot or something worse. That sort of thing usually didn't bother him, but hearing it from her had his back teeth grinding together. "It's a normal reaction."

"You're familiar with normal?"

He stepped out of the kitchen area and walked toward her. Didn't get right next to her because he needed her to be sure she wanted his comfort. "Tell me what you need."

"I don't know." She let out a shuddering breath. "This doesn't make sense."

"This?"

"I have friends and my dad lives close," she said as she took step after step. "I should have called one of them."

Not him. That was the unsaid ending of that sentence.

She stopped in front of him. Despite her mighty personality and the way she stood up to him, she looked tiny to him right then. Probably had something to do with being in her bare feet. With the way she curled her purple painted toenails under.

She was pretty tall at five-eight or so. There was nothing fragile about her. She didn't come off as easy to cry or break down. And her body . . . all curvy and hot.

So interesting.

So fuckable.

Right now he needed to forget that last part. "Why didn't you ask someone else to stay with you?"

"I have absolutely no idea." She lifted her hands as if she was going to touch him again, but then let them fall.

The memory of her touch still burned through him. The way she reached out, seemingly without thinking, and formed a physical connection when she needed it. He liked that side of her. All sides of her actually.

This time he took the lead. He'd peeled off his suit jacket earlier and now stood in front of her in the rest of his usual outfit, right down to the perfectly knotted tie.

He rested his hands on the sides of her waist. "You're going to be okay."

"You don't have to stay." But she moved in, leaned her weight against him and the side of her face against his shoulder.

He could smell the soap she used. Feel the softness of her skin. They combined in gentle torture. The kind he couldn't walk away from.

His fingers slipped through her hair. "You should eat something."

"I'll throw up."

He winced, but not that she could see. "Or we could skip food."

Vomiting and crying—he wasn't really great at handling either. The sound of gagging made him join in, and that was the kind of thing that ruined a guy's tough image.

She glanced up at him with a frown. "Do you want something?"

Now, there was an open-ended question. He went with what he guessed was her actual intent. "I do eat, you know."

She didn't look convinced. "There's leftover Chinese food in the refrigerator."

The magic words.

"My favorite." If the rice didn't result in extra gym time, he'd eat Chinese food every single day. Easy, fast and didn't require more than a fork. It appealed to the time management part of his brain.

She pulled back as the frown deepened. "I don't think of you as having a favorite food."

"What do you imagine me doing?"

"That sounds a bit naughty." Her hands clenched against him as she talked.

Some of the blood left his brain. "Does it?"

"You come off as the type to go out and have power dinners. Sit around with the other rich guys, smoking cigars and talking deals."

That was about as far from how he lived his life as she could get. "Never."

Her fingers all but massaged his muscles now. "Which part?"

He took a second to clear his throat. Tried to ignore the feel of her lower half resting against his and how her face was *right there* in front of him. "All of it."

"Surely, you have friends."

At first the conversation struck him as strange. Mundane yet weirdly personal at the same time. It took a second for his brain to catch up and for him to realize she was trying to get to know him. Not a bad plan since he was standing in her apartment and danger did seem to be knocking at the door. He just wondered if she realized it.

Not one to play games, he tested. Ignored the tension ratcheting up and dove in. "You know that in some conversations you like to highlight how different I am. In other conversations you seem to want me to be like everyone else."

"Oh, I don't think you're like anyone else." She flattened her palms and ran them across his shoulders. "I just wonder about the everyday things."

The nerve endings kicked to life everywhere she touched. "Like?"

"I can't see you standing over the sink, eating food out of a white container."

That's exactly how he did it. "Should I use a plate?"

"It's just . . . well, the sink thing sounds like something I would do."

Were they really talking about food? He couldn't tell. "Maybe we have more in common than you think."

"That's scary."

Yeah, no kidding. "For both of us."

She jabbed a finger into his chest. "See, I think that was a joke."

"I have the ability to form them now and then." He was quickly losing the will to talk, but that was something else. Had more to do with the pounding need to strip her naked and see how all that fire inside her translated in bed.

"Now I think you're trying to make me forget about the police and what happened tonight, which I'm still not sure was an actual 'thing,' but who knows." She brushed her fingers along his jawline. "That's sweet actually."

He felt anything but sweet at the moment. Hot, punishingly turned on, half-ready to dunk his head in the ice cube tray. Those fit.

Despite the need growing inside him and how much he wanted her, he focused on trying to level her out. He'd never considered himself selfish when it came to women. He aimed for satisfaction and all that, but admittedly, that was sex. He did fine there. Talking? Not his strongest skill.

He tried anyway. He rubbed a hand up and down her back. "Emery, you had a scare. You are allowed to feel shaky."

"Do you ever feel shaky?"

"Other than right now?"

"Oh, please." She laughed, but then her hand flew to her mouth and she stepped out of his hold. Kept moving until a good three feet separated them.

This was new, or rather it was a return to their first meeting. "Problem?"

"Do you have a wife?"

He had no idea how her mind got there . . . or why. "What?"

"It just hit me." She rubbed a hand over her forehead as she went back to walking in circles.

"My marital status?"

"Oh, my God. I'm rubbing my hands all over you." She shook her head.

He watched her, fascinated by the amount of energy that must surge through her. She seemed to get nervous and then every muscle needed to move. The pacing started. She traveled back and forth in front of the love seat, nearly tripping over the boxes she had stacked there.

Watching her gave him a bit of a headache, but he couldn't look away. "Any chance you could stop moving around for a second?"

"This is ridiculous." She stared at him. "I don't know anything about you, starting with the basics like your marital status and actual name."

"Is it possible you're fixating on all of this to avoid your concern about the break-in?" First, she thought he was a criminal. Then creepy, which was a term she still threw out now and then, and now married. He was quite the catch in her eyes.

He knew he should be offended, but he got it. He hadn't exactly opened the doors and provided a wealth of information to her.

"How about a real answer?" Her eyes grew wider. "Is there a wife?"

"Not anymore."

"Is she dead?"

What the hell? "That is quite a question."

"Feel free to answer it." She still looked ready to bolt. Never mind that this was her apartment.

He didn't talk about his personal life—ever. Not just because he coveted privacy, though that was a substantial part of it. He didn't want to put anyone else's life in danger by association. The people he dealt with, some of those who found themselves on the wrong side of his negotiating tactics, grew desperate fast. Landing anyone else in the crossfire due to his work choices was not a risk he was willing to take.

"We're divorced, have been for years," he explained. Shauna had remarried and been out of his thoughts for years. His office kept tabs on her, only to the extent they knew where she was and that she was safe.

That was a different time in his life. He lived under a different name and focused on different things. Back then he was emotional, driven for answers about his mother. On the edge and always a single step away from doing something that would turn his life inside out and destroy it forever. With the benefit of age, he now considered Shauna collateral damage to that life. He repaid her for all she lost by leaving her alone.

Emery's half glare and all that wariness hadn't abated. "But she's alive somewhere?"

He was starting to get annoyed. "I didn't kill her, if that's what you're asking."

"Can you really blame me for wanting a straight answer? The surveillance and all the secrecy." Some of the tension left her body and the fidgeting decreased. "You're an odd man."

"I guess that's better than being called 'creepy.' " Or a killer. No wonder he was so good at his job. Apparently his mere presence scared the crap out of women.

"I'm serious."

"Being different doesn't make me a killer." He was starting to feel defensive and that never happened to him.

"It does make you feel a little dangerous. Maybe in a sexy way, but I can't tell yet." She winced. "Okay, I didn't mean it that way. I just—"

"We married in college." He broke in because if she used the word *sexy* again or went even a little farther down that road he would be all over her. Forget that she saw him as this hulking mess who didn't eat food or do anything normal people did. He could overcome that. Getting through what would happen if they slept together was a different issue. One he hadn't worked out in his head yet.

But he would.

"Okay." Something in her body language changed. It was as if each cell sparked to life. She definitely listened and turned over every word.

"We were too young and did it for the wrong reasons." She didn't say anything. Just stood there, as if waiting for the next sentence. For some reason he decided to give her one. "We knew each other since we were kids and it was safe. We should have been friends and left it there."

"It was a mutual split, then."

He couldn't figure out if that was another way to ask if he murdered Shauna or not. "She left me, but I've come to realize I deserved to be left."

"What does that mean?"

"If you think I'm difficult now you should have seen me then." A vast understatement, but sufficient to make his point.

Emery stepped closer again. Treated him to a flirty little walk. "Was that so hard to tell me?"

"Yes."

She grinned. "Did you give her your name or was it a big surprise back then, too? I'm trying to figure out how you said your vows without mentioning it."

"Are you asking for my full name?" He liked how she made the move. The confidence proved very sexy.

"I think I've asked a bunch of times since we met."

She stopped right in front of him, so close that he could look down and see the vee to that shirt and the edges of the lacy light blue bra beneath.

She was going to be the death of him.

The woman tempted him on every level. The body,

that mouth. The brain. The way she moved and how she signaled her interest. It didn't amount to a flashing green light, and he required one of those, but she called out to him in fundamental ways. Something raw and primal awoke inside him.

He'd cut himself off from so much. Sex was an act he shared with like-minded women who wanted a release and no strings. He was honest about that much even though he never gave his real name. He was sure that made him a complete asshole, but he couldn't shake the need to control and protect his identity.

He also couldn't explain why he'd relaxed every personal rule when she came along. He didn't have an excuse, but he did have a choice not to drag her further into his fucked-up mess of a life. "You really should eat something."

"I don't want to eat. I don't want to settle down. I don't want protection." She played with the buttons on his shirt. "I can't even explain what it's like."

Her mood morphed again. Back to sharing with a hint of vulnerability. "The worry about the break-in?"

"Tiffany. The idea that she could be out there and I'm not working fast enough or making people care enough." She balled his shirt in her fist. "It's like this constant, sickening spinning you can't stop."

She absorbed it all, the guilt and the pressure. He understood her personality. He'd stomped out that part of him long ago.

"I'm more worried about *you* right now." He skimmed his fingers over her hips and around to the small of her back. Held her there, close with their bodies barely touching.

"Meaning?"

"Someone came in here. Someone who didn't break a window or trip your alarm." He hated to bring that up now, but the facts would not leave his head. He needed her on guard and thinking about herself and not just about Tiffany, though he was pretty sure whatever happened tonight was related to her friend.

Emery bit her bottom lip. "The police think I left it off."

Then the police didn't understand her. "Did you?"

"No."

"Because you never do." He would bet on it.

"You think it's silly."

He thought it was damn smart. Repetitive actions drummed them into the head. "I didn't say that."

She smoothed out the wrinkles she put in his shirt. Brushed her palm over his stomach then did it again. "After it happened . . ."

She had so much going on that he wasn't sure where the next comment would take them. "What are we talking about?"

"Do you have any idea how many nights I slept on the floor of the closet because I was sure whoever took Tiffany would come back for me?" The color drained from her face as she talked. "Everywhere I went people would whisper. Some insisted I saw the kidnapper and wasn't talking."

Jesus. "Emery."

"That's just the tip, and it's the part that's about me,

but this touched everyone. Detective Cryer pushed and pushed until it almost cost him his job. Uncle Gavin was never the same. My aunt drank herself into a stupor until she finally disappeared. Teachers were shell-shocked. Our best friend, Tyler, was questioned over and over again because Tiffany had written about him in her diary." She blew out a long breath. "Everything was different in the space of one night."

"Your trust in adults, in people in general, changed." He knew the drill. He had lived through a version of it.

"And life never bounced back. I still assume the worst. God, if I had met you a few years ago and you came on with the heavy-handed approach I would have tasered you and called the police."

If she knew some of the thoughts bombarding his brain she might do it now. "But you're calm."

She looked around the room then focused on him again. Those big eyes stared at him, as if willing him to believe her. "You can't really understand what it's like to live through something like that."

The truth sat there, the words damming up in his throat and begging to come out. Of all the things he did not share, this was the biggest. Garrett knew. People from his old life knew. No one else.

He settled for an abbreviated version that he hoped sounded like just another comment that made her huff at him for being strange. "Don't assume."

She blinked. "What?"

"There was a time . . ." The rest of the comment stayed jammed up inside him. He couldn't do it. The buzz of his phone helped derail him. He'd never been so grateful for the damn thing, even though he hated the subject of the text. "Someone is coming."

She pulled away from him and headed toward the window. "Your men?"

He grabbed her arm before she could make herself an open target. "Wait here."

The doorbell chimed, which meant the unexpected guests either made it to the door or his men did. Either way, he would be the one to open it.

He walked over and, after a glance out the peephole, unlocked the door. His men had a guy, probably about Emery's age, pinned against the wall. Sandy blond hair with an athletic build. His gaze flew to Emery and stopped there.

Wren hated the younger man on sight.

He heard a gasp behind him. Emery rushed past, straight for the doorway. He stopped her again, but this time she struggled and pulled away.

"What's happening?" She reached out for the guard holding his arm against the young man's neck. "Stop!"

The yelling and thudding against the wall brought a neighbor into the hall. Much more of this and the police would get a second call. Wren had enough drama for one night.

"You know him?" he asked Emery.

She'd calmed down but tension still radiated off her. "Yes."

He nodded to his men and they immediately released the guest. When they still lingered, looking ready to grab him again, Wren dismissed them. "You can go. We're fine."

The guy made a big show of jerking out of the hold that no longer existed. "I'm sure as hell not fine."

It appeared the drama was not over. To at least stem it a bit, Wren talked to his men again. "I've got this."

"You do?" The guy brushed past Wren, straight into Emery's apartment, grumbling every second. "Then do you mind telling me what the hell that was about?"

"Wait here." Wren ignored the question and closed the door, leaving his men as backup in the hallway. Once inside the apartment again, his position with his back to the door allowed him to watch Emery, to see the interaction. To get pissed off for no good reason.

"You're back." Emery wore a bright smile and she gave the man a big hug.

"That was quite a welcome," he said, still bitching about the scene in the hallway. When he finally stepped back, he didn't let go of Emery. Then he turned to Wren. "You are?"

Annoyed. But he still had the presence of mind to slip back into his fake persona. "Brian Jacobs."

"This is Tyler Bern," Emery said without letting go of the guy.

"The childhood friend." Wren knew exactly who this guy was. He'd hung out with Tiffany and Emery. They'd been inseparable.

The detective's notes suggested both girls had a crush on young Tyler and that Tyler had wanted to date Tiffany, but she said no, a fact that made him a suspect. Apparently the kid had a bit of an overactive ego back then and was the star of some team. Basically, not the type who took rejection well. The notes had actually said that.

And now he was touching Emery. It was all Wren could do to keep from punching the guy. The days of being moved to irrational anger should be behind him. Wren thought they were, but they seemed to flood through him now.

Tyler smiled as he looked at Emery. "You've been talking about me?"

"Sort of." Emery dropped her arm from around Tyler's back. "It's hard to explain."

The smiling, the ease between them—yeah, Wren couldn't watch this. Didn't want to. He did a quick look around for his jacket and grabbed it off the back of the family room chair. "I should go."

She took a step in his general direction then stopped. "You don't need to leave."

"You have a friend here now." Wren pulled his gaze away from her and looked at Tyler. "Someone tried to break into the house tonight."

Tyler frowned. "So, those guys in the hallway are . . . ?"

"They're with me."

He snorted. "Nice friends you have."

"Good night, Emery." Wren nodded to her when he wanted to do much more. "Call if you need anything."

He rarely said those words as anything more than a way to end a conversation with a work client. This time he meant them.

CHAPTER 13

Emery stared at the door as it closed behind Wren. Her emotions flipped around, nearly knocking her over. She didn't know how to think about him.

Even as she stood there, listening to the mumble of his deep voice through the door as he talked to his men in the hallway, she rubbed her fingers together. Remembered the feel of the scruff around his cheek and the smooth flatness of his stomach.

One question kept flipping through her mind—why did she touch him? She'd slipped in close, ran her hands over him. Flirted. None of it fit with who she was or her initial response to him. But something about him lured her in. She found him compelling. Sensed that under the whiff of danger and all that brooding he was a decent man. And that didn't even touch how hot he was. She'd always had a thing for blonds. Not anymore.

"I think I walked in on something," Tyler said.

She'd almost forgotten about her friend and his poor timing. She plastered a smile on her face and turned around to face him. "No, it's . . . actually, I don't know what he is."

She looked at Tyler, her first real crush. She loved

him with all the intensity of a teen high on hormones. He sauntered around the school halls and hung out at his locker while the other kids practically lined up to talk to him. Everyone loved him.

Living only a few streets apart, they'd grown up running around the neighborhood together. They joked and had fun and as they grew up he fell for Tiffany. That broke Emery's heart, but it had long healed. The exaggerated teen angst over him washed away when Tiffany disappeared. What mattered to Emery changed that day.

So many people had pointed to Tyler as a suspect. He'd been questioned until his parents balked and refused one more interview. He switched schools, first to a private one then to a boarding school in Connecticut. After that, they saw each other during vacations and wrote now and then. He moved away and moved on.

Truth was, in a way, she never forgave him for not mourning enough for Tiffany. That sucked and it wasn't fair, but it was how she felt.

There was talk about him being embarrassed about Tiffany insisting they only be friends. They fought the day before someone took her. Still, Emery refused to believe the guy with the dimple, the one who kissed her—really kissed her in her garage for the first time ever—would hurt Tiffany.

Tyler walked around, scanning the room as he went. "That guy's not really your usual type."

She used to think that. "There's an understatement."

The lanky boy had grown into a man. One with an MBA on the road to a big-time financial career. Emery realized despite the height and self-assurance, he didn't compare to Wren. Not even close.

Tyler shot her a questioning look. "You're being cryptic."

She waved off the concern in his eyes and amped up her smile. "Sorry, it's been a weird night."

Tyler finally stopped checking around and leaned against the back of the love seat. "Because of the boyfriend?"

She didn't bother to deny the relationship. Wren wasn't that, but she really had no idea what he was or why she'd wanted to burrow against him and not let go. She'd never been the needy type and was not thrilled that she moved in that direction now, but she'd grown weary and more frustrated by the case than ever before. It was as if she'd journeyed this far and this was her last chance. Nothing in the evidence suggested that, but battling alone just wasn't working. The idea that she might not be able to find the answer for her friend wrecked her.

"It's about Tiffany." Everything, most of her life, had been about Tiffany. Her father complained about it. Her boss, Caroline, worried about it. The detective warned her about it. Now she could add Wren to the list of people who looked at her differently when she talked about what happened back then.

Tyler stood up again. "What?"

"Never mind." She couldn't think of a good reason to inflict her madness on him.

"Emery, come on." He stood in front of her. "Don't blow me off. Not on that topic."

The zing didn't hit her. This close to Wren she'd been all but jumping on top of him, dying to move in. With Tyler all she wanted to do was find that leftover Chinese food and sit on the couch and eat it.

Before she could get there, she did owe him an explanation. She was talking about his friend and his childhood, too. "The investigation is stalled."

His head shot back as he made a face. "I didn't even know it was ongoing."

His shock sent her temperature spiking. It was probably unfair to judge him, but come on. "She's still missing."

"Look, I know I haven't been here, but . . ." He winced.

Her patience expired. It had been a long-ass day and it was getting longer by the second. "Just say it."

"It's been thirteen years."

He acted as if she couldn't count. Talked to her like she was a child. She didn't appreciate either.

She walked around him to the couch. She had a feeling she'd need to be sitting down for the rest of this conversation. "Is that supposed to mean something?"

Instead of taking the chair perpendicular to the couch, he slumped down next to her. Stretched his arm out across the back of the cushions. "It's a hell of a long time."

And imagine if she's alive how long it's been for Tiffany. "Other kidnapped people have been found in that time."

She was about to reel off a list of names, but stopped herself. She worked in this field. She saw the miracles but nowhere as often as she saw the tragic endings.

Lobbying Tyler, or anyone else, to believe Tiffany could be one of those rare cases was a lost cause.

He just kept wincing. "Yeah, but—"

"I thought you were in New York City." There. A nice, safe topic that didn't make her want to lecture or fear her head might explode in rage. She knew he got the hint when he smiled.

"So, we're done having a rational conversation about Tiffany and your ongoing—"

"If you use the word *obsession* I will be pissed." That was her breaking point. Wanting closure and answers didn't mean there was something wrong with her. Worse, using that word shifted the focus from where it should be—Tiffany.

"Okay, how about we call it your drive for answers."

She shrugged. "It's my job."

"Tiffany is not your job."

She wished Wren were here. He might annoy her and say odd things, but he didn't condescend to her or write her off or hint that she'd crossed some sort of line. "Cousin or not, I help bring people home."

"Emery."

"About New York?" She sank back into the cushions and tucked her feet under her.

Tyler sat there for a second, not saying a word. The silence lengthened, but she didn't do a thing to fill it. If talking about Tiffany made him upset then he'd get mundane conversation, but he needed to join in. Talking about nothing important was safer, and right now she welcomed the mindlessness of it.

After another second of hesitation, his big smile returned and he started talking. "I've been back for a few days. I should have called first before just stopping by."

"Nonsense. You're always welcome here." That wasn't completely true. Tonight she wished he were somewhere else, but Wren had already gone. Having company wasn't a bad thing after the night she'd had.

"Then fill me in on what happened here and the men who threw me into a wall."

Ah, that. How in the world did she explain anything about tonight? "Did they?"

"Yeah." He snorted. "When did this become a bad neighborhood?"

"We're going to need wine."

CHAPTER 14

Wren's eyes were about to cross as he sat at the conference table across from Detective Cryer and Garrett. He'd spent half the night and most of the morning studying files, followed by the last hour meeting with these two for some in-person questioning and more in-depth analysis of the case. The idea had been to test the notes and hear directly from a source close to the case about any stray thoughts that didn't make it into the official file.

The meeting likely would have been more effective if he didn't keep yawning. Not one to need much sleep as a general rule, Wren didn't know why the limited two hours last night had made such a big impact.

So much for being in control of the room.

"I still can't believe you're Wren." Rick shook his head. "That he's you. That you kept that secret."

"Some of us can't believe he spilled it," Garrett mumbled.

"He's not going to tell anyone." Wren looked at the detective. "Are you?"

"Never."

In the past week he'd expanded his circle to include

two more. That wasn't like him. He blamed Emery for his sudden openness. For the lowering of walls. He hated giving up any control, but he did trust the detective. And for whatever reason he wanted Emery to know.

But that was enough people and secret spilling for the rest of the year.

With that issue over and resolved, Wren pushed forward in an effort to wipe out the memory of how Emery felt in his arms and that stupid grin on that guy Tyler's face when he breezed in her front door. The familiarity between them plagued Wren all night. He didn't share that sort of history, common nostalgia, with anyone.

Wren didn't see an obvious answer to the mess in front of him now either. They'd gone through everything. The case was as cold as a case could be. He ticked off his mental list. "You had the usual neighborhood pedophiles checked out."

Rick closed the last file and stacked it on the pile in front of him. "Yes and any case with a similar MO within three states, plus tried to match the facts to other cases nationwide."

"Nothing panned out. Right." Wren had been hoping for a clear hole, one he could point out and keep from getting dragged in deeper. He didn't see one.

He'd done some behind-the-scenes work for the department, but it came years after, and was unrelated to, Tiffany's disappearance. His job centered on a too-close relationship between a detective and someone in the governor's office that ended up with political capital being used to influence cases. Wren tracked the connections and put the pieces together.

At Wren's suggestion, the governor left office for "personal reasons" and Wren helped clean up the rest of the mess he left behind. All quiet, but the case helped forge a bond between him and Rick, the one who noticed the problem in the first place.

"It's a thorough list. Tiffany's father. A teacher at school. A guy at the church two streets over who had been on the wrong end of some nasty rumors." Garrett lowered the pages gathered in his fist and stared up at the detective. "Why is Tiffany's father all over the files and questioned several times?"

"The usual 'look at the males closest to her' protocol. Plus, he waited to report her and had some excuse about wanting her to sweat it out wherever she was as some form of punishment." When Garrett started to talk, the detective held up his hand and kept going. "A stupid way to deal with a teen girl he had no idea how to handle. Pushing his wife away then losing her the way he did. The guilt ate at him until the day he died."

"And Emery." Wren knew he'd see her name in the file, but he wanted to see the detective's reaction now. "She was a suspect, too?"

"There was a love triangle thing, and she was supposed to meet Tiffany." Rick shook his head. "She was cleared."

"It looks like everyone was, including the friend, Tyler." Wren dropped the reference just to double-check. He had his own reasons for wanting the guy to get another look. Not attractive reasons. Emery would not be impressed if she knew. "What about his parents cutting off his questioning?"

"That raised a flag, but the kid had an alibi. A cousin and another friend. They had a pickup basketball game."

"Sounds fishy." Wren hadn't meant to say that out loud, but there it was. Out in the open.

The detective laughed. "Sounds like normal kids."

Garrett closed the file he'd been studying and threw it in the box beside him. "He's not that good with the term *normal* so I tend to define it for him."

"Which brings me to my question." Rick leaned forward with his elbows resting on the table.

The faint ringing of office phones could be heard through the walls. People walked by. The usual busy office day, except for what was happening in the conference room.

Wren longed to be back in his office where he could think. "I fear whatever you're about to say will piss me off."

"Why did you agree to take this on?" Rick asked.

The chair squeaked under Garrett as he leaned back even farther. "Fantastic question."

Being the boss, Wren had the distinct advantage of deciding when to call a meeting over. He thought about it, but then took a good look at the determined expressions on the faces of the men sitting across from him. No way was he getting out of here clean by playing the I'm-in-charge card.

But he could tailor the response, keep it short. "Emery kept digging. I thought stepping in might keep her from running into trouble."

Rick, sitting there all gray-haired and distinguished

with his usual take-no-shit attitude, did not look impressed. "That's it, then?"

But that didn't mean Wren was ready to give up control of the conversation or the room. "Excuse me?"

"Look, I've known her a long time. I've come to care about her and about what happens to her." Rick winced as he looked like he was searching for the right words. "I'm concerned about the intentions here and what happens next."

Wren turned the words over then it hit him. "Wait, are you giving me *The Talk*?"

"This should be interesting," Garrett mumbled under his breath.

"Her own father isn't particularly protective." The detective stopped there. Waited a few seconds. "I'm just making sure you're not taking advantage."

Wren didn't know if the detective was worried on a personal level or on a work level, but it ticked him off. "By assisting her in gathering more information about Tiffany's disappearance?"

Rick didn't back down. He threw Wren one of those man-to-man looks. "You know what I mean."

"I don't."

Garrett cleared his throat. "He thinks you're being nice just so you can sleep with her."

"I got that much." Wren barely spared his friend a glance before looking at the detective again. "But truth is she came looking for me and that was your fault."

"Don't make me sorry I gave Wren's name . . . your name . . . to Gavin."

"That's exactly my point. I told you not to give my

name to anyone." It was as if he'd stepped into an alternate universe where the explosion of paperwork in front of him was somehow his fault. That wasn't even close to reality. He got yanked into this case and was staying as a favor . . . in part.

Some of the tension eased from the detective's face. "But you're happy I did."

Garrett laughed. "He's got you there."

The game of two-against-one worked on Wren's nerves. He didn't know what he had with Emery, but he sure as hell knew it was private. "Emery is interesting."

"Oh, Jesus." Garrett kept right on laughing. "Really? That's the word you're using?"

"She's not like you," Rick said.

Garrett shook his head. "No one is like him."

Wren wanted to threaten to fire Garrett for that, but he ignored it instead. "She seems to like me just fine."

"That's my concern."

Wren admired Rick Cryer, but there were limits. "What do you think I'm going to do to her?"

"She didn't seem to know much about you last night, yet you have men following her."

This again. Wren thought he'd ended this issue when he explained it to Emery. Now he had to fight on a second front. "For her protection."

Rick shook his head. "I'm just making sure your interest is business related."

"Even though we're not getting paid," Garrett added.

Wren had a point to make, so he cut through the bullshit and made it. "For the record, my interest in Emery, what I do or not do with her, isn't your business."

"She's been through a lot. I don't want her to be hurt."

Rick's concern got through. Wren didn't tend to dwell in emotion, but he understood the detective's attachment to the case. His drive to see it through likely rivaled Emery's. That kind of dedication Wren could understand. "Then we're agreed because I don't want that either."

"Okay." Rick didn't sound convinced of anything.

Wren wasn't convinced he'd won that round. "You still look concerned."

The older man shrugged. "Do you blame me?"

He really didn't. Wren knew he wasn't an easy man to read and that sometimes his methods might seem unorthodox. "Emery and I understand each other."

The detective's gaze narrowed. "What does that mean?"

Good fucking question. He'd been in the process of figuring that out when Tyler arrived last night. "I'm not sure yet."

Garrett slapped his hand against the table with a thwack. "And with that illogical comment I think we should get back to the business of suspects."

"I'm not sure I made my point," Rick said.

Garrett nodded. "Welcome to my world."

CHAPTER 15

Emery carried two water bottles and tried very hard not to drop one and bounce it across the family room. It had been that kind of night. She got home from work, paced around. Turned the television on and off again. Changed into lounge clothes then the fumbling really began.

She should have gone down the street to the gym or eaten dinner. Anything to burn off the excess energy zipping around inside of her. But none of that happened. Nope, she jumped in the shower, changed into jeans and called Wren, after searching the Brian Jacobs name a hundred times today. She'd used every database available to both law enforcement officials and to regular people hunting down information on someone. And nothing helpful popped up.

When she started working the keyboard she'd feared she might be playing the grown-up equivalent of scribbling his name in her folder. By the end of the day she was frustrated by the lack of information. It was as if the name existed only in Wren's head.

But that didn't explain who the very real man sitting in her family room was.

She handed him a water bottle and sat down on the opposite end of the love seat, as far from him as possible, which amounted to a half-cushion away. "I wasn't sure you'd come over when I called."

The bottle made a crinkling noise when he grabbed on to it. "Why not?"

He didn't mention that she'd used his emergency private number for a nonemergency, so neither did she. "You kind of ran out of here last night."

Then she'd thought about him all night while Tyler sat there talking about his new job and the new city he loved. Emery had been happy for him, even as a part of her grumbled that it had been so easy for him to move on and never mention Tiffany.

For most of the night she'd been guilty of the same sin. As he talked, her mind switched to Wren. The sound of his voice. The way his muscles felt through his shirt. She certainly wouldn't have won any Good Friend prize for her mental wanderings.

When Tyler finally did get around to talking about Tiffany again it was to declare her gone and it time to move on. Emery had ushered him out the door right after that. She heard enough of that nonsense from her dad. Another voice wasn't really welcome.

"You had company. Something and someone else to occupy your time." Wren didn't look at her as he set the unopened bottle on the coffee table.

She took in the stiffness of his shoulders and the fact he hadn't even bothered to take off his suit jacket. He walked in and went to the couch because she told him to have a seat. Very little else had transpired except for her why-am-I-doing-this panicked race to the kitchen for water. "Don't do that."

He leaned back on the cushions and faced her. "What?"

Gone was the easy flow of conversation from last night and the touching. Yeah, he didn't look even a little interested in touching, which was a damn shame. "You sound all haughty and businesslike."

"You may have just summed up the majority of my personality." He smiled but the gesture didn't quite reach his eyes. It looked forced and disappeared right after it happened.

She tugged on the wrapper around her water bottle. Picked at the end until she could rip off a nice long piece. "I don't buy that. Not anymore."

His gaze bounced from her hands to her face. "What changed?"

"I don't even know. Maybe it's a sense or a hope." Of course, neither of those explained why the air in the room was all but suffocating her.

"Ah."

Talk about an unhelpful response. She put the bottle on the table next to his and sat back again, just inches away from him. "Does that mean you get what I'm saying?"

"Not even a little bit."

She would have laughed at that if the tension strangling her in a bear hug would ease. "Any chance I could get you to take off your jacket? Maybe loosen that tie."

"You still seem overly concerned with my wardrobe." But he relaxed a little. Sank back into the cushions and rested his arm across the top.

"It's like armor."

His fingers tapped against the love seat. "It's wool, I believe."

"Now you're being a gigantic pain in the ass, just because you can." The guy could not take a hint. She was dying to get him out of the suit. She could pretend this had to do with wanting to know he was human and to loosen him up. Yeah, there was some of that, but this was really about wanting more from him.

She liked sex and didn't apologize for that. But she had no interest in random hookups or one-night stands with strangers. That meant getting to know a guy and she hadn't made time for that in more than a year. The last relationship, if she could even call it that, ended with him leaving for the west coast and graduate school. Neither of them cared that his shipping out meant them ending, which said something about her ability to handle any sort of serious dating.

She hadn't been heartsick when he left, but she had been lonely. She filled in nonwork time with friends, but truth was she worked a lot more these days. She buried herself in it. She made connections all day, traced this missing person to that John or Jane Doe photo. The detail-oriented work was both satisfying and infuriating. She could go for weeks without making any progress so that when she did, it spurred her to do even more, to push harder.

That amounted to a lot of late nights. Plus, not many guys wanted to hear a woman on the other side of the dating table talk about dead bodies, and the ones that did were not the type you wanted to date. Ever.

But little by little she discovered that the man in front of her did interest her. Not just in a what-makes-him-tick way. No, this went deeper. She truly wanted to dig around and *get* him. To figure out how that complex mind worked. "If it's any consolation, I'm kind of used to the pain in the ass thing. It's oddly endearing on you."

He stood up and she was sure he was going to leave. She toyed with the idea of being sensible and letting him go. Abandoned that entirely and shifted, about to jump in front of him when he stopped.

He stripped off his jacket and folded it. Laid it across the arm of the chair. Then his long fingers went to his tie. He tugged on the knot and slipped it open. The slide of material against material filled the room as he peeled it off and dumped it on top of the jacket. Next came the shirt button. He undid the top two, until the tip of a white undershirt peeked out.

His eyebrow lifted as he looked down at her. "Better?"

Lordy. That sort of slow striptease should be illegal. Should but thank God it wasn't. Her only regret was that it stopped. "Do you sleep in the suit?"

"Are you asking for personal reasons or are you taking a poll of some sort?"

"You make me want to scream." His name . . . over and over. She dug her fingernails into the seat cushion next to her to keep from doing anything even remotely like that.

She'd never had need shoot through her like this. She'd had great sex before. A guy in college was into the up-against-a-wall hot-and-dirty type. She sure didn't hate that. But Wren seduced in a much more subtle way. His presence wound around her until all she could think about was how it would feel to have his hands all over her.

"Interesting." He sat down again, this time closer and angled so he faced her. "How was your visit with Tyler?"

The quick change in topic threw her for a second. She got whiplash as she struggled to keep up. "Random."

"I'm not sure what that means in this context."

"I didn't know he was in town. I didn't expect him . . ." She'd come to the go-for-it point in the conversation and decided to plunge ahead. "I didn't want you to leave."

She slipped her hand over his knee. Thought about telling him that she didn't get why and she shouldn't even like him, but she did. All those comments and arguments went through her mind. In and right back out again when he slid his hand over hers.

"Let's talk about that last part." He lifted their joined hands.

"It's a mystery, to be honest."

He kissed the back of her hand. "Maybe you find me charming."

More so with each passing second. "Every now and then."

"That seems about right." He laughed against her skin.

The rich sound vibrated through her. "Thank you for coming to the rescue last night."

She let her fingers brush over that scruffy chin she adored so much. Then he ran his free hand down the soft inside of her arm and an explosion went off in her head. The tingling reached every nerve ending.

His mouth followed his hand in a trail of nibbling kisses that extended to her elbow. "I get the sense you don't need rescuing very often. In fact, you strike me as the rescuer rather than the rescuee."

She wrapped her arm around his head and plunged her fingers into his hair. The strands slipped between her fingers. "Do you need to be rescued?"

"From the darkness you think plagues me?"

"That seems like a dramatic way of putting it, but is it a fair statement?" The air conditioner clicked on, but there was no other sound in the room. For a second she thought she heard a song, but realized the sound likely escaped from an open window from the floor below.

"I made the choice of this life long ago."

She let her arm drop and sat back a little to get a better look at him. "So, you came out of the womb wearing a suit and barking orders."

"Hardly." The warm sound of his voice filled the room. "I was the soccer-playing, drinking-behind-the-school type in high school, but eventually grew up a bit."

"Wait." Her mind went blank for a second. Not a single thought bounced around in there until a rush of young Wren images ran through. "You're saying you were a bad boy?"

"Very."

She might never get that image out of her head. "I'm trying to imagine you with a naughty side."

"Oh, I can still be naughty. I just get my thrills in other ways now."

Her heart did this weird bouncing thing. She was pretty sure in any other situation she'd need a surgeon and a hospital, but this bounce hit her with a rush that she didn't want to end. "I think you're flirting with me."

He put their joined hands on his lap. Right there on his upper thighs. "Is it working?"

She could feel the outline of his muscles through the material. That was just impressive. No other way around it. So much so that she almost got lost in the feel of him. Only the thought of all her fruitless investigative searching today and the very real sense she still didn't know his actual name stopped her.

"Yes." She squeezed his hand but didn't let go. "But . . ."

He made a humming sound. "I had a feeling there would be a 'but.' "

"Let's say I wanted you to keep stripping those clothes off." She shook her head. That is not at all what she meant to say.

She had a little speech prepared about them needing to be honest with each other and how he could trust her. Forget all that. She leapt over logic right to the naked issue that kept running through her mind.

"Do you still?" he asked.

His voice sounded deeper, but she decided that was all in her head. "Am I too forward for you?"

"I like a woman who knows what she wants."

From another man that might come off as a line. Not him. He sounded genuine, maybe even a little excited.

That didn't surprise her. He was different from other guys in so many respects, why not this one. "Some men don't."

He rolled his eyes. "Some men are fucking idiots."

"No argument there." The amusement in his voice, his smile—the combination sent a bolt of happiness shooting through her. It took every ounce of control she possessed to stay on track. To not waver and drag him into the bedroom with her. "Well, before one stitch more comes off of either of us—"

"Wait, are you talking in hypotheticals or are you serious about the undressing thing?"

He still held her hand. The heat radiated off him contrasted with the cool air blasting through the room from the air conditioner. "I got the impression you were attracted to me."

"I'll rein it in and say simply, yes."

Her finger pressed into his wrist and his wild heartbeat thumped against her skin. She took that as a very good sign. "And if you didn't rein it in this time?"

"The need to strip you naked and spread you out on that mattress is kicking my ass."

What was she even saying before that? "Subtle."

"There's nothing subtle about how much I want you."

She thought back to the first time they met and the warnings he'd issued while pretending to be someone else. "You hid it well."

"I really didn't."

"Well . . ." She'd lost the ability to form intelligent sentences. "The feeling is mutual."

"That sounds like a 'go' signal." He leaned in. Looked ready to finally kiss her.

She longed for the moment but still forced her hand to come up and press against his chest. To hold him off. Not with a lot of strength. More like she rested it against him. Even that had her heartbeat thundering in her ears.

"Except that I need to know a man before I get naked." He could tell her just about anything and she'd consider it good enough. "Something real, and I mean that. Tell me something few people know about you. Like your name."

He didn't hesitate. "Levi. Levi Wren."

She'd expected something else, but she wasn't sure what. "Really?"

"That's it. You're one of about ten people in the world who know it."

Finding out felt almost anti-climactic. "Huh."

"You don't think it fits?"

"I do." The more she thought about it, the more it worked for her. It was a good name. Solid and a bit sexy. "Levi. May I call you that?"

"Only when we're alone. I mean it. Just the two of us and very private, then it's okay."

He made that sound sexy. "That's your real name?"

"It's my legal name."

Even on the verge of sex he proved to be exhausting. "Are we saying the same thing? I did ask for something real."

"I gave you my name."

She sighed at him. Drew it out and made it loud to let him know she wasn't impressed. "Wow, really?"

"That's bigger than you think."

"What if I told you that I didn't believe Levi Wren was your birth name?"

He didn't even flinch. "I barely know Levi anymore. I've been just Wren and now Brian for years now. Before that I went by other names. The distance between me and Levi is very long."

She had to give him credit for being honest. He didn't even try to trick her. But still . . . "Why?"

"Maybe I can find another way to impress you. Like my shoe size?"

Now she really wanted to know what was going on with his name. Not that she'd admit it. She guessed the more interested she acted, the less likely he'd be to share it. But he wasn't getting off without sharing something. "You went from carefree jock to someone else. Tell me how that happens to a guy. How do you become a different person?"

He leaned his head against the back of the love seat. "It's a long story."

Finally. She curled her legs under her and watched him. "We've got nothing but time."

"You're ability to prolong pleasure is . . ." He lifted their hands one more time and kissed hers. "Let's say annoying, though I'm tempted to use a stronger word."

"Wait until you experience my stamina."

"Okay, you win." He let go of her hand.

She hated the loss of his touch but understood. He needed some space and she respected that. "I thought that might do it."

"It isn't pretty." He rubbed his palms up and down on his thighs.

For a guy who held it together and thrived on conflict and danger, the idea of spilling secrets made him twitchy. Some of his usual rock-hard control faltered. She could see it in the way he moved. The fact that he moved at all.

"I don't want pretty. I want truth." She touched him then because *not* touching him proved too hard. She reached out and rested her hand on the cushion by his hip. Let her fingers make slight contact. Through his pants, but still they touched.

"You say that, but—"

"If I knew who took Tiffany I would kill the person myself. I dream of doing it and don't feel an ounce of guilt." There it was. Every ugly word about how fury and the need for vengeance pumped through her. She didn't share it often, but with him it felt right. Like some odd form of encouragement. "Is your past less pretty than that?"

"About the same." He didn't move, but he seemed to slouch down until his shoulders rested against the cushions. "The best way to describe it is to tell you a story."

"Nice."

"Let's hope you think so in a few minutes."

For the first time since she met him, she sensed wavering. The dip in his usual confident demeanor shook her. Still, a rush to know more caught her in its wake. "Try me."

For a second he didn't say anything. Stray noises from the downstairs apartment and a slam of a door in the hallway blurred in the background. The usual hum of apartment living didn't throw her off. She blocked it all and focused on him, willing him to talk. After another almost minute of silence, he did.

"There once was a very angry young man." He seemed to be searching for the right words, but then shook his head. "Not the usual hormone-driven entitled type. He wasn't angry about something stupid that happened on spring break or some slight in the weight room. Rage filled him, consumed him. Guided every decision."

The sharp whack of his words echoed through the room. Tension encircled her, pressed on her like an invisible hand until the weight on her chest threatened to explode.

"How old was this man?" She didn't bother to ask who he was because she knew. While she couldn't imagine a younger, less assured version of him, he didn't hide the fact there was one.

"Twenty-one."

"A boy." Not that much younger than her, but she rarely thought of the guys she knew in college as grown men. Half of them seemed to be mentally stuck in high school, reliving the glory days. Not that she saw him like that at all.

"One who had grown up fast and ugly." He sank deeper into the cushions as his usual perfect posture and knife-sharp control faded. "During class, he'd plot. His attention centered on one man."

"Who?"

"A man who didn't deserve having even one person thinking about him. An evil piece of shit." The words punched out of him as the anger he spoke about seemed to snap to life and curl around him.

A mix of frustration and wariness clogged her throat. Her mind stayed trapped in the hazy middle ground between fearing what came next and the driving need to hear more. She brushed the back of her hand up and down the outside of his leg. The move wasn't sexual. She just needed a connection with him, to give him a sign of silent support.

"The angry young man made plans. Lots and lots of plans. He ran, worked out, bulked up, performed drills. He practiced at the gun range and became an expert shot." His hands lay on his lap and every now and then his fingers would clench and unclench on the front of his thighs. "He ignored everything else and stoked his fury until it blocked out every other emotion flowing through him."

With each word, the anxiety grew inside her. It bounced and pinged until her muscles begged for her to get up and move. But she sat there determined to listen to every word. To chip away at the painful information packed away inside him.

He blew out a long breath. "Then he met someone."

Her stomach took another wild turn on its roller-coaster ride. "A woman?"

"A man named Quint."

She was already half lost in a story that didn't fit how she saw Levi or Wren or whoever he was now. "Isn't that a fruit?"

"That's quince, but Quint is not his real name anyway."

"Of course not. I guess that's where you learned that trick." Fearing the way she blurted that out amounted to a huge miscalculation, she rushed to keep him talking. "Sorry. Go ahead."

"Quint ran a very specialized company. He . . . made things happen." For just a second the corners of Wren's mouth curled up in a smile but then disappeared.

The heaviness of his words contrasted with the lightness of his expression. Like so much with him, she didn't know how to analyze the barrage of information in front of her. "That sounds a little scary."

"It was." After one last balling of his hands into fists, he let them fall open, palms up. "For a price he set up very awful people. Turned their lives inside out, ruined their reputations. Broke them."

"I don't get it." She couldn't ferret out the good from the bad in the story.

"He served as judge and jury. Once he determined guilt, he acted."

She knew she should ask if this Quint guy physically hurt people or made them disappear. Should but didn't. For a few seconds longer she wanted to hold on to the fiction that Wren—Levi . . . it was going to take forever to switch his name over in her mind—might talk tough but never stray to the dark side.

"So, Quint was a criminal of sorts?" This time her stomach flipped and she had to swallow back the rush of bile that threatened to overcome her.

"To the public he was a solid, very successful businessman. A financial whiz with all the right contacts and many brilliant people working for him." Wren lifted his hands then let them drop again. "No one questioned him. No one doubted his professionalism or his commitment to the community."

A strange panic slammed into her. "But . . . ?"

"But he had this side business based on vigilante work. For it, he recruited angry young men like myself. Guys on the edge. The kind of desperate that ended in chaos. Young men who were about to do something very stupid, and would have without his intervention."

She couldn't dance around this anymore. "Including you."

Wren looked forward and stared at the wall separating her family room from the bedroom area. "Me and a few others. We were the Quint Five. We worked for him, trained with him. We were employees, but it was much more than that. He gave us a sense of family."

She could almost envision them. Boys on the edge of full adulthood with more ego than common sense. "I'm guessing this was some sort of secret group."

Levi looked at her then. "As you said earlier, I learned many tricks from Quint. Privacy was one of them. So was loyalty. But really, it was the place I learned a lot of my skills. We all worked for Quint and he provided more than money and supplies."

"You said *was*?"

"Quint sold his company and retired to Mexico years ago after we all took other positions and found our own careers."

"He must have hated to lose you."

"Not really. He viewed his job as sort of a teacher. A

lethal one, but still. He wanted us to succeed and move on to find what interested us."

"So it was almost like foster care."

"But we weren't kids and we earned paychecks. We also played with guns."

That part sounded so normal. Well, except for the guns. Wren described this self-appointed guardian and vigilante who functioned on the outside as a businessman but behind closed doors as some sort of enforcer. The idea of that guy selling his house and sitting on a beach wouldn't come together in her head. "And the other members of the group? Where are they now?"

"All successful and no longer desperate. None in jail."

In other words, businessmen like Levi Wren. Secretive, powerful. "But are they dangerous?"

"Some more than others, but probably not in the way you think." His hand fell to the cushion right next to hers, but he didn't reach out to touch her. "Some, like me, walk the line between what others consider right and wrong. Some ignore the line completely."

"So, the Quint Five no longer exists."

"Not in any sort of formal business way. We help each other now and then. We meet."

"In other words, you act like family."

"I don't know because I don't really *get* family."

"I have about a billion more questions." About Quint and the anger and what started Wren spinning in the first place.

"The bottom line is Quint taught me skills and gave me focus. He did it for all of us. Saved us."

The words brought her winging back to reality. The idea that he might have taken a different turn in life and not be sitting in front of her nearly dropped her to her knees. He'd almost sacrificed everything. For what, she didn't know, but she was clear that nothing in the story bordered on exaggeration. If Wren stated he'd been on the edge then he really had been.

"Quint also provided me with this group of people like me who I know I can count on, even today, if I need anything."

"Does that ever happen?" She couldn't imagine him reaching out for help, despite the history he may share with the other person, but he acted like the bond had never been broken.

He nodded. "Now and then. We work in different areas of business, but we trade intel and feed each other leads."

He might deny it or not understand it, but this was his version of family, which made her wonder about his actual one.

"We now think of ourselves as Quint Associates. It's sort of an informal social club. An ode to the old man." A note of affection weaved into his voice. "But I do use what I learned from him to fix problems."

The fixer thing. A murky concept even without the history. "By ruining people's lives and reputations?"

"By finding weaknesses and exploiting them."

"You're the judge and jury these days?" There wasn't any heat behind her question. True, the concept of vigilantism scared her. There were so many risks and the idea of being wrong paralyzed her. But she'd seen awful things in her job. She knew well that evil lurked out there, ready to pounce. She didn't exactly hate the idea of a group of competent men waiting to even the score.

"I'm not Robin Hood, Emery. I don't pretend to be a saint either. I get paid to solve problems, and I'm damn good at that job." His hand lay open, palm up, right next to hers. "So?"

The question hung there as she stared at his palm then at his face again. "What do you expect me to say?"

"I'm waiting to see if you kick me out and run as far away as possible."

She waited for that instinct to kick in, for the wailing alarm to scream in her head. But nothing. She didn't feel fear or worry. Watching him now, with his protective wall lowered just enough for her to peek in, the driving need to know more plowed into her. The thought of walking away, abandoning him, came into her head and left just as fast.

Not being either a danger or adrenaline junky, her reaction didn't make much sense. He was all but telling her how he lived his life in the gray areas. The reality didn't scare her at all. "I don't want to."

His eyes narrowed. "Is that sufficient to let me stay?"

The time had come for a decision. She could step out and keep their relationship about business and Tiffany. That would allow her to watch over him and make sure he stayed on the right side of the line. Or she could plunge in.

When it came right down to it there wasn't much of a debate in her mind. She knew what she wanted. A self-made man wrapped in a mystery. A true lover of secrets. Imperfect, determined and flawed. She wanted him.

She stood up.

He looked up without making a move. "Am I leaving?"

Silly man. She held out a hand. "We're going into the bedroom."

"This isn't the reaction I expected." But he was up with his arms around her, her body folded against his.

This felt right. Perfect even.

"Don't talk." She eased her body deeper into his. Let her fingers slide around his shoulders to the back of his neck to slip into his hair. "For a few minutes I don't want to think and analyze or regret the past. I just want to enjoy. Feel."

All the tension and worry eased from his face. "I think we can do better than a few minutes."

That lightness inside her came zinging back. "I was counting on that."

"If my clothes are coming off we're going to make it worthwhile." He winked at her.

That did it. "Enough talk. Now is the time to really impress me."

CHAPTER 16

Wren hadn't meant to share any of that. He'd stopped before spilling every last detail, but still. He'd run on about the life he had before. The life he declared over when he dropped his father's last name and moved out of Michigan years ago.

Now that he talked about Quint and the past, his mind dwelled there. Memories lingered. The splash of blood his father burned off the wall with cleaning products. To this day, the sharp smell of bleach started a rapid punching in Wren's gut that he had a hard time controlling.

Then there was the rug that disappeared from his parents' bedroom, along with every photo that proved it ever existed. All the questions from detectives. The way his father drummed his version of their family life into his head until the line between truth and fiction blurred and blinked out.

He'd been young when it happened, but Wren remembered it all. A therapist once told him about how some people blocked out emotional trauma. The pieces slipped away and never came back. He'd never been that lucky. He'd never found anything to drown out the memory of the camera lights and all those microphones as the press descended.

But now he had Emery, at least for a little while. Looking at her, standing there so vulnerable yet so strong, he noticed the hope that usually filled her eyes had been replaced with something else. Sympathy, maybe? He hated that.

Pity was wasted on him. The last thing he needed was for her to see him as one of the victims she worked with every day. He wasn't her client. He wasn't a case or a problem she needed to solve.

That's why he held most of the story back. He'd walked right to the edge, ready to let it all come tumbling out for the first time in years, but stopped. Emery wasn't part of Quint Associates, a dysfunctional brotherhood of like-minded men he knew and trusted. The few he could call on if he needed a favor or help on a case. Powerful men with drive and impressive resources. Men with fractured backgrounds, just like him. Some far worse than him.

Emery wasn't like Garrett either or even a friend. Not really. But she did haunt him. The need to be inside her, taste her, pounded him. No way was he going to forfeit the chance now in exchange for hand-holding.

He walked her backward. With each step, their bodies rubbed together. Her breasts crushed against his chest as his hands slid down her ass. He nearly threw her over his shoulder at the thought of how she'd feel when he was inside of her.

Digging deep, he found a reservoir of control and tapped it, but the dance continued. Their legs tangled and his gaze stayed locked on hers. The urge to kiss her, to peel that T-shirt up and off her, nearly strangled him. But he waited. The taste would be so much sweeter if he drew this out, made every second tick by like an eternity.

Her back pressed against the wall and he leaned into her. His mouth hovered right over hers. "I spent all day thinking about fucking you."

Her arms slipped around his neck. "Sounds like you were a naughty boy at work."

"Good thing I own the place." Right then he would have signed it all over to her in a bargain that ended with him ripping off her underwear.

A feverish need gripped him. The pros and cons of taking this step fell away. He didn't care if it was smart or dangerous. He just wanted it to happen.

She shot him a sexy smile and his mouth crashed against hers. The kiss, hot and wild, burned through him. Blood roared in his ears and raced in his veins. She seduced him just by standing there. Those sweet curves. The slip of her tongue against his. The wet heat of her mouth.

His fingers slid under the band of her shirt. He opened his hands, loving the way his palms spanned her soft skin. The scent of her shampoo wound around him as the kiss pushed on. Not sweet and not lingering. No, this was demanding. All-consuming in the way she lured him in and made demands without saying a word.

His fingertips brushed against the edge of her bra. With two tugs, he had the clasp open. He cupped her breasts in his palms, gently massaging as he captured her gasp in his mouth. Still, the kiss raged. Hands, mouth and a drumming need building inside him.

He had to see her. All of her.

Pulling back, he gave her one last chance to break away. The silence to come to her senses. To grab control and walk away.

She unbuttoned his shirt.

Opening one then the next, those fingers undid each one until she reached his waist. "Levi?"

Jesus, the way she said the name he'd all but wiped from his memory. He had no idea how much he ached to hear it on her lips until he did. "Yes?"

She eased away from the wall, just enough to press her mouth against his ear. To lick her tongue around the outside rim then whisper, "It's time to be a naughty boy."

Her breath, that voice, pinged across his nerve endings. Need pummeled him now. Forcing his hands to stay steady, he lifted the thin fabric of her shirt. Up and over, stripping her, almost tearing it.

The light bathed her skin in a soft glow. He rubbed his palms over her shoulders. Skimmed across the tiny straps of the light blue bra balanced there. "So fucking beautiful."

"Take it off."

He flicked the straps to the sides, until they fell down and rested against her arms. The front gaped and he slipped a finger just inside the cup, tracing her nipple— back and forth. With each circle her breathing kicked up. Her chest rose as her fingers clenched against his biceps.

The need to get her naked hit him with a fierce urgency. Every muscle shook as he tried to throw on the brakes and make this moment last. With one push, the bra dropped down and she whipped it off, letting it fall to the floor somewhere behind them. Then she was on him. Her foot traveled up the back of his calf as she wrapped her body around his.

No way could he stop now. Lifting her off the floor, he carried her the rest of the way into the bedroom and fell onto the mattress with her. Tiny moaning sounds escaped her throat when their mouths met in another flame-inducing kiss. His hands roamed as he kicked off his shoes. The thuds against the hardwood echoed around them. He ignored the faint sound of music and knock of the bed against the floor and concentrated on the touch of the woman beneath him.

Her hands moved as she tugged his shirttails out of his pants. After a few yanks she had him sitting back and taking it off. Then the undershirt. Stripped to the waist, he slid over her again. Forget finesse. His control fizzled out under the force of that stamina she'd bragged about.

The woman knew how to kiss. Knew where to touch him to send his temperature spiking.

Just as he settled between her raised thighs a thought hit him. *Condom.* He'd put one in his jacket then took it out again. Something about she'd be upset about the break-in and him not wanting to take advantage of her. But he'd underestimated her. She wasn't fragile or unsure. Her strength—her need—washed over him, igniting his own.

"Fuck chivalry." He mumbled the words against her neck.

She pulled back and pinched his shoulder until he looked at her. "What?"

"I didn't bring a condom." It took all of his will-power not to race up and down the hall begging her neighbors for one. "Trust me, I'm kicking my own ass over that decision."

"Damn."

"Exactly."

"I haven't dated anyone in a while. I don't have any, so no protection." She groaned as her head fell back into the pillow. "That's a no-go for me."

"Agreed." Now if only he could breathe.

Ducking his head, he balanced on his elbows and looked down the length of her. If he were younger and more of a dick he might try to convince her with the old "I'm clean" speech. He was, but that wasn't the point. He respected her and her decision on this issue. They were smart people and needed to act that way.

Drinking in one last look, his gaze hesitated on the top curve of her breast. Slid over her nipple and across her skin. Clearly his attraction had him locked in a haze that made him slower than usual. They had all sorts of options. Great options.

He smiled as he lowered his body again and nuzzled her neck. "Good thing there are so many other things I can do to you."

"Tell me more." She stretched her arms above her head. "Use as many words as you want."

As if he could talk. "I might be limited to grunts."

"I love the idea of having that kind of power over you."

"You do." But he couldn't think about that now. How big that was and what it meant . . . later.

He moved down, stopping to lick his tongue across her nipple and watch it tighten. When her back lifted off the mattress, he did it again. Kept going until her body shifted on the bed, looking as if every nerve jumped and quivered.

Continuing, he trailed a line of kisses down her stomach. His fingers worked on the button at the top of her jeans. His hands trembled with the need to yank the last of her clothes off her. He settled for peeling them down inch by inch, kissing each peek of skin he uncovered.

The rustling of material as he gave it one last tug and ripped it off. That left her and the thin blue bikini underwear. He lowered his head and placed a kiss in the dead center. Smelled her. Rubbed his cheek against her until she widened her thighs even farther.

Her fingers slid into his hair and held him there. He didn't back away. One hand slipped under the elastic band of her underwear while the other skimmed the underside of her leg to the back of her knee. He folded the edge of the underwear back, baring her to his gaze. His tongue pressed inside her as her heels stabbed into the mattress.

"Take them off, Levi."

Damn, he loved the sound of his name on her lips. "I want you to beg."

Her head whipped from side to side on the pillow. "Please."

Moving to his knees, he pushed her legs back and grabbed for the edge of her underwear. He dragged them down and let them fall. No way was he looking away from her. She had his full attention. Then she opened her legs, letting them fall to the sides.

Her confidence was just about the sexiest thing he'd ever seen.

"I'm going to make you scream." He barely got the words out. Heat rolled over him and his hands shook with the need to touch her again.

"I'm counting on that."

Moving in slow motion, he slipped down again, angling his body and slipping back between her thighs. This time he didn't play. He slid a finger inside her. Pressed in and out, going deeper each time. Licked his tongue along her seam, found her place that started her squirming and flicked against it.

Her breath came out in gasps, but he didn't relent. The taste of her had him wanting more. Using his hands and mouth, he kept up the sensual torture until her muscles shook. Her legs pressed against his shoulders as she grabbed for the comforter, twisting the material in her clenched fists.

He varied the speed of his finger then added a second, scissoring them inside her until her shoulders lifted off the mattress. Her hips bucked. Her toes curled and uncurled. Her tiny inner muscles tightened against him as he pulled his fingers out of her and thrust them inside again.

"Yes." Her body stiffened as she started chanting his name. "God, Levi. Yes."

She made him feel like a hero. Her body reacted to his touch and she didn't hide any reaction from him. She let him see her desire and it was fucking glorious.

With one last pass of his tongue, her body let go. Her fingers shifted from the covers to his shoulders. She pressed against him as her muscles squeezed and her body pulsed against his tongue. He could almost feel the waves of pleasure move through her and had to fight to keep from losing it right there.

Calling on his control, he rolled to the side. Kept the connection with her body by draping his hand across her thigh. Thought he might have a fighting chance not to spill it until her fingers slipped into his hair, gently caressing.

A man only had so much control in a situation like this. "Uh, Emery."

"Will you tell me something?"

If he wasn't careful, he would show her something. That wasn't exactly how a guy wanted to come his first time with a woman. There, in his suit. Not impressive.

"Sure." His answer sounded strangled even to his ears.

"Why were you so angry?" The mattress dipped as she turned to her side and slid down to face him. "Back then, I mean."

Okay, that killed his erection. He guessed he should thank her for saving him from an embarrassing teen flashback. But this subject sucked. "Is now the time for this conversation?"

She traced her finger over his lips and down to his jaw. "This strikes me as the perfect time to share."

He wasn't sure how to answer that without pissing her off. Pointing out that he'd already shared a secret about his life and then went down on her seemed especially dickish. "It's not really something I talk about."

"You don't give out your name either, but you told me."

He'd forgotten most of his personal rules when it came to her. "Hard to argue with that logic."

"Then don't."

He debated telling her another story and keeping the facts hidden. He might have done it if she weren't right there with her leg sliding along his, naked and trailing her hand down his bare chest. "There was a woman."

"Ah." She nodded. "There always is."

"My mother." When she frowned but stayed quiet, he pushed on over his reluctance and every ounce of common sense that told him to stop. "I was training and plotting and learning to shoot because I was angry about my father."

She frowned. "I don't understand."

He reached out to rest his hand on her hip but stopped. This wasn't a time for touching or joy or anything good. "I wanted him dead."

Slowly, she sat up. "I don't get what you're saying."

"I think you do. He was the one I wanted to punish. Worse, actually, but I settled for ruining him." He leaned on his elbow and stared up at her. "Because he killed my mother."

"I . . . Oh, Levi." Emery crossed her legs in front of her and dragged the edge of the comforter across her naked body. "I don't even know what to say."

He didn't either. It wasn't as if he told this story often. Quint knew. The other members of the group knew, and that included Garrett. But the universe of the people pretty much ended there. He'd walked away from his father, that life and his name almost a decade ago. Got his revenge and left. Killed off the young man he once was and started over with his acquired skills.

On the verge of telling her he couldn't talk about it the words started to flow. "The market turned and his business was in trouble. Between the margin calls and the panicked clients demanding to withdraw their money, everything fell apart."

She balled the comforter on her lap. "Okay, but . . . I mean, murder?"

"He had a two million dollar life insurance policy on my mom and a mistress waiting for him to break free. I guess with those pressures his choice sounded like a good idea."

"Damn." She reached out and touched the side of his face. One slip of her fingers then the warmth was gone again.

"He wasn't particularly original about it. They were supposed to meet at a work party that night. She never showed." Wren sat up then because lying down didn't feel right. Nothing about this moment did.

They'd flipped from pleasure to serious and he didn't know how to get the pleasure back . . . but a part of him didn't want to. There was something about purging the information that felt right. With her past, through all the pain she'd experienced, he knew she'd get it. She'd at least understand it.

"You're sure?" She rested a hand on his knee.

Rather than fight the comfort, he dove into it. Picked up her hand and held it in both of his. "I know he did it."

"How?"

He caressed her fingers, stunned by the contrast of the harsh memories and her healing touch. "He says she ran away. Her mom, my grandmother, was Japanese and had returned to Osaka years before to take care of her sick sister. My father insisted my mom was miserable as a wife and left to join her long-lost family in Japan because nothing in the US held her back."

Emery shook her head. "Except you."

"He could go into great detail about how awful a mother she was, too." Wren put her hand back on his lap and covered it with one of his. Didn't break the bond. "None of it true, of course. At least nothing that matched my memories of her. And she'd never actually lived in Japan or talked about going there, but he didn't let those facts get in his way."

"The police thought he did it?"

"Almost everyone did, but it took years for the police to collect enough evidence to arrest him." The prosecutors were *sure* he'd been found guilty, but they underestimated people's biases and willingness to believe a woman of Japanese descent would value her Asian mother and that family over her own and just leave without word. As if her ethnic background meant she loved her child less. It was all so sick and unbelievable that Wren still couldn't process it. "All but the people on his juries."

Emery's eyes widened. "Juries, as in plural?"

"There was a trial followed by a mistrial because the first jury couldn't reach a decision. The second time around he was acquitted." By that point the news had been saturated by his father's lies about his mother being disconnected and yearning for something else. He'd painted himself as the victim and loving father. All lies.

Emery's hand squeezed his. "What about your mom?"

The cold pit he covered and buried and tried to ignore formed again in his stomach. The icy branches ran through him, cutting through his defenses. "Never found. Her social security number has never been used again. The bank accounts and credit cards in her name went untouched. I've looked and traced every piece of evidence. My dad was thorough."

Emery moved then. Slipped over and settled on his lap with her arms wrapped around him. "I'm so sorry."

For a second, he just sat there. He didn't even realize their bodies were rocking back and forth until he felt the slight sway. Something about her warmth and the concern in her voice broke through. Instead of running from his past and the truth, it rushed out of him.

He wanted her to know. He *needed* her to know that he got it. He understood the hollowness and emptiness that went along with not knowing. With craving answers and never finding them. "No witnesses but a trail of alleged sightings that put her at airports then out of the US."

She brushed a hand through his hair. "You don't buy it."

"Later, when I was older, I tried to track the sightings and they didn't pan out. The intel seemed to be planted."

"By your father."

"Of course." No matter what his father said there was no other viable suspect. There were no other explanations. "Their bedroom rug was gone the afternoon she disappeared. So were all of the photos that suggested there ever was one. He insisted I was wrong, but I knew."

Her arm tightened around him. "How old were you?"

"Nine when she disappeared. Twelve when he was arrested. Sixteen when he was acquitted. Twenty-five when I ruined him."

"Ruined?"

"An all-out assault on his life. Leaked evidence that supported his guilt. Made up other stuff. Separated him from friends. Made it impossible for them to publicly support him without looking as if they were supporting a killer." He blew out a long breath. "Used shell companies and stole what little money he had left. Made it impossible for him to work and earn more."

"That's quite an attack."

"I let him live." A fact Wren regretted more than once.

"Which is how you became a fixer."

"Quint was a successful businessman. He also knew a lot about walking on the wrong side of the law in order to get things done." Wren decided to leave it there because details would only confuse the conversation and lead them in an odd direction. "I saw what worked and how to apply just the right amount of pressure. By the time I moved to DC I had my degrees and contacts and the money to get started. I built the rest."

A stark silence fell over the room. He waited for her to bolt. Hell, in her position he would. Get out and not look back.

She turned and straddled his lap. "You're not like your father."

The move, the intimacy of the position, shocked him, but it settled him. The way the comforter had dropped until only his pants separated them did the exact opposite of settling him. "I sure as hell hope not."

"For the record, you're not creepy." She smiled as her arms went around his neck.

"You sure? Even I have to admit that story is pretty creepy." And she didn't even know the worst or how bad he got before he exacted his revenge.

"You're a survivor."

Her word had his defenses rising. "I'm no hero. Please don't make me out to be."

"No, you're really human."

He specifically remembered her saying otherwise before but didn't remind her. Not when her eyes had gone soft and her body leaned into his. "No one has ever accused me of that before."

"They don't know you."

"You do?"

"Let me show you what I've learned about what you like." Her hand snaked down between them. "Unless you object?"

Her fingers slid over him, caressing and cupping him until his erection started to fill her hand. Next, she turned to his zipper and the pressure of his belt eased.

So fucking tempting. "We still don't have a condom." He almost hated reminding her of that.

"Then I'll have to use my mouth."

The last of the tension and the horror of the memories fell away. They'd be back, but for now he planned on concentrating on her. On the tick of his zipper as she slowly lowered it. "For the record, I have no objection to what you're doing right now."

"I thought not." She shoved him until his back hit the mattress.

"Nice."

"Oh, it's about to be." She leaned down and her hair brushed over his skin. "Your turn."

For this, he'd concede control.

CHAPTER 17

After everything learned last night, everything they did, Emery had wondered how and when they'd see each other again. Would things be weird . . . would he be even weirder than usual? Then she spied him at the coffee shop table in the back by the bathroom. He sat with two cups in front of him, looking at something on his phone.

She should have figured he'd top off a night of expert going down on her with coffee. The man did savor his caffeine.

As she walked through the line of people and got closer, she tried not to think about how her body had moved under him. Or that tongue. At least he proved one thing—Levi was not all work and no play. The man knew his way around a woman. Understood pleasure and was not one bit selfish in bed.

He got hotter by the second.

She ignored the happy memories pinging through her body and watched him concentrate on his cell. How he cradled the phone with those long fingers . . . yeah, remembering those had a flash of heat moving into her cheeks.

She pulled out the chair across from him, wincing when it screeched across the floor, and sat down. "You're here."

He put the cell down. One button click and the screen went dark. "Where should I be?"

"Excellent question."

He looked delicious. The bright green tie perfectly matched his eyes. He had the dark suit on and wore a slight smile. He looked more relaxed than during their usual meetings. A little more approachable, maybe.

When the conversation stopped, he sat back in his chair and watched her. His gaze never wavered. "I'm not clear what's happening right now."

That described most of her relationship with him. "How does it feel to be lost in the conversation? Strange, right?"

"Maybe we should start over." He pushed one coffee cup closer to her. "This is for you."

Every movement, every time he shifted or his fingers wrapped around something new, something inside her crackled. She felt every gesture as if he were touching her.

"Is that what you want? After last night, I mean." She hadn't really meant to say that. To just bring up the evening without the customary chatting and flirting first.

His smile faded a bit. "I feel as if I missed a text."

She was starting to think she was the only one walking around in a haze today. If this whole crackle thing only ran one way she was going to be really embarrassed. So, she tried again. "I wondered if you'd do that whole hard-to-get thing."

"Does that really strike you as something I'd do?" His eyebrow lifted as he took a sip from his cup.

She conducted a quick glance around. Some people waited in line. Others pushed and shoved their way around the congested shop. No one seemed to notice them, but she leaned in and dropped her voice anyway. "Some men get weird after sex."

He leaned in, meeting her halfway across the small table. "Technically, we didn't have sex."

The teasing words eased some of the tension zipping around inside her. "How would you describe it?"

Part of her *really* wanted him to describe it. To go into great detail and maybe foreshadow what other bedroom tricks he possessed. The rest of her wanted to push him. There was something about him sitting there, all proper and businesslike, that made her feel extra naughty.

"From the look on your face I assume you don't think I'll talk dirty in public." He slid his arm across the table and turned his hand palm up. "You are absolutely wrong."

She wanted to take the dare and reach out and touch him, but she hesitated. "Doesn't seem to fit with that fancy suit."

"Don't let the jacket fool you."

"Oh, really?" She traced her fingertips over the lines on his palm.

His fingers curled around hers, but he kept the touch light. "Underneath is an actual man."

"Do tell." And she meant that in every way. He'd shared something so personal, so difficult, for him. Now she craved more.

"Who wants to see you naked again."

All the air left her body. She could almost hear the whooshing sound. "Subtle."

That smile came back. It lifted the corner of his mouth, making him look even sexier. "Did you want me to play games?"

"No." She loved that he didn't. He ignored the whole "act cool and don't contact her for days" idiocy. He was clear he wanted her last night and showing up today, acting like it was the most natural thing in the world, showed her he still wanted her today. She couldn't think of anything hotter.

He brushed his fingers over hers, barely touching yet caressing all the same. The skimming of skin over skin was a stark reminder of all his talents and the glimpse he had treated her to last night.

"What do you want?" he asked in a voice that seemed even deeper, smokier, than usual.

Underneath the very public foreplay, memories of the evening before crawled through. What happened between them blew past a simple release. The sharing dove much deeper.

"Last night was a good start." The way he opened up surprised her and gave her hope. She feared that door would slam shut. At the very least, that he'd regret he ever opened it.

The tension in his face had hinted at the battle waging inside him. He'd crossed a line back then. Him, with his reserve and that wall of control that smacked into her every time she saw him. He did something to track that man down and it had cost Levi something.

Maybe everything. She got the impression who he was and how he dealt with people—at a distance and in cryptic conversations—formed back then.

His fingers froze for a second. "Now you're hedging."

He must have heard it in her voice. He seemed to pick up on the fact they'd crossed from sex talk into something else. He might claim not to get people, but he could read them.

"Frankly, you scare the shit out of me." On a very fundamental level, he did. Not for her safety, but she wasn't sure his sanity was secure in his hands.

His hand slipped away. He didn't move back, but his mood changed. Slight but the heat had receded and now he wore a blank expression. "You're back to thinking I'm dangerous."

She kept her hand on the table and didn't move back. She tried to show him without pleading what she meant. "This has nothing to do with being afraid of you or anything you told me yesterday."

"You're sure?"

"Definitely."

Some of the tension seemed to leave his shoulders. "Then I'll take that as a sign of progress."

"Wow, you're really talking sexy now."

He laughed. That fast the tension broke. They'd shifted from flirty talk to serious and now hit a level of comfort.

She'd never really experienced all those stages with one person. She went out with a guy who was great when the clothes came off but always gave off a whiff of "I'm on the lookout for something better." She'd gone out with really nice guys who didn't get her heart-beat revving. She didn't run toward danger, but she now knew the flawed, intense type rang her bells. She didn't love that realization and sure didn't want to psychoanalyze where that came from.

"I could go into vivid detail about where I want to put my fingers." His gaze traveled over her face then down her neck. "My tongue."

The woman walking by the table glanced over and smiled. Emery smiled back before turning to Wren. "We're in public."

He shrugged as he picked up his coffee again. Acted like the conversation didn't affect him at all. "You issued the challenge. You seem to forget that I'm a man with questionable boundaries."

He wanted a challenge? Fine. She put her hands on either side of the table and gave it a little shake. "Do you think this table could hold us?"

He didn't even blink. "I'm willing to test it."

Okay, that was pretty hot. This side of him proved tough to resist. Emery wondered why she was even trying.

Her fingers slipped over the top button of her silk dress shirt. "Tough talker, but I bet if I undid even one of these you'd get all huffy and storm out."

He put the cup down and held out both hands. "Try me."

The noise in the café behind her faded out. In that moment all she saw was his face and that kissable mouth and she wanted to dive over the furniture to get to him. "Really?"

"When it comes to this topic, I am not restrained."

She could hear her breathing echoing in her head and tried to relax. This was just talk and they were in public. Nothing could happen . . . yet. "Admittedly, you're a bit of a wild man in the bedroom."

"I'll be whatever you want."

"Dominant." She didn't even know how she choked the word out.

He rubbed his fingers along his jaw. "Is that what you want or are you saying it's a problem?"

"Not a problem. Not even a little." On him taking the lead proved to be a *very* good thing. "I'm just saying—"

"Wanting to be in control and making sure you get what you need are not mutually exclusive. I promise I can do both."

She could barely concentrate. His fingers moved back and forth over that scruff around his chin. The same scruff that rubbed over her bare thighs. She jerked and knocked into her cup. He caught it right before it fell. Drops streaked across the table. She stared at them while she tried to clear her head. "Well, now that we're on the same page on that point . . ."

"I'm willing to continue the conversation."

She rummaged through her bag until she found a tissue and used it to clean up the coffee around her. "I bet."

"Maybe over dinner?"

Forget cleaning. Her head shot up and she looked at him. A promise lingered right there in those eyes. Then she remembered the text she read first thing this morning. "Damn."

He reached over and finished cleaning up the last of

the coffee. "I do eat meals, you know. I thought we'd established that."

"I have to meet my father."

Wren stilled. "Is that a real thing or an excuse not to see me?"

"Very real, I'm afraid." She didn't love spending hours of unstructured time with her dad even on the best days. Now she'd be sitting there, thinking about where else she'd rather be sitting. *Great.*

"You sound thrilled about the visit." He leaned back and threw the wet ball of tissue in the garbage can behind him. Made it in one shot, of course.

"He's . . . difficult." She had no real way of summing up her father in one quick sentence, but that came close.

"Interesting." Wren nodded to the woman who knocked into his chair as she passed by and mumbled an apology. He shifted the chair away from the open aisle. "I'm pretty sure you've said that about me."

"Wow, I really don't want to draw parallels between you and my father." She'd spent enough years in therapy in college, working out her family issues and survivor guilt. She didn't want to return. "Let's just say he hates what I do, who I am and how I spend my time."

Wren whistled. "That covers a lot of territory."

"I mentioned Tiffany during our weekly dinner the other night and he didn't take it well." Emery stopped when she heard a noise. She realized it was her foot banging against the table leg. With that, she stopped moving around. "I ended up leaving early."

"He didn't like Tiffany? But I thought she was his niece, or did I get that wrong?"

"No, you're right. But the issue is more about what he believes to be my obsession with her being missing."

"She *is* missing."

"Right? You know that and I do, but he wrote her off long ago."

"Despite his view, you're going to see him."

She didn't notice she'd been holding her breath until right then. Instead of lecture, Wren sided with her. The relief nearly knocked her over. "He's my dad."

"Ah, well. I'm not sure what that means, but it matters to you, so I'll pretend to get it." Wren made a face. It looked like he wanted to say something then stopped. Then he started again. "Did you need me to come with you?"

And there he just got even sexier. Who knew that was possible? He tended to overdo, but on this point she appreciated the gesture. "You don't like people or being in public."

"Yet, here I sit."

"You've come a long way in a few days." She didn't want that to mean anything . . . but then she did . . . or not. He had her mind spinning until her common sense all but scrambled.

"My personal rules have taken a beating since I met you, yes." He slipped his fingers around his coffee cup then let go again. "Still, if you need backup, I would assist."

She watched his hands and the uncharacteristic shifting of his weight. From the minute she met him he'd been solid and in control. Talking about her dad seemed to make Levi squirm. She couldn't help but find that adorable. "Are you good with dads?"

"I have no idea." He snorted. "Probably not."

"The offer is sweet." Sweet, sexy, charming. The whole conversation, the fact he was here and not hiding or pissed off because he'd shared so much about himself yesterday, had her aching to be alone with him again.

"*Sweet* is not the word people usually use to describe me."

"It fits now, and I appreciate the offer, but I should probably handle this one myself." Wren might take on countries and fix corruption, or whatever it was he did. That didn't mean he deserved to have her father inflicted on him. "Dad can be intense."

"I could see where intensity might be a problem."

Something in that tone had her thinking they'd changed topics again. "Are we still talking about messed-up families?"

"No."

"Now you're just toying with me."

"I'd like to, but apparently you have plans this evening."

She laughed. "Drink your coffee like a good boy."

"And I'll get a reward?"

"Maybe." Most definitely.

EMERY RUSHED HOME after work that night. Her dad had insisted on coming over. She thought a neutral restaurant would be better, but he refused to lose the argument.

She slammed the door behind her and threw her bag down. The keys clanged as she threw them in the bowl on the table by the couch. Next came the kicking off of her heels, her favorite part of the day and why she usually wore sneakers to and from the metro. She'd been in too much of a hurry to get out of the office and home to clean up the apartment. She blamed Wren for that.

The night had been wilder than she expected. The man knew how to use his tongue. *Mercy.* She didn't have a single regret about what happened when her underwear came off, except for that whisper of frustration that came in wishing he'd stayed. That he would have let go of some of his control and let her take the lead.

But enjoying that side of Wren and not being embarrassed about how much she enjoyed the hours didn't mean she wanted to accidentally announce what happened to her dad. That meant she needed to figure out where her clothes had landed as Wren undressed her last night.

She scurried around the space, sliding across the hardwood in her bare feet when she thought she saw a peek of blue under the bed.

"Got it." She leaned down and snatched up her bra right as the doorbell rang.

Underwear. Underwear, underwear. She had no idea where the bikini underwear got to. She just had to hope they didn't make a surprise appearance while Dad issued whatever lecture he planned on giving.

At the second set of rapid knocks, she got to the entry. A quick look through the peephole and she opened the door. Her father stood there in dress pants and a long-sleeved shirt without the sleeves rolled up, despite the sweat-inducing humidity. "Hi, Dad."

He didn't move. "You're out of breath."

Always the champion of fun conversation, her father didn't disappoint this time either. "I just got home."

She backed up so that he could pass in front of her. As usual, he glanced around her apartment with a look of confusion on his face. He had the whole furrowed-brow-sighing thing down. She never knew if it was the general look of just about to tip into chaos that upset him or the fact she rented, which he found financially irresponsible. Either way, him coming here only heightened an already tense situation.

His gaze fell on the stack of boxes. Her copies of all the material she could find about Tiffany's case. "Is all this necessary?"

Emery sighed but somehow managed to keep the sound inside. "It's easier to keep the material in boxes than spread it all over the floor."

He sat down on the edge of the love seat. "You know what I'm talking about."

"This topic got us into trouble just a few days ago."

"That's what I'm here to talk with you about." He gestured toward the chair across from him. "Sit."

Never mind that it was her chair and her apartment and she'd paid for everything in it without his help. Money led to strings, and she never wanted to be in the position of owing her father anything. The relationship was rocky enough without adding in that factor.

Still, she'd stomped away from him the last time they met. He deserved it, but she'd long ago figured out capitulation on the easy stuff made her feel less guilty about how frustrated she got with him about everything else. "I'm sorry I walked out on our dinner."

He waved off her halfhearted apology. "I get that you're emotional about this subject."

"The subject of my cousin and best friend being missing for more than a decade? Yeah, it makes me cranky." Like right now. Just a few sentences in and anxiety churned in her stomach.

"Cousin and *childhood* friend. The two of you were already moving apart, and I'm telling you her father was about to send her away to school."

"That's not—"

"Believe it or not, Emery. I'm not here to fight with you."

Certainly sounded like he was. The talking-over-her thing was a big clue. And it sounded as if he'd come loaded with all the same arguments. The ones sure to send her anger spiking. But she would play along. He deserved that much respect. "Why are you here?"

"I think it's time I stepped in." He pulled a folded piece of paper out of his shirt pocket. "I am going to hire a specialist to come on board, take over all of this and provide us with a fresh look at Tiffany's disappearance."

Emery knew it killed him to say that last part. He was absolutely convinced Tiffany had run away and he blamed her for driving her own father to an early death. Her father had a habit of blaming the victim for not being careful enough, or in the wrong place, or with the wrong people. He did it while talking about things he'd heard on the news. He did it the few times she'd tried to talk about her work with him. She learned early not to do that again.

The only new thing here was the idea of an investigator of some sort. She knew she should feel grateful, even though the move was pretty clunky in light of how much time had passed and all the comments he'd made. Still, she couldn't shake the sense that this was a way of scolding her.

"I've hired a professional who will study every one of your files and provide us with a report. We can finally have some objective comments and then put this matter to bed."

"No." There were reasons and arguments, but she didn't bother with any of them. Didn't take the paper either.

He dropped it on the coffee table in front of him. "What is that supposed to mean?"

She would not let him control this and shift the answer in the direction he wanted. Rather than question his version of "objectivity" she went with a more neutral explanation, one that happened to be true.

"There already is a private party investigating the entire matter. He's talked with me and Detective Cryer. He has all the paperwork and files." Hyperbole seemed to be called for here, so she went with it. Her father was not one to back down easily. He had to be whacked.

His scowl hit full force. "Who?"

"Someone Senator Dayton recommended." Again, a partial truth, but Emery felt fine using it. "In fact, I met with her and the investigator. Everything has started. We have the best people looking into this."

"What is the man's name?"

Of course he assumed it would be a man. He just happened to be right this time. "That's not important."

"Of course it is. I need to talk with him."

That was never going to happen. "You can't until he asks to see you. He insisted on anonymity. That's the way he works. It's so he's not improperly influenced and conducts a totally objective review."

She kept skirting the truth, something that should make her feel guilty. She didn't even experience a twinge. Her father planned to come in, take over under the guise of "relieving some of the burden" and then control it all. Well, she wasn't in the mood for that game. When it came to Tiffany, Emery knew she couldn't let her father's demanding nature win.

"That's ridiculous," he said in a voice growing more agitated by the second. "I was there. A grown-up. You were only a child."

"Then you'll likely be interviewed." She tried to imagine Wren interrogating her dad and her mind refused to go there. "Hey, he's in charge, not me."

"You can't possibly afford the proper kind of review." Her father looked around as he said the words, as if to drive home the fact she had limited resources.

"I'm not paying for it." She'd finally said the first completely true thing . . . which got her wondering as to how Wren was going to get compensated. She doubted he ran his business and paid for those suits by performing tons of unplanned-for pro bono work.

"Who is?"

"The point is that you don't need to worry about this issue." She spied what she feared was the corner of her abandoned underwear tucked under the side of the couch. "It's out of my hands. The investigator has started and will eventually go through all of this." She got up and walked in the opposite direction of the underwear. "We should go."

"What?"

She slipped her shoes back on, almost groaning at how the tops pinched her feet. "I thought we were having dinner."

"This conversation is not over." He didn't even stand up.

"It actually is." She grabbed her keys and walked to the door, keeping her back to him and not watching to see if he followed. She turned around at the last minute. "You can use the meal to tell me everything else I'm doing wrong with my life. That should be fun for you."

"Emery."

"I can tell you about the attempted break-in." She knew that would get his attention.

He stood up slowly. "Here?"

She didn't intend to explain about her round-the-clock bodyguards, so she just answered the question he asked. "Yes."

"And yet you continue to sleep here by yourself?" He shook his head. "Absolutely not. You need to come home and stay with me."

"I'm staying with Caroline." What was one more lie in a series of many? And this one saved her from being pulled back to her father's house, the absolutely last place she wanted to stay. "I was just stopping here to check the place and meet you."

"That is not good enough. Your safety comes first."

She opened the door. "No, food does."

CHAPTER 18

His private line rang a little after ten that night. Wren was still in the office because the morning coffee runs and evenings spent digging around in Tiffany's case meant he had to put in extra hours on his company's cases. If the result turned out to be another night like the last one, sprawled across Emcry's bed, he'd go without sleep for a month. That woman was absolutely worth the overtime.

He picked up on the first ring. No need to play games when he knew the identity of the caller. Could almost smell her just from seeing her name come across his cell screen.

"Are you home?" Because he could swing by for a few minutes, or hours.

Emery laughed on the other end of the line. "Almost."

The answer didn't make much sense. He glanced at his watch. "That was a long dinner."

"Dad dropped me off at Caroline's house after because that's where I told him I was staying. I've been visiting with her for an hour or so." When Wren started to question, Emery talked right over him. "Don't ask about the staying-over thing. It's a long story."

"We'll come back to that. How was dinner with Dad?" Wren couldn't imagine having more than three words for his father—go to hell. No need for a long, drawn-out meal. Wren doubted he could choke down food if he ever saw the man again or had to sit across from him at a table.

No, watching from a distance was good enough. So long as his father followed the rules and didn't stray outside of a hundred mile area in Belize, exactly where Wren dumped him all those years ago with little money and under the threat of killing him if he tried to come back to the US. There, he got to live his broken life. All alone. It killed Wren to let his father live, but he promised Quint he would stick to this plan. Something about how it was a better solution because it punished his father and saved Wren's soul.

"I would describe the night as trying," she said.

Keys jingled in the background and the thump of footsteps echoed on the line. The woman never stopped moving. He smiled as he leaned back in his chair and balanced his shoes on the edge of his desk. "What exactly are you doing?"

"Is that a modified version of asking me what I'm wearing?"

The lightness in her voice eased the tension of his long day. "You should feel free to answer that question first."

"Nice try." Her voice faded out as a sound that suggested she was fumbling with the phone came over the line. "Walking into my building."

She called before she was even home. He didn't hate that. "Are Keith and Stan with you?"

"I would have to know who those two people are to be able to answer the question."

Now she was just playing with him. No way did she keep from asking her unwanted shadows their names. Hell, she probably knew before he did because he hadn't bothered to ask Garrett until two nights ago. "The men stationed outside your house."

She'd refused to accept the bodyguards. Wouldn't even talk about it when he called this afternoon and told her they'd continue to follow at a comfortable distance. Also told her good luck losing them. She'd hung up on him.

"Ah, yes. Them."

He could almost hear her roll her eyes. "I told you I was keeping them on duty."

"That's not heavy-handed at all."

Her spirit reeled him in and drove him mad. He couldn't remember the last time a woman had him spinning and changing his schedule and offering up his name. Then there was the following-her-around thing. That one was downright embarrassing. "I thought I was being fairly thoughtful in not insisting they come inside and sleep on your couch."

She snorted. "Never going to happen, but good thing they sort of blend into the neighborhood with that impressive dark sedan because I have no idea how I would have explained their presence to my dad."

Since she wasn't exactly fighting him about protection, Wren took it as a sign she didn't hate the idea. She might be independent and strong, but she was also smart. Someone got too close to her place the other night. He'd been prepared to press his point and argue about this, but he wasn't sure he had to.

But there was an issue he did want to discuss. "How about saying, 'Dad, the guy I'm sleeping with assigned bodyguards to me'? Or is that too much?"

"Sure, that sounds like something I'd say to my *father*." The laughter moved back into her voice. "And, as you pointed out, we haven't actually slept together yet."

Speaking of things he'd rather talk about . . . "You mean haven't had sex, because we did actually nod off for about an hour after the oral."

She sighed loud enough to blow out his eardrums. "Yes, Levi. Sex."

"I can come over right now and fix that for us." If she said yes he'd break the sound barrier getting to her.

"Subtle."

Not exactly the answer he wanted. "You need to stop thinking I intend to be subtle." They'd get back to the idea of sex and a visit, but first he needed one issue settled for the night. "Are you inside the apartment yet?"

"In a second." The keys jangling grew louder. "Keep your pants on."

Not the phrase any man longed to hear. "Do you mean that?"

"Not even a little."

"I can be there in—"

"Oh, my God!" Her voice broke into his then choked off. For that second, fear vibrated in her tone. A thud and then something like racing footsteps sounded in the background. "Not again."

"Emery?" Wren jackknifed and his feet hit the floor. "What is it?"

"My apartment . . . I don't . . ." Her words stammered and her breathing came out in short staccato puffs.

"Inhale." His hand curled around the cell and tightened until the plastic dug into his palm. Panic flooded through him. He hadn't felt the sensation in so long that he barely recognized it. "Talk to me."

"Someone's been here."

He stood up, dragging the phone and the file on his lap with him. "Where are the guards?"

Hearing the quickfire of her words and the gulping in of air touched off something inside him. A harsh breath hiccupped in his chest. That giant, churning ball of anxiety in his gut did not ease. He couldn't stay neutral and disconnected. She was not just a job.

"Right behind me." Her voice faded then started up again. "In the hall."

He walked around the side of the desk, knocking a stack of paperwork to the floor. Documents crunched under his shoes as he doubled back and opened his top drawer to find his keys and wallet.

He had to get to her. Now. "You do not leave them. I'll be there in a second."

"Okay." She exhaled into the phone, loud and shaky. "Just hurry."

Wren blew through a red light and took more than one corner too fast. The wild ride matched the pumping inside him. Anxiety rolled over him as he drove, roaring past the speed limit and earning both stares and honking.

Finding a spot to park on her street proved impossible, so he stopped in the middle and called for Stan to come down and take care of the car while he checked on Emery. He threw open the door and bolted for the front of her building. He didn't miss a step as he crossed paths with his man and passed the keys before heading for her door.

She stood in the entry. Seeing her there, with her arms crossed in front of her while she gnawed on her bottom lip, had him rushing down the hall.

"Emery?" He didn't realize he'd said her name out loud until she spun around.

Her face crumpled as she pushed away from the doorframe and lurched toward him. "You're here."

"Of course." He caught her and wrapped his arms around her. Inhaled the familiar scent of her shampoo. She was safe, but he still had no idea what happened.

He maneuvered their joined bodies until her back faced the inside of her apartment and he could peek in. His mind spun as he looked around. One of his men stood in the center of the room, taking pictures. The rest of the room waited in shambles. Ripped papers and crumpled files. The boxes of information she kept on Tiffany's case were overturned and emptied out. He hadn't looked inside those, but if her collection mirrored his then most of it was gone.

Slowly he came back to the present. Held her until his muscles ached, but there was no way he'd let go. Not when he could feel the material of his jacket bunched in her fists and puffs of air against his neck from her labored breathing. His mind flashed to comfort and he fought for the right words to say. When nothing came to him, he went with smoothing his hand up and down her back while the other one kept her locked against him.

Wren glanced at the bodyguard in charge, Keith. "Anything missing?"

The man stood up, all six-foot-four retired marine of him. "I checked the entire apartment. I can't speak as to personal items, but these boxes took a hit."

"He's back." She mumbled the words against Wren's shirt.

He still heard them. Lifted her head. "Who?"

"The person who took Tiffany." After gulping in a huge intake of breath she stood back with her hand still resting on his arm. "That's the only thing that makes sense, right? I asked around about you, bugged the senator. Made someone nervous."

"That suggests Tiffany knew her attacker. That it wasn't a random act by someone passing through." Which was exactly what Wren feared after the first break-in. A second could not be considered a coincidence.

"I know." A shiver had Emery pulling her body in tighter.

"Do we call the detective?" the bodyguard asked.

"No." Emery almost screamed the reply.

Wren wasn't sure that was the wrong answer for right now, but he doubted they had the same reasoning on that. "Because?"

She pulled back, not the whole way but enough to put some space between their bodies. She took one step then another, all while holding on to Wren's jacket and the arm underneath. "I just want to go through what's here and what's missing."

"There could be prints," the bodyguard pointed out.

"Did you . . ." Before Wren got the rest of the question out about having filmed, photographed and gotten the supplies to check for prints, Keith nodded. Wren looked at Emery again. "He's handled it."

She swayed a bit but stayed still. "I don't know what that means."

"We should leave."

She burst into action. Shuffled across the floor, crouching down to look at this paper and that one. Before he could catch her arm, she maneuvered around the couch. Every muscle sprung to action, like a bundle of exposed nerves. The walking, the scanning, the studying. Emery unleashed an amount of energy that had the whole room tilting in response.

"I have to look through these." She bent over by the edge of the couch and scooped up two fistfuls of papers. She looked at each one, reading and then dropping when she got to the end. "We can tell what he wants by seeing what's no longer here."

"Emery."

She waved him off. "It's okay. I have it all memorized."

That's the kind of comment that scared the hell out of him. "I think you should sit down."

She stilled and her arms fell to her sides. "How can I?"

Watching her now he could see the pain. Her body listed to one side and her mouth screwed up in a look of concentration. All the color had left her face and the easy banter disappeared. She hovered right on the edge. He sensed it as much as felt it.

"Okay." He waited until she nodded to turn her attention to Keith. "You can wait in the hall. We're fine."

The other man dropped his camera into his pocket and eased back toward the door. In another few steps, he walked out, closing the door behind him. That left Wren alone with Emery, who had turned into a little ball of energy. She whirled here and raced over to there. By the time she collected more papers and they filled each fist again she'd touched almost every corner of the floor.

He was about to call out her name again when she stopped. Just powered down in the middle of the room. Stood there with drawn cheeks and a wall of desperation thumping off her.

She shook her head. "I don't know where to start."

He had no idea what the right answer was, but dragging her body and mind through this exercise over and over had to be terrible for her. A person could only take so much. She hunted evil and tried to bring answers to victims. She stood as a survivor amid the mess.

But the bigger problem was getting her out of there. There was a possibility the person who broke in still waited nearby. He could be listening in. Wren needed the place searched, the police called in and new alarm equipment installed, and all without talking about Tiffany and potentially drawing the wrong people out into the open before he could put the proper protections in place.

She would balk at all of that. That left him few options, none of them particularly new to him. None dangerous to her, but all came with a heavy dose of asshole behavior on his part. Weighing her safety against her temper, he decided to take the risk.

"With wine." He used a lighter tone, hoping to bring back some of the life in her eyes.

She shook her head, her eyes narrowed in confusion. "Are you a big drinker?"

"Not particularly, but I can tell from the collection that you like it." He nodded at the two wine racks on the table behind her couch. Both full. "White or red?"

She followed his gaze then went back to staring at him. Her expression stayed blank, but she finally seemed to focus on him more than the chaos around her. "Red."

"Sit." He had to work fast. Get her relaxed and move in.

She started to ease down then shot back up again. "I don't really want to touch anything."

He couldn't blame her, but that didn't make his job any easier. "Then how are you going to look through—"

"I was going to beg you to do it." She shook her head. "I know you have a lot of the files. With your help I think we could figure it out."

"Ah." That sounded like trust to him, which made what he planned to do even shittier. "You only have to ask."

"I think I just did."

"Good enough." He moved around behind her and started massaging her shoulders. Rubbed along her tight muscles and down to her biceps before traveling up again.

Her head fell forward on a groan. "That's one of your hidden superpowers."

"I decided it was time to let you in on my secret."

"Your hands feel so good."

"Good." He made a mental note to give her a massage again when he wasn't in the middle of manipulating her.

She said something he couldn't hear and he asked her to repeat it. The second time the words came louder. "I blew it."

His hands stilled on her neck. "Meaning?"

"I made it known I was looking for you. Searched you out, mentioned you—well, the name Wren—on a message board that tracks missing people."

The message board piece was news. Bad fucking news. "You did?"

"The senator, the police. A reporter I know."

And now a reporter. Jesus, they needed to go through all of this at some point. Not today and not now. She needed to be out of there and away from the confusion that had descended on her life. But at some point they needed to talk about all she'd done to investigate his identity so that he could try to undo any of the potential damage. "That's very enterprising of you."

She pushed away from him and started pacing. Her balance seemed off and she mumbled to herself, breaking now and then to say something to him. "I can't stop shaking."

He saw the tremors move through her. Tense and on edge, waiting for attack. "You need to rest and I need to get you out of here."

"I don't . . . what?" She shook her head. "No. It's fine. I just need to concentrate."

She seemed to go over some invisible edge. She didn't stop moving. Her eyes stayed wide and she didn't blink. Then she started to babble. She said something about her uncle and started listing out all the documents that should be in her boxes.

She stopped walking around in circles and rubbed her hands together. "No, that's not the right order. I'm missing some and I can't miss any."

Jesus. "Emery."

"I'll start over." She waved her hand and then went back to the beginning of the list again, stopping only long enough to mention the names of potential kidnappers, of the men the police had already excluded.

Seeing her this way, so detached from reality and removed from her usual strength, killed him. He needed her calm and rational. He wanted her somewhere safe.

He also wanted his guys in there, doing a thorough search, checking every corner and every fingerprint. Setting up as much surveillance equipment as possible. That meant taking her out of there and keeping her away until the panic washed away and he could be ready to prevent another attack. Not an easy task.

After a quick run through his options, he went with the easiest one. The one guaranteed to piss her off later when she slipped back into being herself, but he'd take the heat if it meant figuring out who was trying to blow up her personal life.

"You're going to . . ." He pressed on the right spot.

Careful and quick, but it had her gasping. Then nothing. "Fall over."

The papers in her hands fell to the floor and scattered as her body went limp. He caught her in his arms and lifted her off the floor. For a second, he just stood there, holding her in the silence. Enjoying the feel of her. The warmth of her body.

His gaze roamed around the room. He looked for any evidence no matter how tiny that would clue him in about the danger haunting her life these days. From what he could tell, she'd gone a lifetime without being pursued and watched. Now this.

Someone kept getting into her building and this time into her most personal space. There were scuff marks around the lock on the door, but Wren wasn't convinced they showed a forced entry. The person came by when she wasn't there. Possibly a coincidence or maybe someone who knew her schedule. Add in Tyler's sudden reappearance and her public attempt to get Tiffany's case back on anyone's radar, and the threat of danger became all too real.

"Keith?" The door opened as soon as Wren called out.

The bodyguard stood there frowning as he looked at Emery's sprawl with her hair hanging over his arm. "What happened? Is she okay?"

"She's asleep."

Keith's frown only deepened. "She was walking around as if—"

There was no need to tiptoe around this. "I knocked her out."

This time Keith made a face. "Was that wise?"

Oh, hell, no. He might have trouble with people and knowing how to act and what might upset others, but Wren knew this move was not going to go over well. He was not a complete dumbass. He'd pay for this no matter how well intentioned the move was. "Definitely not. She's going to be pissed and rightly so."

"Then why do it?"

Wren had asked himself that question so many times. He should be able to treat Emery like any other client in any other case—with cool detachment. But he couldn't maintain the separation. She smiled and he felt it deep inside. She took him on, pushed back, and his attraction to her flared.

But he wasn't about to explain any of that. Not when he didn't understand it at all and wasn't ready to analyze it. "She was spinning."

"Sure."

Wren wasn't used to being on the defensive. "I want her safe and she wasn't exactly in the mood to listen to logic and accept my protection."

"I see."

That was the least convincing response Wren had ever heard. "Do you?"

"Yes, sir."

"Which is your way of telling me I'm in deep shit?"

Keith nodded. "Yes, sir. Absolutely."

"I was hoping you'd disagree with me." Sometimes Wren wished he'd surrounded himself with people who told him what he wanted to hear. Doing the opposite had been a sound business decision, but damn, it sucked to have people right there telling him when he screwed up. "Finish whatever forensics you need then call Detective Cryer. Tell him Emery was out when you found her apartment like this."

"The police will look for her. They might worry she's been harmed or taken."

They better or he'd work behind the scenes to have them fired for incompetency. "Tell them she's with me. The detective has my contact information and can call."

"You think that will be good enough to keep them from asking more questions?"

For the detective for now, yes. For Emery, no. He'd have to start explaining the second she woke up. Even then . . . "I'll make it be."

CHAPTER 19

Emery heard noises. Voices. Somehow they lifted above the ringing in her ears. She shook her head and realized she sat up, lounged in a chair . . . or something.

Her eyes popped open and her heartbeat kicked up to a gallop as she glanced around the unfamiliar surroundings. Beige leather seats. The oval windows. She was on a plane, a private plane. That could only mean one thing.

She sat up straight. "Levi Wren!"

He stepped out from behind her but didn't say a word. So much for hoping she'd gotten locked in a dream. No, this was very real. She remembered being in her apartment and the tie. Him talking about wine. Then that massage . . . The clouds cleared and reality snapped into place. She had to grab on to the armrests of the plush seat to keep from strangling him.

His need for control was annoying. This . . . well, she didn't know what this was. She should be afraid and worried and demanding to see the pilot. She didn't feel any of those things. Except confused. And pissed. She was really pissed.

"You're awake." He didn't sound too happy about that.

Smart man. "What did you do?"

"Now, wait a second." He sat in the seat in front of her. "I can explain."

He'd likely take fifteen sentences and all sorts of fancy words to do it. She wanted the truth—now—so she started with the basic facts. "We're on a plane."

"Yes."

"Yours?" She didn't know why she bothered asking it as a question since that was the only explanation for how he got it so fast and had no trouble getting her limp body on board. That part was astonishing, really. A man in a suit carries a drugged woman to an airport and no one stops him, or at least that's what she guessed since she was actually in the air and not in her apartment or at a police station.

"I share it with . . . okay, the specifics don't matter." He frowned at her. "There's no need to make a growling noise."

"Why?"

"Because I intended to answer you."

That could only be a stall. No way was he that clueless. "I mean, *why are we on a plane?*"

He had the good sense to wince. To not pretend to misunderstand. "Oh, that."

Amazing how he seemed to have lost a few IQ points now that they'd left the ground. "Yeah, that."

"You were upset." That's it. He actually stopped talking. Sat there with his arms draped over the sides of his chair. All relaxed and natural in his big-money environment.

"You can't possibly think that explains this." She

looked around, wondering what in the world could explain *this*.

He had the nerve to frown at her. "I just wanted you out of there, somewhere safe."

"And you thought we should get on a plane instead of using a car? That you shouldn't at least ask first before flying me across the country?" For some weird reason that didn't surprise her. His reasoning made zero sense to her, but she imagined this made sense to him . . . somehow.

"We're just circling DC."

She hit him with sarcasm because that's all she had at the moment. "Oh, okay, then."

"It's not a big deal." He started to shrug but stopped.

"How old are you?"

He winced. "Uh, thirty-five."

"So, old enough to know better." By about twenty years.

"I wouldn't have taken you out of the metro area without your permission."

She saw him visibly swallow and took that as a sign that he realized he may have taken a wrong turn in his thinking on this one. "Because that would be outrageous, right?"

"I'm not sure if you're still being sarcastic."

Good Lord. "I am. I assure you."

"I wanted to take you to Garrett's place in upstate New York for a few days." He stared at her as if he was saying something reasonable and obvious. "Until we could figure out the reason for these break-ins."

Who the hell was Garrett? She had so many questions. "But instead you . . . actually, I give up. What's going on here?"

"I wanted your permission before we left the metro area. I needed for you to wake up for that."

It was as if he wanted her to throw him out a window. "So we're flying in circles."

"Basically."

Basically. *Sure.* "But you did drug me."

"Of course not. That's ridiculous."

She pointed at him in warning. "Not the smartest word for you to use right now."

"I wouldn't drug you." He sounded appalled at the idea.

She felt as if she'd stepped into a black hole. "As opposed to whatever this is?"

She settled back into the soft leather chair and studied him. His quick response qualified as a bit too much denial. He did something to get her on this plane without her remembering it, and she'd figure out what. She just needed a few minutes to adjust to the fact that he put her on a plane. An actual plane.

The real question is why her anger had already begun to fizzle. She wasn't screaming and kicking. She didn't have a response to that. Not one she understood. Despite the caveman behavior and messed-up people skills, Wren charmed her. She sensed he meant well. He just had absolutely no idea what he *should* be doing to impress her. But this wasn't it.

"You don't like to fly?" he asked.

"Honestly, you are ten seconds away from getting punched." Maybe that would make him understand how big and risky this move was. Whatever he hoped to accomplish couldn't be worth her wrath. Lucky for him, she was more curious than anything else at the moment. Though his frustrated frown was pretty cute. "And that sad face won't help you, so tell me why I'm really here."

"Like I said, I wanted you out of your apartment and safe until I could figure out who broke in and why. So, I used a pressure point to knock you out."

"Normal people would ask before taking me out of my house." Then again, most people wouldn't knock her out. At some point she needed to find out what he did because that struck her as a skill that could come in handy now and then.

He glanced out the window into the dark night with the blinking lights below. "As you've told me several times, with that one notable exception, I'm not all that normal."

The tone. The lack of eye contact. The combination made her wonder if the throwaway comment, made to sound half-joking, really bothered him. "I think you may be abusing that insight."

"I don't know what that means." He turned back to face her with a renewed intensity in his eyes. "But the point was to get you out of there, scour the place, check nearby security cameras. And, honestly, to keep you from being subjected to more police questions. In my experience, after the police are called to one house several times for break-in charges they start to question the victim and what he or she is doing in the house that's causing all the trouble."

"That all sounds sort of reasonable, which has me concerned about my own sanity." She leaned her head back and sank deeper into the seat cushion. "Also makes me think there's a part you're not saying."

"I knew you'd fight me on leaving the house and I wanted you out."

That sounded exactly like something he would do. "So, this is about your bossiness."

"I don't think—"

"Levi Wren." She needed him to at least admit he'd overstepped.

"Fine. Yes. I generally just handle things rather than ask for permission, and that's what I did here. Clearly that wasn't the best choice." He spoiled the pseudo-apology by grumbling under his breath. Then he peeked up at her and treated her to a heated half smile. "I like when you say my name, by the way. No one has said it, including me, in a very long time."

"Don't try to adorable your way out of this." Man, he was right on the edge of making her forgive him without more begging. "Can we land?"

"Do you have your pilot's license?"

She bit back a laugh. "I'm going to assume that was your version of a joke." She cleared her throat. "Will you have the plane land if I ask you to?"

"Of course." He shot her one of those what-are-you-thinking frowns. "You're not a prisoner."

From the look on his face she thought he probably believed that. "We'll debate that and your boundary issues later."

"Must we?"

As if she would let him off the hook that easily. From her limited time with Wren she understood that he worked better with clarity. If she gave him a fuzzy edge or wavered in her words, he'd find a loophole. He was not going to be that lucky this time.

But first they needed to get on the ground, which led to her other question. The one she hadn't answered before the night took its weird turn. "Is anything missing from my apartment?"

"From your filing system, we think some parts of the Tiffany files. But you'll need to confirm that."

"The break-in is about my renewed investigation." Her heart tumbled and a heavy sadness moved over her. The not knowing weighed on her every day. The thought Tiffany could be out there, pleading for help and praying it would come, fueling her mind on empty hope, chipped away at Emery's confidence. Shaped how she led her life.

He nodded. "Clearly."

The honest answer delivered a slap, but she welcomed it. Wren was a mass of imperfections, but every word he said appeared to stem from the truth.

Adrenaline pumped through her. "Which means the person who took her is nearby. Tiffany could be alive."

"Let's not get ahead of ourselves." He leaned forward with his elbows balanced on his knees. "It means someone is watching and concerned. That's the only conclusion we can jump to at this point."

She understood him now. Sometimes he threw out the convoluted sentences as a way to get her to focus on something other than the topic. Other times, he cut right to his reasoning and kept her expectations low. He'd performed the two tricks over and over. It only took a heavy dose of plane air for her to work it through. "Are you afraid I'll get my hopes up or are you really thinking this might not be the attacker?"

"Both, possibly."

The gobbledygook option. "Thank you for that definitive answer."

"It kept your mind off the fact you're on a plane." He pointed to the window off to her left.

"It didn't." She glanced out at the horizon. A pattern of lights outlined the DC metro area. She made out a twisting river and rows of lights from cars still piled up on the highway south of DC, leading into Virginia.

The world was quieter up there. The questions didn't matter. She didn't possess stacks of files and need to search for answers. She floated and relaxed and concentrated on the soothing sound of his deep voice. But it wasn't real and the world below them called.

"We need to land," she said, wishing it weren't true. She'd much rather linger up there, soaking up the romance of the starry night.

"Okay. It will take a few minutes to get to the private airport and get permission, but this should be pretty fast." He reached over and grabbed a telephone hanging on the wall. He issued a few orders then nodded to her lap. "Seat belt."

"Just like that?" That seemed far too easy. Few things with him so far had run that problem-free.

"I'm in charge, remember?" He exhaled. "And I need to make a call."

"To?" She fumbled with the metal clasp. It took two clanking tries to get the locking mechanism to work.

"My second-in-command. He'll need to meet us since your guards dropped us off and they're back at your apartment."

"That sounds reasonable." Which made her skeptical. "So, what aren't you saying?"

"The other goal for taking you out of the house was to be out of range in case your apartment had a listening device planted in it or, worse, the person who keeps breaking in—regardless of whether this relates to Tiffany—was nearby."

"There are so many scary pieces to that sentence." She tried to take it apart and analyze it and still couldn't make it all work.

"Hence the reason we're in the air."

Her stomach took flight when the plane started to descend. "Not for much longer."

"Correct."

"And you're not going to pull a stunt like this again. Not ever." Though she really doubted he could top this one.

He shook his head. "I'm not promising that."

She rolled her eyes. "What a surprise."

CHAPTER 20

The plane bounced to a stop almost a half hour later. The engines still roared and bells dinged in the background. She could hear Wren's side of the conversation on the phone with the pilot. It sounded like flight stuff, but she had no way of knowing. She also wondered what came next.

Before she could ask, the cockpit door opened. She spied a flash of the sleeve of a white shirt and a man's gray hair. A few more bangs and the plane's door opened.

She glanced out the window in time to see someone coming up the stairs. Then a face appeared. Looked younger than Wren, but not by much. A tall, handsome dark-haired man in a fancy suit that looked all too familiar in its tailoring.

She watched him step closer, struck by Wren's lack of urgency and absence of concern over their guest's arrival. This must be the guy who worked with Wren, but she wanted to be sure. "Who are you?"

"His friend, Garrett McGrath." He sat across the aisle, facing them. "The person he'll call as a character witness at his upcoming kidnapping trial, though I honestly don't know what I'll say to excuse this stunt."

Wren glared at the newcomer, an obvious friend. "She wasn't kidnapped. I was keeping her safe until I knew the area was clear."

Something about the ease of conversation and the way Wren didn't fight Garrett's presence told Emery what she needed to know. They knew each other well. Well enough for Garrett to step in and not stumble, which meant he was all too familiar with Wren's misfiring behavior.

"Does he actually believe that?" she asked Garrett.

He smiled at her with more than a little compassion in his eyes. "Unfortunately, yes."

Wren tapped his fingers on the armrest of his seat. "I landed the second she told me to. Well, as soon as was feasible."

"Well, there. Totally reasonable behavior." Garrett leaned in closer. "Who could fault you?"

She liked Garrett. She knew little more than his name, but she sensed the attachment to Wren. That made Garrett someone she wanted to know. The amusement in his voice and hint of wariness in his eyes reminded her of how she dealt with Wren.

Mostly, she wanted Garrett and Wren to know she didn't understand what happened tonight but was willing to chalk it up to Wren's oddness. "I'm fine."

"See? She's fine." Wren pointed at her but talked to Garrett.

That was more than a little annoying. Rather than tell him, she tried to appeal to the more logical of the two. Shifting in her chair, she tucked her legs under her and faced Garrett. "My sense is that he doesn't understand the enormity of his controlling behavior."

He nodded. "That is a kind way of putting it."

Yeah, she liked Garrett more every passing minute. He could be a great asset in helping with her Wren-deciphering skills. "What would you say?"

"He pays my salary, so let's go with your words."

Now that was interesting. "You work for him?"

"Yes. I'm second-in-command at Owari Enterprises."

She'd learned more information in two minutes from this guy than she had the entire time she'd been asking Wren questions. Wasn't that interesting? "What's that?"

"The name of his business." Garrett looked at Wren. "What did you two talk about on all those coffee dates?"

Something clunked in her head. The idea of Mr. Top Secret spilling date information . . . well, she couldn't even imagine that. "He told you about those?"

"No." Wren finally talked but that's all he had to offer.

Garrett chuckled. "I didn't give him a choice."

Maybe Garrett was a little too much like Wren after all. "I don't understand."

"He's overseeing the bodyguards and has conducted surveillance on you," Wren said.

Garrett winced. "That sounds worse than it is."

"I'm assuming he ordered it." There was something freeing and quite enjoyable about talking around Wren while he sat right there. She wanted to rapid-fire questions at Garrett and get all those answers she craved.

"Smart woman," Garrett said.

"I used to think so." But her attraction and ready forgiveness for Wren had her wondering. "My biggest concern right now is that the whole unconscious-and-on-a-private-plane thing isn't more upsetting to me."

The initial wariness and being ticked off gave way to something else. Wren did this for her. To protect her. On one level she loved the attempt. It was the execution that turned out to be an abject failure. But she sensed she could fix his aim if his instincts were good.

But maybe that was wishful female thinking. It was possible she'd seen one too many happy-ending movies where the love of a good woman could change a man. Thanks to her life experience the idea never held any appeal to her. Now, the idea held more promise for her.

Wren glared at her. "You knew I wouldn't hurt you."

Only he would think scowling was a good way to get out of this mess. "Is that the point?"

"Yes."

Garrett shook his head. "If you would have met him a few years ago you'd realize that this is such a better version of him than before."

"What was he like?" God, she wanted to know. She'd sit on the plane for hours if it meant getting a peek into the real man behind the black suit. Start with his actual name and the rest of his personal story and she could spin the rest from there.

Wren offered the answer. "Fine."

A tsk-tsking sound filled the plane as Garrett continued to shake his head. "Hard to resist that charm, isn't it?"

It actually was. The play of light and dark. The stack of flaws that combined to make Wren so compelling. And yes, the charm. He buried it deep, but it snuck through sometimes.

"How long have you known each other?" she asked Garrett since asking Wren questions about what he considered private information hadn't helped her all that much.

Wren's frown deepened. "Why are you asking him?"

"Because you never tell me anything."

He shrugged. "You know more than most."

Two steps forward, ninety-two steps back. "Honestly, that's your response?"

Garrett exhaled as he stood up. "I'm just going to go ahead and issue a blanket apology for his behavior and general cluelessness."

"Is that necessary?" Wren grumbled the question under his breath. Added in some impressive swearing while he was at it.

Garrett kept talking directly to her. "This is usually the point where he pretends to fire me."

"Does that happen a lot?" For some reason that made her laugh.

"Daily. Whenever I disagree or tell him he can't do something."

She could totally see that happening. "Does he get angry?"

Wren waved a hand in front of her face. "I'm right here."

"Not in a yelling and screaming kind of way," Garrett said, talking over Wren.

This time Wren stood up. "Are you two almost done?"

Garrett didn't back down. He put a hand on the back of Wren's seat and stood there. "Just about."

"I have more questions." She raised her hand. Since she was the only one still sitting, she didn't know if they even saw it, so she just talked louder. "And I would love to hear the conversation that goes along with the firing."

Wren ducked his head and glanced out the plane window. "Too late. He's getting out."

That got her to her feet. She guessed Garrett didn't need a shield or someone stepping in to fight his battles. Still, she felt pushed and wanted to push back. "You can't just kick him out. I don't even know if we're in Virginia, Maryland or DC."

"Thank you for being offended on my behalf, but that's my car." Garrett pointed at one of the two cars sitting near the plane. "Do you need a ride?"

"She's coming with me," Wren said.

She didn't have time to figure out where they were or how the cars got there. No, Wren dove right in and had her head spinning. "Since you asked so nicely?"

"The guards are finishing the sweep and installing a new security system at her house so we don't have a repeat of last night."

"You're not good at asking for permission from me, are you?" Forget that she didn't have money for that and had no idea how she'd keep up the monthly charges. Her bigger concern was his ongoing insistence that he knew how she should lead her life.

Yes, the break-ins scared the crap out of her. The implications, the connection to Tiffany, had panic eating away at her stomach lining. But she'd survived all these years and been able to function because she took control. She wasn't ready to hand that over now.

Not that Wren looked convinced. He shot her one of those you-know-better expressions. "That's not really my style, now is it?"

"A supremely tone-deaf response." Garrett clapped Wren on the shoulder. "Well done."

She ignored the show of male bonding and thought about the safety issues. She was not one to take that for granted. She'd lost so much and almost lost everything. Only lucky timing and a heap of teenage anger kept her from being in the wrong place when the horror came. Saved her from crossing the line into victimhood.

One point Wren was trying to make did get through. New alarm system or not, she couldn't stay in her apartment.

Questions flooded her brain and she started asking them. "Is the plan to take me to a hotel or a secret cabin or—"

"My house."

Garrett whistled.

Emery forgot how to breathe. It took all her concentration to get even a partial sentence out. "Where you live with . . . ?"

"Alone." Wren morphed back into the brooding guy she met the first day. Brooding with a big splash of grumpiness. "I'm not going to kill you, if that's the concern."

"That's . . . wow." Garrett whistled again. "We need to work on your dating game."

On that, Emery disagreed. She also wanted to stay on track, so she kept her focus on Wren. "I'm impressed you live in a house and not a bunker or hole of some kind."

Wren glared at her. "You continue to be confused about whether I'm human."

"Gee, I wonder why that's confusing for her," Garrett said.

She was too busy thinking about where he would live and what it would look like to get derailed. "This house doesn't have one of those panic rooms, right?"

Wren shrugged. "Actually, it does."

Of course it did. It probably also had an elevator and staff. Yeah, going anywhere near the place would be a mistake. She was about to tell him that but another sentence slipped out of her. "Let me put it this way. Do you plan to lock me in it?"

"You can go anywhere and do anything you want in my house, which is in DC and not out in the middle of nowhere."

"You being invited into the inner sanctum is huge," Garrett said. "Hell, you knowing his name is a stunner."

Wren never broke eye contact with her. "Emery, your answer?"

"While I'm impressed, you're acting as if you're giving me a choice—"

"I'm trying not to make another misstep."

She believed him. He knew he'd gone too far. For the right reasons, maybe, but he'd crossed a line. Now he was walking it back and doing it in a way that made much more sense. She decided to view that as progress. "Fine, but you should know I hate when you talk to me in that tone."

"You've made that clear."

Just when she was on the verge of giving him what he wanted he said something like that. "But yet you keep doing it."

"It's the only tone I have."

"No, it's not." But she saw the way he curled his hands into balls and held his body so stiff. He was waiting for a blow, expecting her to refuse. That wasn't going to happen. "You're impossible, by the way."

He must have sensed that he'd regained the upper hand. Some of the stress left his eyes and the frown tugging at the corners of his mouth eased. He barely spared Garrett a glance as he issued an order. "Get out."

"On that note, I'll leave you." Garrett reached out and shook her hand. Held it for an extra second. "As long as you're sure you're okay."

"I am, thanks." She gave him a smile then let go.

She watched him walk to the front of the plane. Wren's gaze nearly burned her cheek.

"Emery?"

Her gaze moved to him. Strong, determined Wren. "Fine. I'll go with you."

A look of satisfaction spread across his face as he nodded. "Excellent."

"You're not going to blindfold me, are you?" Though she wasn't sure she hated the idea.

A smile lit his face. "Only if you ask very nicely."

CHAPTER 21

Wren tried to see his house through Emery's eyes. The layers of security. The cameras. The lead-in through the garage. It probably struck her as a cave. A place someone *not normal* would choose to live.

They walked in silence to the main floor as he turned on lights and music using his cell. The trail led them to the oversized great room, which opened to the state-of-the-art kitchen. She bypassed both and stopped in another room at the back of the house, the dining room, with its soaring windows and papers strewn all over the tabletop. Papers that outlined and analyzed a horrific part of her life.

Emery walked by the built-in bar and stopped at the head of the table. She shuffled a few pages around before moving them to the side. Scanned the document left on top. "You've been working."

That sounded neutral. Sort of. "I promised you I would help."

She looked up. "And you keep your promises."

He had no idea where this conversation was going or even what it was about, but he needed to face the spur of the moment choices he made earlier. Grabbing on to the top of a chair, he stood directly across from her. "Look, I know I messed up tonight."

"How?"

Her head tilted to the side in that sexy way that had his breath stuttering inside his chest. She had that power. The strength to push on over unimaginable pain. The smarts to build a life outside the shadow of her well-respected father and the girl who vanished in an unspeakable instant. The drive to find him, to make him step up. She could read him and had him reorganizing parts of his life to include her.

He'd never met another woman like her. Never had one sneak under his defenses. Never been pulled in and whipped around. Never lowered the shields. And never had more trouble keeping up with a conversation. Her mind moved and he struggled to match her. "I don't understand the question."

"I'm wondering if you really know what you did wrong." She pulled out a chair and sat down. Looked comfortable and right lounging there in his house.

"It's the control thing." He thought that summed up most of his personality.

"See, I think you really don't understand how far over the line you stepped." She drummed her fingers on the nearest paper stack. "I mean, you get it on some level, mostly because I got angry and your friend Garrett seemed shocked by your behavior. But I think you'd do it again."

If it meant keeping her safe? Hell, yeah. "I wouldn't use the plane a second time."

Her eyebrow lifted. "You think the only issue was your choice of transportation?"

She didn't sound angry, but he wasn't taking any chances. "No."

"Good guess." The chair creaked as she got up again. She wandered into the kitchen, dragging her fingertips along the stone countertop, and slipped behind the island to stand by the sink. "Water?"

"Right." Of course she needed a drink. He could use something stronger, but water worked. He joined her, stopping only to open the refrigerator and grab two bottles. "Do you want a glass?"

"No need." She unscrewed the cap and took a long drink. Playing with the cap, she looked around. "This isn't what I thought your house would look like."

"You were expecting a cave?" He turned around to lean against the counter and face her. His outer thigh brushed against hers, but neither of them moved away.

"More like a bunch of cold marble and fancy expensive lights."

"I strike you as fancy?" He fought the urge to scan the open area. Not that he needed a reminder. He'd picked out everything that went into his house. Moved in, stripped out all the shiny mirrors and stone floors. Replaced every slick surface. Switched to weathered hardwoods and furniture he actually wanted to sit on.

He wasn't home all that often, so when he was he wanted it to actually feel like a home. Something he never had growing up. A place to relax, not a prop for his father's court case.

She shook her head. "Not really."

"Then I don't understand this conversation." A usual occurrence with her. He was growing accustomed to the sensation of being one step behind when dealing with her. At first it bothered him. Now he waited for the what-the-hell-is-she-talking-about moment to arrive every time he saw her.

She stepped in between his outstretched legs. "Did your wife decorate it?"

Ah, that's what this was. An information-gathering session. Made sense. He could handle this. "She never lived here. We were divorced long before I started Owari, back when the only money I had was what I'd earned working for Quint."

She glanced behind her then back to him. "The comfortable chairs and big stone fireplace are all you?"

She seemed to be confused about the concept of him living alone. "Who else would they be?"

"A designer."

Now there was a nightmare thought. "I barely let Garrett in here."

"Good point." She set the water bottle on the counter next to him and eased in a bit closer. "What was her name?"

He didn't pretend to be confused. "Shauna."

"Do you still love her?"

A smart man would hedge, throw out a line, but he promised he'd never do that. Shauna deserved more respect than that. He blew it, not her. "I'll always love her."

Some of the light left Emery's face. "I see."

"You don't." He set his bottle down next to hers and rubbed his hands up and down her arms. "The problem was that I was never *in* love with her. We were friends who survived shitty upbringings. We gravitated toward each other. Got each other out and away from the mess."

The tension drained from Emery's face. "She knew about your parents."

"She was there through it all, including the time when I wanted to kill my dad."

Emery blinked a few times. "You mean you thought about it."

"I mean I tried to." Forget wading in. He dove right off the cliff. He skipped over the details about the nights of hiding and following. All the time he logged on the shooting range. The stacks of paper outlining plan after plan for getting the job done. But he hit the highlight. The part she might never forget, and he had no idea why he took that risk.

"That's what Quint saved you from doing." She didn't touch him, but she didn't bolt either.

"He got through when Shauna couldn't." As soon as he said her name her face flashed in his mind. The wounded expression he had to claim. He promised never to hurt another woman like that again, which meant staying detached. "You can imagine how that blows a marriage apart."

"I'm sorry."

"She's much happier now." She had to be because she was pretty miserable with him.

"Are you?"

No one ever asked him that before, but he still didn't hesitate. "Happiness hasn't been all that important to me."

Emery shook her head. "You scare me when you say things like that."

He'd never had anyone state a preference for something other than honesty before. "Why?"

"I think a part of you truly believes that nonsense." She moved in even closer, bridging the gap between them. Shutting out the distance until their body heat swirled around them. "People deserve happiness, Levi. You deserve it."

"Okay." He increased his stance. Brought her right between his legs until she leaned against him.

"Tell me your real name." Still she didn't touch him. She tucked her hands in her back pockets but maintained that last bit of emotional distance.

He should have seen that one coming. Dancing around questions about his past. Talking about mundane things like the house. She'd been moving in, circling as she waited for the right time to ask the one thing that mattered to her.

He applauded the skill. But that didn't mean he wanted to cough up the information. "Why?"

"Because I want to know it before we have sex."

Well, damn. She picked the one comment guaranteed to smash his guard to pieces. "Is that going to happen tonight?"

"We're going to go upstairs and get naked. What happens after that is up to you, but I'm hoping you'll pick the choice that involves condoms." She finally rested her palms against his chest. "You do have some, right?"

"Bought them today." Because he wasn't a complete dumbass.

"Nice."

He didn't want to be an asshole either. He put his hand over hers. Caressed the back of her hand as he said the words that almost killed him to spit out. "You've been through a lot tonight and you don't have to—"

"I know what I want and what I need." Her hand moved under his until her thumb brushed his fingers. "The answer to both questions is you."

That was it, then. No other woman he saw in the time since Shauna even knew to question the name he gave them, that being Brian Jacobs. Emery did and never wavered. She made it clear she wanted to know the real thing. An idea that scared the hell out of him, but she hadn't balked or panicked no matter what bit of truth he dropped on her.

"Levi Wren Upton." He hadn't said it all together like that in years. Hell, he never even used Levi these days. The three together were so disconnected from who he was now and how he led his life. When he held a memorial service and said his final goodbye to his mother he buried Levi Upton, too.

She smiled. "So, just the last name is different."

Warmth radiated off her. The comfort of touching her and soft acceptance in her voice made the admission easier. He never planned to say the name again. One more thing that changed since meeting her.

"I didn't want any part of my father to linger. The judge understood why I didn't want to share a name with my mother's killer." He blew out an uneasy breath. "I left Michigan and very quickly became someone else."

"I'm not sure changing your name is the same as changing who you are." She pressed a finger against his chest, right above his heart. "In here."

To him they were. The anger stayed, festered. He funneled it all into his business. Into growing it, making it thrive. Becoming successful in a way that wiped out all the insecurities and fears Levi Upton had. Eventually he found stability, the kind that only came with time and the false veneer of moving on. "Wren originally came from my mom because her mother had an aviary in Japan. Wrens were her favorite, so it seemed right to keep it."

"One of the few connections to your past." Before he could ask what that meant, Emery spoke again. "What did Shauna think?"

"That I'd likely end up in jail for murder." When they weren't fighting about money, they fought about that topic.

Emery's hands slid up to his shoulders. "Do you miss any part of your old life?"

Something about this position filled him with a sense of contentment. Her breast pressed against his chest and their bodies met, and he sank into her. The happiness shooting through him contrasted with the rough subject. For a second, guilt slammed into him. Whenever life smoothed out this feeling of not deserving, it rushed in behind. It had been that way his entire life.

But he didn't want to stop with a partial story. Emery had the pieces, and he wanted her to understand the framework. To fully understand the man in front of her, the one who wanted to touch her, kiss her . . . be inside her. "I was filled with rage and desperate for revenge. I stalked my father, hunted him down. Tried twice to kill him."

"And now I know you're not exaggerating when you say that."

"Not even a little." Was ten seconds from firing the gun on the second try.

"Oh, Levi."

He expected revulsion or at least a wave of wariness. She offered him empathy. Openness showed on her face. She listened and accepted and either ignored the reality of who he was then or didn't notice the underlying evil that still ran through him as he stood right in front of her.

The need to make her understand punched him. "That's the man you say you want to have sex with tonight."

Her arms wound their way around his neck as her fingers slipped into his hair. "That's the man I want. Period."

Those words. "Be sure."

She lifted up on her tiptoes and pressed her mouth against his. A gentle kiss that promised so much more. "Where's the bedroom?"

They barely made it upstairs. Lights clicked on around them as they moved, as if on some unseen timer. They tripped and fumbled their way up the steps through blinding kisses. They spun and their hands toured over each other as they tugged and pulled at each other's clothes.

By the time they crossed the threshold to his bedroom she was ready to rip her pants off and jump on the bed. But she forced her breathing to slow, her body to calm down. She wanted to savor this. If the last time they got naked was any indication of the heat they had together, she planned to string it out. Not let go until the very end.

Then her back hit the oversized mattress. It spanned half of the large room. A super-king-sized bed, if there was such a thing. While she watched him undo his belt and whip it out of his pants, she saw bits of her surroundings. A small couch and a large television. It all blinked out when his shoulders blocked her but, oh, what a welcome view.

She slid her palms over his bare chest to his biceps. She wasn't even sure when or how he stripped off his shirt, but she was not sorry. His muscles bulged under her fingertips. Not the kind that were pumped up from hours in the gym. No, he was sleek and lean.

He had the body of a runner and the hands of a genius. Right now he swept them down her stomach to the top of her jeans. She lifted her hips as he pulled them off. Down went the pants then her underwear, until she was naked and open to him.

Instead of diving in and taking pleasure, he gave it. His fingers skimmed over her sensitized skin. Her cells burst to life as first his hands then his lips traced over her. When he settled down with his shoulders between her thighs she almost lost her mind. Memories of his mouth and what he could do with it had plagued her all day.

Real time proved so much better. His tongue moved over the very tops of her inner thighs. He licked and sucked, teasing her skin and bringing her breathing to a stammering halt. When he finally shifted, dragging his mouth over until he feasted on her, she had to grab on to his shoulders then his head to keep from shimmying all around.

He kissed her there. Used his tongue and his fingers to ready her body for his. Plunged in and out, flicking and enticing, as her hips lifted on a steady beat.

"Levi, please." She didn't even know what she was begging for. She'd say anything, do anything, to reach release. But she wanted him inside her first, making love to her. Theirs bodies touching everywhere.

But he didn't stop. Not until her hands dropped to her sides and her chest rose and fell on harsh breaths. Not until she groaned and chanted his name. Then he moved over her. She barely heard the rip of the condom wrapper. She knew she should find the strength to lift her arms and help get his pants the rest of the way off, but her muscles wouldn't move. She hovered the fine line between tightening to the point of breaking and sensual lethargy. She craved both. Wanted it all.

She closed her eyes, just for a second. When she opened them again she could feel the rub of his bare legs against hers. The hair there tickled the backs of her thighs. "You got your pants off."

He laughed and the rich sound floated through the room. "Barely."

His erection pressed against her. She glanced down and watched him slide the condom on. He rubbed the tip back and forth across her opening until she lifted up, bringing her legs toward her chest. Half on his knees now, he put his hands on the backs of her legs, right by the knees, and began to enter her.

There was nothing hesitant about the way he filled her. He sank into her on one long thrust that stole her breath. Pulling out, he hesitated for only a second then plunged again.

Something inside her snapped. Forget the slow mating and seduction of her body by his. She wanted wild and out of control. She wanted to see him out of breath and on the edge.

Pushing on his shoulders, she got him to ease back. When he looked at her in confusion, she shifted her hips. His smile wasn't hard to read after that. It lit up his face. With an arm wrapped around her back, he spun them. Turned them over until she straddled his hips and rode his erection.

She needed this. Craved this.

Bracing her hands on his chest, she lifted then fell down again. The push against the tiny muscles inside her had her gasping. Her breath hitched and she fought to drag in enough air. She would have inhaled, but he pulled her head down and kissed her. Enveloped her in his heat.

And then she heard it. His soft panting. Felt the tremble in his hands. He wasn't immune to her and didn't pretend to be. She loved that a man so hell-bent on control could let go in the bedroom. Give in to his needs and let the moment touch him. Not pretend otherwise.

She wanted to vary the speed and torture them both. Make it last. She couldn't.

They fell into a steady rhythm that wound her up and tightened every muscle. Desire churned deep in her belly. She pressed her knees tighter against his sides and sank down harder and faster. Reveled in the feel of his hands massaging her breasts while his erection stretched and filled her.

The orgasm slammed into her. Broke right over the dam and had her head falling back. She kept moving, kept milking that incredible sensation. Every nerve ending tingled and her heart hammered in her ears until she could barely hear.

When the waves finally stopped pummeling her, she fell forward. Let her hair drape over her shoulders and brush his skin. Watched as his head pushed into the pillows and his hands clamped down on her hips. He came while her body still pulsed.

He finally stopped and she let her body ease down to rest against him. For a few minutes the mix of their breathing echoed in the still room. A sheen of sweat covered both of their bodies and her muscles turned to liquid. She didn't care about any of it. All that mattered was the frantic thump of his heart under her ear. The way he combed his fingers through her hair and smoothed the other hand up and down her back.

She may not always understand him, but she understood this. Their needs matched. Their bodies fit.

"I should kidnap you more often." His deep voice was filled with amusement as he talked.

If she could have moved her hand she would have

pinched him. She settled for turning her head and giving a little nibble to his chest. "That is not the lesson you were supposed to learn."

"I will do pretty much whatever you want right now."

She peeked up at him. The uneven rise and fall of his chest. The closed eyes and satisfied expression. "A second round?"

His eyes popped open. "Damn, woman."

"Is that a no?" She somehow doubted it.

He let out a long exhale. "Give me a few minutes."

Since she couldn't actually move that wouldn't be a problem. "I'm not going anywhere."

With a groan, he moved. Flipped her over onto her back and balanced his body over hers. "Until we're ready we should practice kissing."

Just when she thought he couldn't get sexier he said something that lured her in even more. She wrapped her arms around his neck. "I think we need lots of practice."

He lowered his head until his mouth skimmed across hers. "But it turns out I may not need too many minutes to recover."

"Let's see if we can set a record."

CHAPTER 22

Emery insisted on retrieving clothes. Wren had been tempted to feed her a line about buying her new ones. He could and he would, but he knew her well enough to sense that the offer would meet with an eye roll.

Unfortunately, getting enough supplies to stay at his house for a few days meant leaving the bed. He'd been prepared to call in sick for the first time in his grown-up life. She blew that apart over breakfast. He'd managed to usher her out of the house before Mrs. Hayes appeared to clean up. That introduction could wait until Emery felt more comfortable being with him. No need to hit her with more parts of his life until she adjusted to the secrets he'd already told.

Still, roaming around the city did not strike him as smart. Not until he had a better handle on who would take the risk to break into her place not once but twice. That was all he could think about as she unlocked the outside door to the apartment building. Well, almost. But the text from Keith saying the place was clear on their last check and no one had entered the complex in the last ten minutes kept dragging his focus back to the safety issues.

He tried one more time to make it clear he planned to be in her apartment for only a short amount of time. "Since this is a terrible idea, we'll get in and out fast."

She didn't even look at him, but she did shake her head. "Or I can decide how long we stay once I decide what I'm packing."

Clearly his approach did not impress her. "This is an unnecessary risk."

"I can't go to work naked."

It was as if she was trying to torture him. To get him to whisk her back to bed. "You could take some time off."

"Because that's what you would do in my position? Hide and not go outside?" She ended the comment with an eye roll.

He had to admit she had a point. "Okay, you win that argument."

That earned him a big smile. "I like that about you."

The happiness flowing through her was a big improvement from the wariness that wrapped around her as they'd stepped out of the car a few seconds earlier. Still, he was smart enough to wade in carefully to any conversation. "What?"

"You know when to concede."

"Only to you." He never did it any other time or with anyone else. It might damage his reputation if it got out, but he doubted the people he dealt with on a daily basis would believe her if she tried to explain it to them. They tended to be more of the we-rule-the-women misogynist crowd. The assholes.

She winked at him. "Nice answer."

He was so busy soaking in her smile that he almost

tripped over the idiot waiting in the hallway by her door. "What the hell?"

Emery stepped in front of Wren, as if to protect him. "Tyler?"

Tyler glanced around her smaller frame and focused on Wren. "I was going to ask where you've been, but I guess I know."

Wren wasn't in the mood for an intrusion from a twenty-something annoyance. "Then you can save time and skip to telling us what you're doing here."

"Inside voices, gentlemen." She unlocked her door then pointed to it. "Both of you, go."

Wren waited until Tyler went inside to follow. He sent a quick message to Keith to let him know he should stand by. The unwanted guest would be leaving soon, but the bigger question for Wren was how he got in, in the first place.

Emery stepped into the family room then turned around to face the men. Her confusion was obvious as she looked at Tyler. "Did I forget that you were coming over?"

"I just—"

"What?" Wren asked, not willing to hear the kid ramble on about nothing. Forget that he was only a decade younger and actually a grown-up, the guy came off to Wren as a kid.

"What is your problem?" Tyler made a scoffing sound before turning away from Wren. "Really, Emery. This guy is not your type."

"I'm not convinced you know what she wants."

Wren did. He'd spent all night learning what she liked and didn't like. What made her moan.

"Enough." She put her hand on his chest before glaring at him. "Play nice."

"Could I talk to you alone for a second?" Tyler asked as he walked toward the kitchen. "Just for a second."

"No." The dislike for this guy hit Wren full force. He didn't have a reason, really, but there was something smarmy about him. All swagger and little substance. Sure, he was supposed to be smart and a financial up-and-comer. Wren knew because he'd checked on the guy's background as part of the case. Checked and still didn't think all the pieces connected.

Bottom line: Wren had no idea what Emery saw in Tyler. Wren chalked the long-ago attraction up to teen angst.

Her fingers wrapped around Wren's tie and she tugged for a few seconds before letting go again. "You understand that sort of response tempts me to say yes even though I intended to say no, right?"

"I do now," he said as he smoothed the material out again.

She turned to Tyler with her arms crossed in front of her. "What's going on?"

"I was worried about you." The anger clicked off and the charm came roaring back. "The other night you talked about a break-in. We had a nice time together, so I thought you might like some company."

Wren really wanted to punch the guy. The fact Tyler kept glancing over then looking to the door, like he was sending a subliminal signal for Wren to leave, sure didn't help. "I think he wants me to go."

"I wonder why." Emery spared Wren a quick glance before focusing on her friend again. "Tyler, I'm fine. Really. The break-in was a weird thing, but you have to expect it when you live in the middle of a city."

He smiled at her. "I live in a big city. You live in DC."

Whatever the hell that meant. Wren couldn't really ferret the meaning out, but he thought it was some sort of New York versus DC battle that only Tyler seemed to be playing.

"Look, I'll call you later." She reached out to touch the side of Tyler's arm. "I have to get to work and there are a few things we need to do before that."

Tyler's gaze switched from her to Wren and back again. "Maybe we can have dinner this weekend?"

She nodded. "Sounds good."

Not to him. Wren thought that sounded pretty fucking terrible. "Does it?"

She ignored the comment as she ushered Tyler to the door and waved goodbye. "Talk to you soon."

Then she turned on Wren.

"That glare could melt steel." He might not be great with people, but he knew that was not the expression of a happy woman.

"Really?" That's all she said.

He got the point. "What? I let him live."

She let out a lingering sigh as she walked around him and grabbed a duffel bag out of the hall closet. "You could have been nicer."

"Not really." He thought he was rather controlled

compared to what he wanted to do to Tyler. The guy had a grating personality. Fine on the outside. Supportive family. Right schools. Big job. But there was something. A chill that moved underneath that made Wren doubt the sincerity of anything the guy said.

She glared at him again, this time from over her shoulder. "Levi Wren."

Fine. He would let it drop. After all, he was an old friend of hers and . . . nope. He couldn't do it. "Tyler is entitled and annoying."

"You don't even know him."

"I'm familiar with the type." Wren noticed she didn't exactly argue with that point. He should have let the topic drop, but there was one last thing he needed to know as he followed her to the bedroom closet. "You're not actually going on a date with him, are you?"

She dumped the bag on the bed and started filling it. Put enough clothes in for about two days. "Who said anything about a date?"

Wren wanted to dump all of her clothes in there but refrained. "He did."

She sat down on the bed and stared up at him. "He said dinner."

"We've had dinner."

She frowned. "Did we actually eat that Chinese takeout the other night?"

As if that were the point. "And we've had sex. Have you had sex with Tyler?"

"I think you're regressing. You sound like you're twelve."

She wasn't wrong, but he pushed ahead anyway.

"Probably true but, for the record, getting naked means we're seeing each other."

Silence screeched through the room after that. Her mouth dropped open and Wren could almost hear her thinking, which was good because his mind had gone blank. He'd said words he never intended to say. He felt them to his soul, but that didn't mean he meant to spill like that.

"Seeing each other?" She hesitated between each word.

Shit. Yeah, forget the plane. Now he'd really messed up. That comment had been an overreach. It also shook him that he even thought it, let alone said it out loud.

"I'm not sure what that means to you, but I'm wondering if I get a say in what we are and what we're doing," she said in a monotone voice.

He wasn't sure how to respond, so he went with honest. "Unfortunately."

One of her eyebrows lifted. "You'd rather order me?"

This was not going well. "Is that option open to me?"

She stood up. Something that looked suspiciously like a smile started to form on her lips. "You, Mr. Loner. The big brooding guy who values his privacy so much that no one even knows who you really are. You want us to date?"

Now it was his turn to be knocked speechless. "Did I use that word?"

"I picked it. Now, answer the question."

She'd actually backed him into a wall physically . . . hell, in every way possible. He didn't know when it happened, but there he stood, pushed against the doorway with his one arm tangled in the clothes on one side of her closet, with her *right there*.

"Admittedly, I don't sound like much of a catch in your description." Any smart woman would run. He kept waiting for her to do just that.

"I'm surprised you want to put a label on what we're doing."

He wasn't sure he was the one who did that, but bringing that up struck him like a bad idea. "Anything I say now will sound dirty."

"Be serious."

"I was. Was being honest, too." This part he was very clear on. "I don't like the idea of you seeing anyone else."

"And in exchange you'll say we're dating."

Damn, she almost stood on top of him now. "The direction of this conversation has me nervous."

"I refuse to believe you actually get nervous."

When she said things like that he wondered if she knew him at all. Either that or he was a much better actor than he thought. "Again, I am human."

"You seemed pretty human last night."

This he could handle. Some of the tension eased from his shoulders. A ball of anxiety still kicked around in his gut, but the memories of the night helped with that. "I thought that went well."

"That is the least romantic thing I've ever heard you say." She took his hand. "But, so we're clear, I don't want you to see anyone else either."

It took a second for the words to filter through his brain, along with the male panic from the word *dating*, but they got through. He squeezed her fingers. "Then it's settled."

"I'm not a hundred percent sure that's true, but fine." She let go and turned back to the bed. "Let me finish grabbing some clothes and other stuff."

He should have declared that a victory and pulled back. Should have, but there was one more thing. "We have another issue."

She laughed. "You think we only have two?"

There was nothing amusing about this topic. Not for Wren. "Tyler got into your building."

She shrugged as she folded up a T-shirt and tucked it into the corner of her bag. "It happens in apartment buildings all the time. He buzzes another unit from outside and keeps doing it until someone lets him in."

Since he needed her to hear what he was saying, he walked up next to her, facing her. "I meant that the guard stationed outside didn't say Tyler was here."

Her head shot up and she stared at him. "Say it when?"

A strange need to shut this conversation down stole over him. He wasn't the type to ignore problems, but part of him sensed this might be a time where the messenger—namely, him—suffered the brunt of her anger.

He showed her the message on his cell. "No report of a Tyler sighting, which means he got in without coming through the front door."

Instead of getting angry, she held on to his hand and the phone and read through the message on the screen. Looked like she read it a second time before glancing up again. "How is that possible? He shouldn't know about the back exit."

A shot of relief had him fighting to keep from gulping in air. "We'll figure that out when we watch the surveillance tape."

She made a face. "Now you're making me nervous."

"Good."

EMERY COULDN'T STOP mentally replaying the scene from the bedroom. A week ago, even five days ago, with all that happened there she would have gotten stuck on the questions about Tyler. The part about him just showing up, the timing . . . how he got into her building unseen. There was an explanation, of course, but she would have asked for it.

But her focus had shifted ever so slightly. All she could think about was Wren. They were *dating*. That was such a big word. When she mentioned it, tested the word, she'd been so sure he'd run and blow a Levi-sized hole through her front door on the way out. Didn't happen.

He was a constant surprise. So was the fact she'd brought him to work. That hadn't been planned, but then nothing with him had been. He followed her to the coffee shop and he'd been in her thoughts—actually with her—so much since then.

Heads turned as they walked down the aisle separating one side of cubicles from the other. One volunteer winked at her. Another openly stared. Emery got it. Wren's face and confidence. The way he moved, tall and so sure of his place in the world. Everything about him commanded attention.

Not that his ego exploded from any of it. He nodded hello and that was about all. He didn't do that guy thing where he scanned the room for the prettiest woman. He kept his hand on her back and moved them from one end of the room to the other.

They stopped at the entrance to Caroline's office. She had a door, but it was always open. This time was no different. She was up and waiting by the time they got there. Emery figured the strange silence that fell over the room drew her out.

Caroline ushered them inside and circled back to her desk. She stood by her desk and didn't offer them a chair. Right now, there was nowhere to sit. Case files lined almost every inch of the place.

"This is unexpected. I thought you'd stay home, Emery." Caroline glanced at Wren. "And I'm only guessing at who you are. I have to say I didn't think I'd ever meet you, but your reputation is impressive."

To wipe out any awkwardness, mostly hers, Emery fell back on introductions. "This is Caroline Montgomery. My boss."

Wren reached out and shook her hand. "Ms. Montgomery."

"Please call me Caroline." She bit down on her lower lip as if she was trying to keep from smiling. "And I should call you . . . ?"

Wren shot Emery a side glance before looking at Caroline again. "Actually—"

Emery rushed to fill in the blank. "Brian Jacobs."

"Huh." Caroline treated them to a slow nod. "Okay."

"She knows the name Wren." Emery's nerves

twitched until she had to fight the urge to fumble around as she looked at him. "Just that. I told her the day after we met and I . . . well, she's the only one I've told."

Emery didn't expect him to divulge his real name to everyone she knew. In fact, a part of her liked sharing the special secret of his first name and his real identity . . . for now. If their relationship, or whatever it was, continued then they'd have to talk about the name thing in some depth. Until then, she'd call him Brian in public and never say the name Levi to anyone.

"And I haven't repeated it nor will I. Consider it forgotten, Brian." Caroline turned to Emery. "But why are you here today?"

"I still have a job, right?"

Caroline frowned. "You were robbed last night. You can take a day off for that."

"Especially since it was the second time," he added.

"That's not what happened." When Wren started to talk again, Emery cut him off. "Don't help."

She half expected him to butt in and this time not accept the role of second chair in this conversation. But he just stood there, taking in the notices pinned to the board on one side of Caroline's office. The new cases. Then his gaze switched to the whiteboard inside the glassed-in conference room to the left of Caroline's office. It displayed the status of cases and a list of assignments.

Despite his strength and all his resources, all the work he did to "fix" things, at heart he was the boy who lost his mother by his father's hand. Standing there, seeing the evidence of so much similar despair, had to have an impact. Emery regretted bringing him face-to-face with pain that might resonate so much with his past.

"You can work from home." Caroline winced. "Oh, hell. I didn't think. Forget that. You can come stay with me until you feel comfortable going back."

That snapped Wren out of his stillness. He shifted his weight and jumped back into the conversation. "She's staying with me."

Caroline smiled. "Well, that's interesting."

Wren smiled back. "I agree."

"That's enough of that." She'd barely adjusted to the dating thing and the fact he agreed. The last thing Emery needed was to add matchmaking into the mix. "He was just dropping me off."

He looked at her. "You promise that you will either call me or Keith if you leave this building? He and Stan are right outside."

"I'm confused." Caroline leaned against the first of a long row of file cabinets lined up behind her desk. "Who are all these people you're talking about?"

Emery waved the question away, hoping to put off the ones that would follow as well. "Never mind."

"Bodyguards," Wren said at the same time.

Caroline stood up straight again as the corners of her mouth fell. "Emery?"

"He thinks . . ." He cleared his throat and Emery immediately changed course before he could take over. "Fine. We *both* think the break-ins are tied to me digging around in Tiffany's case in a more public way than usual."

Caroline's gaze flashed to Wren. "You think she's in danger beyond a simple break-in?"

"Yes."

That wasn't going to make her life easier. Emery could just feel it. "He's being cautious."

She could almost imagine the safety lectures Caroline would hand down after this. She'd survived violence as a kid and was ruthless in protecting the people who worked for her—the staff and the band of volunteers. Caroline was especially protective of her and she never took that for granted.

Caroline watched Wren for a few more seconds then nodded. "Then we'll all be cautious."

"Thank you," he said. "I can station some of my people here, if you like."

"Do you do that sort of thing often?" Caroline asked.

He didn't hesitate. "I do whatever needs to be done."

She understood him, but that didn't mean other people did, so Emery offered a translation. "He thinks that sort of statement is comforting."

"If you have someone outside, I would like to talk to them, though I'm not sure how it will help. It's an office building with many offices. A lot of people go in and out." Caroline shook her head. "I'm not sure how anyone would track them all."

"Keith is in the hall. His job is to stay by Emery's side whenever I'm not around."

That was news to her. Emery wasn't sure she liked it or the thing where the two of them talked about her even though she was standing right there. "When did I agree to that?"

"You can argue about that later." Caroline searched through a stack of messages on her desk then handed one to Emery. "Senator Dayton's office called. She wants to talk to you."

Normally Emery would think that was a good thing and meant something positive for one of her cases. This time, no. "About what?"

"Maybe she can help, or it's possible she knows something," Caroline said.

Emery looked at the number and showed it to Wren.

He nodded. "We can go over now."

That sounded good in theory, but working around the senator's schedule and time in the district could be tough. "She's a busy woman. I doubt we can just pop in and expect to be seen."

"I bet we can." He took the note and tucked it in his jacket pocket. "You don't need to roll your eyes at me."

She couldn't help it. He brought it out in her. "I'll stop once you tone down the bossiness."

Caroline laughed. "Well, it looks to me like you're in good hands."

More matchmaking. Great. "Don't encourage him."

"Too late." He slipped his hand under her elbow. "I'm encouraged."

Great.

CHAPTER 23

Wren read Garrett's smartass text asking if he'd retired and then turned the sound off on the cell. But his second-in-command had a point. Work had taken a backseat to Emery. Not his usual priorities, but he didn't regret being with her instead of in his desk chair.

He just didn't expect to be in Senator Dayton's office for the second time in less than two weeks. As a general rule he avoided politicians, even the very few he respected. Waiting in the senator's quiet office while she finished with a phone call in the other room he could feel Emery's anxiety. It bounced off her.

They sat only a few feet apart in the chairs set up in front of Sheila's desk. Not on top of each other but close enough for him to pick up on her nervous energy. The fidgeting. The heavy sighing.

"You okay?" he asked.

Emery glared at him. "Promise me you'll behave."

He wasn't sure when he became the issue. It's not as if this was his first time in public. "I am a well-respected businessman, you know."

"About that." She shifted in her chair and the wood

creaked beneath her. "How can that be when no one actually is supposed to know who you are?"

He chalked up the combative mood to her frustration of not knowing why she was there, but she was shooting the wrong messenger. "Your premise is wrong."

She treated him to an eye roll. "Of course it is."

He bit back a long exhale because the last thing this moment needed was more drama. "People know my name, or the name I want them to know."

"That sentence is a mess."

He was pretty sure he'd stepped right into one of those no-win scenarios. Not exactly a new sensation when dealing with Emery. "What's the point of being considered reclusive and mysterious if you can't limit the number of people who really know who you are?"

She leaned over the side of the chair, closing the gap between them. "And that question is ridiculous."

"I see you two are still getting along." The senator's voice boomed through the quiet room as she walked in and circled around to her desk to face them.

Damn, he hadn't even heard her open the door. He also hadn't realized he was leaning in to meet Emery in the space between their two chairs until right that moment.

He stood up. "And good afternoon to you."

"Hello." Emery nodded as she stood up.

"Well, now." The senator's eyes narrowed as she looked back and forth from Emery to Wren. "Now that I see your faces I think you're getting along just fine. Very fine."

He didn't know if women's intuition was a real thing

or not, but come on. "There's no way you can tell that by looking at us."

Emery cleared her throat and plastered on what looked like a fake smile. "You called and asked to see me?"

"Have a seat." Sheila nodded to the chairs they just left. "Now."

Emery's smile fell. "That sounds bad."

"It's never good when she starts a conversation in that maternal tone." Wren knew that from experience, like from the last time he stepped into this office.

"Don't try to gang up on me." The senator sat back in her big chair. "I can have you both arrested."

As a tactic, intimidation didn't really work on Wren. It took a lot to scare him—strangely, his feelings for Emery qualified—but this move didn't. "Actually, you can't."

"Yes, Wren. You know people, but so do I."

"I meant that I'm not aware of a senator's ability to have people arrested."

After a quick scowl at Wren, the senator turned her attention to Emery. "Your father called me."

Emery's head whipped back. "What?"

"He demanded to know who I hired to look into Tiffany's case for you."

"You're the one paying Wren and his company?" Emery's stunned expression didn't ease. She looked pale and confused. The way she gripped the armrests of her chair suggested she was only a few seconds away from ripping the fragile furniture apart.

Sheila shook her head. "Of course not."

At least on this one point, he could offer some insight. "No one is paying me, which is not exactly information I want leaked to the public."

Emery slowly turned until she faced him. "You afraid people might think you're a good guy?"

Some of her color rushed back into her cheeks. Wren took that as a good sign. "I'm more concerned with other clients refusing to pay their bills. You should see what I charge."

"Anyway." Sheila tapped the end of her pen against her desk until she had everyone's attention. "Your father called several times then came in and insisted on seeing me."

That move sounded all too familiar to Wren. "Apparently that trait runs in the family."

The senator talked right over him. "Normally, I would have had him escorted out, but I admit I was intrigued."

"What did he say?" Emery asked.

"He's convinced you've either been taken in by a con man or that an investigator will get your hopes up about Tiffany. Whichever one, he wanted the investigation stopped." The senator scoffed. "I can only assume he thought I'd handle that with an act of Congress."

Tracking down the senator, throwing his weight around. That all struck Wren as a lot of work and energy for Emery's father to expend. He hadn't gotten the impression that the man was particularly warm or loving, but then Wren didn't know a hell of a lot about decent fathers.

"He said he would handle it." The senator moved her

chair closer to her desk. "He also mentioned a break-in and safety concerns. That's why I wanted to see you. To make sure you were okay."

Emery blinked a few times too many, as if she couldn't deal with what she was hearing. "That's impressive constituent service."

"I doubt she makes this offer to every former Maryland resident." Wren sensed Sheila appreciated how Emery had helped her in the past. He also got the impression that the senator just plain liked Emery. That he could understand, so he tried to ease her worries on this subject. "I've had my people take over Emery's security."

Emery made a strangled sound. "That sentence."

He didn't see the problem. "Was accurate."

"You make me sound as if I'm in witness protection."

He refused to argue about his word choice again. He looked at Sheila instead. "I'm assuming you didn't give her father my name."

"I know your rules, Wren."

The comment didn't exactly inspire confidence. "I'll refrain from pointing out that you arranged a meeting between me and Emery without my prior consent and despite those very rules."

Sheila's eyebrow lifted. "That seems to have worked out fine for you."

That's what he liked about the senator. She was smart. In this case, too damn smart. He didn't like that she could read him. Between her and Emery he'd soon have to hand in his misunderstood loner badge. "I've been looking into the case."

"Your message said you figured out why your name was in her uncle's file." The senator tapped her fingertips together as she eyed him. "So, you can imagine I'm surprised to hear you're still working on this."

Emery snorted. "No, you weren't." When he stared at her, she shrugged. "What? She wasn't. She knows you, which means she knew you would see this through. That's who you are even though you seem desperate to hide that side of you."

Yeah, he definitely needed to hand in that badge.

Sheila smiled. "She's a good match for you."

"Okay." They'd gotten way off track. Wren rushed to shove them back on course. "What about her father?"

The senator's mood sobered. "You're going to need to talk with him, Emery. I can't have him coming in here, acting as if I work solely for him and am here to do his bidding."

Emery nodded. "I understand."

"Frankly, he's nothing like you," the senator continued. "While I enjoy seeing you, that feeling of goodwill doesn't extend to your family."

"I'll talk to him."

Wren liked the theory, but he wondered about the execution. "What are you going to say?"

"I have absolutely no idea." She stood up and smiled at the senator. "We'll let you get back to work."

"You're sure you're okay?" the senator asked. "The break-in has me concerned."

"I'm handling it," he said, because he was.

"What more could a woman want?" Emery gave a final small wave and walked toward the door.

She was out and in the reception area before he could catch her. He got a few steps before he heard footsteps behind him.

Sheila snagged the arm of his suit jacket. "Be careful."

He glanced into the hall and figured they had about a minute before Emery came rushing in looking for him. He lowered his voice just in case. "I'm not going to let her get hurt."

"I meant be careful with her or you'll answer to me."

Rather than be offended Wren took the comment in stride. He liked that someone was sticking up for Emery because it sounded as if her father had an odd way of doing so. "She's pretty tough."

"We all have our breaking point." The senator tapped her finger against Wren's chest. "Even you."

"Wait, are you worried about her or me?"

She frowned. "Just don't mess this up."

Yeah, that was the plan.

EMERY MADE IT all the way to Wren's kitchen before asking the question that had been buzzing in her head during the few hours of work she managed to put in today and the car ride back to his house. She dropped her purse on the oversized kitchen counter and turned around to face him. "What was the senator talking about to you in her office right before we left?"

Wren dropped his keys and wallet next to where her hand was braced beside her hip. Next came the tie. He loosened it and opened the top button on his shirt. Looked like he was stripping down after a long workday even though it was barely six. She guessed for him that almost qualified as a half day.

He frowned. "I honestly have no idea."

From his confused expression she didn't think he was hedging. Which meant the senator had said something personal. Something about dealing with people, and possibly feelings. Areas where Wren thought he came up short.

At first Emery agreed, but now she wasn't so sure. A man who dropped his work to help a woman he didn't know and guarded her, albeit a little too closely, but still because he genuinely worried about her, couldn't be as cold and detached as he claimed to be. He insisted the Levi Upton side of him died years ago. But that reserve of patience and decency came from somewhere.

The way he presented his life, as a man who fixed things and stayed clear of people, only told part of the story. Then there was his friendship with Garrett, his relationships with both the senator and Detective Cryer. Most of the people who met him seemed to not only respect him but to want to stay in contact with him. She didn't think that was just about keeping Wren close because he might be of use one day. That's not how it was for her. Not by a long shot.

Their lives intersected. They knew some of the same people, were fighting for the same things. His soft spot for women in trouble might stem from his mother's death, but Emery suspected it was really an indication that he was a good man. A brooding, moody, controlling one, but still good.

The only thing that scared her about him was how

attached she'd become. How right it felt to walk into his house and dream about being in his bed. She didn't normally find the commanding type attractive, but on him she had from the start. She could not fall for him . . . but that urge was getting harder to resist.

She watched him now as he moved around his kitchen. Got them both a bottle of water and checked the stove. That last part didn't make much sense. So much about him was complex and out of reach. So much didn't fit with the rest.

"Poor Wren." When he looked up her heart did this crazy loop. "People are so confusing."

He snorted. "I'm not arguing with that assessment."

Before he walked over to her, she saw the light on in the oven. Then she inhaled. Chicken and some spice. While she enjoyed eating it, cooking was well above her skill level. Still, rosemary? Something very familiar. "Why do I smell food?"

He nodded to the area behind her. "It's in the oven. It's on warm, so it can stay in awhile."

It was interesting he thought that explained anything. She was still pretty confused. "Your house magically prepares food while you're at work. If so, rich people are way luckier than I imagined."

He smiled. "Mrs. Hayes."

Apparently they were just saying random names now. Either that or she missed a *very* big piece of information about who else lived in the house. "Excuse me?"

"I have a woman who comes in and takes care of everything."

He had a woman . . . "Including you."

"If you're asking if she cooks for me then yes." He did not blink. "Her job requirements are limited to household things."

She wasn't sure what to ask next. She'd known he did well and had money. She didn't know he had paying-people-to-tie-his-shoes money. "Does she live here?"

"No."

"But she works for you?"

"A lot of people work for me." His voice took on an edge.

She wasn't exactly sure which question made his defenses rise, but one of them sure did. "It was a simple question."

"It felt like a judgment."

She had to admit that was fair. Living in the DC area she walked around with these stereotypes in her head about men in power. Men with lots of money. Men who lived in this ritzy neighborhood. He actually smashed all of her old theories to dust.

Despite that, she was still a little weirded out by the idea of a woman coming into the house and picking up after her once she was gone. The whole notion kind of made Emery feel like a secret or a trophy or something. She couldn't really mentally nail down why it made her twitchy, but it did.

"Is she here now?" she asked, hoping the answer was no because it meant she was hiding in a closet or something.

"I texted and asked her to make dinner then take the next few days off."

That validated all of her fears. "Because I'm here. Are you afraid I'll scare her?"

He put a hand on either side of her on the counter's edge, basically trapping her between his arms. "I'm hoping we'll have sex tonight and maybe again tomorrow, and I figured you didn't want an audience."

The indignation and frustration, with more than a little hurt mixed in, had been brewing. With that comment and the sparkle in his eyes, it all washed away. Sounded like she jumped to one conclusion too many.

Her fingers went to the loosened knot of his tie. "Good call."

"Thank you."

The rising anger gave way to a very different feeling, still heated but not in the same way. Her heart raced and the need to see him naked again pounded her. She didn't doubt that he was game, but she did wonder if he was a bed-only type. "On all of it."

The corner of his mouth kicked up in a sexy grin. "Meaning?"

"Can dinner wait?" There was no way she could choke down one bite of food. Not now. Not as she stripped off his tie. Not when her fingers settled on the top of his belt.

"I don't see why not." Still, he stood there, leaning into her but not touching. His hands still next to her but not on her.

It looked like the man needed a bigger hint.

"Then I have one question for you." She started opening the buttons of his crisp white shirt. "Are you familiar with the concept of sex against a wall?"

He nodded nice and slow. "I do believe I've read about that once or twice."

Her breathing turned shallow and her brain blinked out for a second. "Any chance you want to experiment?"

"Does it go something like this?"

He moved then. His fingers closed on her waist. She was about to wrap around him and steal one of those amazing kisses when he spun her around. He pressed her chest against the wall and her hands came up for balance. His palms touched against the backs of hers.

His breath skimmed over her neck then to the back of her ear. "I'm going to fuck you right here."

God, yes. "Do it."

"But you have to be ready."

He bit down on her ear, a gentle nip that she felt to her toes. She wanted to say something, nod, but nothing came out.

He used his knee to push her legs apart. His leg slid along her inner thighs and kept going. Up until his knee pressed against her. He rubbed against her through her jeans and his pants. Small circles. Slow then fast. A welcomed sexual torment that had her resting her forehead against the wall.

Just as her hips started to sway in time to the rhythm of his knee, one of his hands slipped inside the waistband of her jeans. His hand spanned the width of her bare stomach, pulling her back into him, then dipped lower. His fingertips eased under the top of her underwear. Then inside her.

She wanted him to rip everything off. Tried to tell him, but her brain kept misfiring. "That's a good start."

"You can still talk, so I should try harder." He plunged his finger in deeper.

"Definitely." Her hands curled into balls against the wall as the muscles in her knees started to give out. He had her limp and wet and ready.

He trailed a line of kisses along the underside of her hair. "We'll do it over and over until we get it right."

"Oh, damn." That finger was almost magical. He hit the right spot then eased back inside her when she gasped. He kept repeating the action until her body begged for more.

"I want you to be satisfied," he whispered.

She reached down and grabbed his hand. Through the layers of clothing, she held it tight against her. "Then stop talking and move."

"Not yet."

He touched that spot one more time and her body started to buck. Her arms shook, barely able to hold her up. She put her cheek against the cool plaster as the pleasure hit her. It rushed over her body in waves. She closed her eyes and bit her bottom lip to hold it back, but she couldn't stop it. She came as she guided his fingers in deeper.

In the background she could hear a zipper. Then her waistband loosened and he tugged her jeans down.

Reality kicked her. "Condom."

"Handled."

"Really?"

"I've learned to always carry one when I'm with you. Just in case."

He put the packet in her hand. She heard the jangle as he undid his belt. Only his body kept her pinned to the wall now, but she wasn't going anywhere. "I knew I could count on you."

"For anything." His hands slipped her underwear down. "You want sex against a wall, you got it."

She wanted to say something, do something. All she could do was close her eyes and enjoy as his fingers moved inside her again. "Then let's get to experimenting."

CHAPTER 24

Wren actually almost worked seven full hours the next day. Maybe a normal day for some. A really light day for him, especially since most of yesterday was spent with Emery's boss and the senator. Basically, it had been an all-Emery day. That was starting to be a pattern in his life, which Garrett pointed out about nine hundred times today.

Never mind that it was Friday and he had the weekend ahead of him to catch up. Not that the goal would be easy since he had no intention of leaving Emery's side. She had hours of nonwork time, which meant she could get into a lot of trouble. He'd really like to avoid being a part of that, starting right now.

He looked over at her from his position in the driver's seat. They sat in the driveway of her father's house with the engine running. Had for the last five minutes. He'd previously volunteered to go with her to see her father. Of course, that was before they slept together. Before he'd trailed his tongue all over her and spent hours kissing and touching her. Amazing how that changed things when it came to meeting her father.

"I can wait in the car." That struck Wren as a smart

idea. He wasn't really a meet-my-dad type anyway. He basically hated fathers thanks to his own.

Emery stopped flicking the lock toggle back and forth. Immediately the annoying clicking vanished. "We both know this will keep ratcheting up until you meet him."

Wren wasn't ready to admit anything remotely like that. Still . . . "This?"

"His poking around."

So, not the sex. Seemed like they were on two different wavelengths tonight. Not the best time for a communications issue. But he couldn't help but point out one tiny issue. "Notice how I'm not drawing comparisons between his behavior and yours."

She switched from shifting on the leather seat to glaring. "That's wise."

Well, if someone was going to look at him like that it may as well be her father. He shut off the car and opened the door. "Let's go in."

She caught his arm before he could slip out of the car. "Before we do, there's one issue we need to discuss."

"Are you having an attack of nerves?" This was one of those times he'd missed the subtle clues. Worry he understood. From all accounts, and Detective Cryer didn't have a very positive one, Emery's dad was a dick. Knowing that as an outsider and being related to that were two different things.

"Hardly."

"Really? Because that's probably normal." He had no idea what he was talking about, but he just kept firing out random thoughts he hoped sounded good or at least helped.

She twisted the strap of her purse between her fingers. "I'm dancing around the dating thing."

"Meaning?"

"You know what I mean."

"I don't, so this should be interesting." He shut the door and settled back into the seat. "Go on."

She sighed at him. The type that telegraphed her utter annoyance with the male sex in general. "We should skip that part. Telling him about it, I'm saying."

As in pretend the talking, the touching and all that sex hadn't happened. On the bed, in the shower, against the kitchen wall.

Not fucking likely. "Excuse me?"

Her second sigh carried on for several beats. "Are you really not getting this?"

"I'm going to make you say it." Because then maybe she would understand how weird and insulting this conversation was. He was supposed to change his life around, come out from hiding—something he never did—and she would keep on pretending he was the hired help. That sounded just great.

"I don't announce my dating life to my father. Ever. He judges and it's not his business."

Uh-huh. "And?"

"He's not a guy you want looking into your background."

Wren wrapped his fingers around the wheel and tried to tamp down on his anger. "I think I can handle covering my tracks. I mean, it is what I do."

"You're ticked off." She gnawed on her bottom lip.

"You picked up on that, did you?"

She put her hand on his knee. "I don't want him knowing."

"That we're having sex?" He guessed the idea between the soft voice and the touching was to calm him down. It didn't work. All he could think about was her wish to tuck him away somewhere. Yes, that's basically how he lived his life, but that was his choice. For some reason it ticked him off when she wanted to do it to him.

"Anything." She sank back into the seat. "If he thinks we have a personal relationship, he'll fixate on it. I'll get lectures about how I'm mixing business with pleasure, which is a mistake."

That took some of the heat out of Wren's anger. He switched from being frustrated with her to not liking her father. And he'd already started out not being that impressed with the good professor. "He does know you're an adult, right?"

"Yes."

"Do you?" Because the way he saw it she had to own responsibility for her part in letting this relationship drag on this way.

"He has a phone and a computer and inundates me until I respond. He can be toxic." She winced. "But he's all I have."

The words flipped the whole situation around on him. She yearned to belong. He got that. On top of that she placated and tried to please. She'd suffered tremendous loss and handled it by trying to make him happy.

When that failed, she did what mattered to her and tried to balance that with what her father demanded. The longer he sat there, the clearer the picture became to Wren.

He felt for her because the situation sucked. "Admittedly, I'm not an expert on relationships with fathers—"

"Stop right there." She lifted her hand. "Look, I know it's stupid, but I learned long ago that the best way to deal with him is to live my life, establish my boundaries, ignore most of what he says, but to not lose contact. It makes him spin when I try to put space between us. He actually gets worse when we don't talk."

No way could he fight that argument. "Fine. I won't announce that I've seen you naked. Now can we go in and get this over with?"

She stared at him for a second longer. "Why do I think I'm going to regret this?"

"You're only just realizing that now?" He opened the door again.

"I continue to underestimate you."

At least she finally admitted it. "Serious mistake."

HER FATHER ANSWERED the door on the first knock. "Dad."

His gaze darted to Wren. "Who's this?"

Skip the hellos. No questions about why she didn't use her key or just try to open the door. Her father being her father, he jumped right to the only thing he cared about. The stranger on his doorstep. At least the man was consistent.

They still stood on the front porch overlooking the

pristine green lawn. The same one she used to lie on as a kid and dream as she watched the clouds stream by. Now, cars passed and the light hadn't faded, so she could see neighbors walking dogs on the street and smell the scent of freshly cut grass.

She was about to do the formal introductions when Wren angled his body slightly in front of hers.

"I'm the man investigating the Tiffany Younger matter." Wren didn't extend his hand in greeting.

Neither did her father. "Your name?"

"Brian Jacobs."

Her father didn't move or invite them inside. "Is that also your agency's name?"

"It's the name I use."

Yeah, this was going about as well as she expected. Lots of tension. Underlying strain. A touch of anger. At least Wren managed to give an answer that sounded strange but was really the truth. Impressive.

Her father looked Wren up and down. "You don't look like law enforcement."

"I'm not." Wren didn't back down one inch. The thread of menace in his voice matched her father's.

"Then I'm confused about your involvement in this matter."

"Dad, could we actually come inside before you start the interrogation?" Because much more of this testosterone battle and there might be blood on his beloved roses.

After a few seconds of hesitation, her father moved to the side. "Fine."

"Thanks." It seemed like a stupid thing to say to her

father, but her nerves were zapping. As it was, she wondered if the pounding headache would ever go away.

They got in and as far as the top of the step down into the family room before her father started talking again. "I'm afraid there's been a misunderstanding, Mr. Jacobs."

"How so?"

"Your services are not needed. I'm happy to pay for—"

"You can't fire him." She wanted to make at least that much clear.

They'd launched into all-out war without bothering to sit down. They stood in the hallway leading to the back of the house and the kitchen. No fanfare. Nothing. Just arguments. She was transported to her teenaged years again, feeling out of place and uncomfortable.

Her father pointed a finger at her. "I'm trying to fix this."

"That's my job." Wren put the side of his hand against her father's finger and moved it out of her face.

She could fight her own battles, but it was pretty sexy to have a guy who wanted to stand up and help. "Maybe we should sit down."

As usual, her father ignored her. "What does that mean?"

"That's what I do. I look into problems and solve them." The explanation didn't exactly say much. Wren stood there with his arms folded in front of him, not looking like he intended to offer more.

Her father scoffed. "That's not a career."

Wren smiled at her. "I've heard that before."

She immediately felt lighter, more confident and secure. "I told you that you need a better explanation of what you do."

He nodded. "Apparently."

Her father stepped up, right in Wren's face. "This is a serious situation."

Wren didn't move. "I assure you, I know that."

Another exchange and her father might run right into Wren. Emery really didn't want to see that, so she rushed to give some context. "He usually takes on much bigger matters."

"Actually." Wren's deep voice commanded the room. "I don't think there's anything bigger than a missing loved one. But the point is I have the resources needed to complete the work."

If she hadn't been falling for him before that statement that would have done it. The intensity of his voice, the purity of his words. He wasn't giving lip service or trying to win anyone over. He stepped up and helped with Tiffany because she mattered to him. A young woman he never met. A person he didn't have any responsibility to, yet he took it on.

Damn, she loved everything about that. Everything about him.

"Do you have references?" her father asked in his usual businesslike way.

The question might have sounded reasonable, but she was done. She put Wren in this position, so it was time for her to do a little rescuing. "That's not necessary. He works with me and I'm satisfied."

"I'm afraid that's not good enough." Her father

looked over her head at Wren. "I'm sure you under-stand."

He shook his head. "I don't."

"My daughter is too close to this situation."

"She also hates when men talk around her," she pointed out. Not that her father ever noticed how she felt about anything.

Wren looked as if he were trying to hide a smile. "She strikes me as intelligent and practical. I'm comfortable with taking direction from her. I trust her instincts."

Well, that was just about the sexiest thing. If this were the time to properly show her appreciation she'd touch him, but she banked it for later. "Thank you."

"Let me be honest." More man-to-man talk. Her father threw in some concerned hand-wringing as he talked this time. "You are not the right man for the job. Frankly, I'm not convinced this job is even needed. It's clear what happened—"

"It is?" That was news to her.

"—but if Emery is going to pursue this, I at least want it done right. That way we can end the inquiries and move on."

Enough. Emery stepped in front of Wren. Blocked her father's view of him as much as she could with her smaller size. "It's not your decision. Besides, you've never helped with anything relating to Tiffany. Why start now?"

Her father's face flushed red with anger. "This proves my point. You're too emotional."

"I'm not," Wren said. "And, so that we're clear, I'd

expect Emery to be passionate about finding answers about her cousin. She has me to provide the realism. What I need from her is her drive to solve this. Her dedication."

"That doesn't sound very professional."

Her head wouldn't stop spinning. She volleyed back and forth between loving everything Wren said and wanting to shake her father. It had always been that way with him. It was no surprise this time followed the same pattern. "It's fine for me, so stop bothering Senator Dayton. Don't call Caroline or any of my friends. Back out of this case. Now."

"I wasn't aware you still had friends," her father said, stepping right into a subject they'd battled about for years. "I was under the impression you pushed them away, including Tyler. I hear he's in town."

The shot qualified as the one too many. Emery shut it all down. "We're not arguing about this. We are absolutely done here."

Her father looked at Wren. "Do you have a business card?"

"No."

She stepped back, almost slipped her arm through Wren's but stopped herself in time. "We're leaving."

"Emery, stop. We need to talk this through like adults."

Wren started to leave then turned around and looked at her father again. "One question. Where were you the night Tiffany disappeared?"

Her father stilled. "Excuse me?"

Wren shrugged. "It's a fair question."

"In the house with Emery."

"All night?" Wren asked.

Emery had never seen her father thrown off that fast. She felt a kick of guilt over how much she enjoyed his wide-eyed stammering.

Her father walked to the door and opened it, ushering them out. "You had your one question. I'll leave the rest of my answers to the person who actually takes over the investigation."

"A change in investigators is not going to happen." That was one issue she would not budge on.

"Sorry." Wren smiled. "She's the boss."

"We'll discuss this later." Rage vibrated in her father's tone as he talked to her.

"No, we won't." And she vowed to make that true.

They hit the outside and the fresh air. Despite the start of evening the weather hadn't turned. Heat still rolled off the driveway. Not that she felt much of anything anyway.

Her fingers were trembling so hard that she fumbled with the car door. She was about to give up when Wren's arm reached around her. He opened it, and watched her climb inside before closing it again. She sat there, waiting for him and ignoring her father as he stood on the front porch scowling.

Wren didn't say anything for a few minutes. Started the car and backed out onto the street. Half a block later he pulled over and put it in park. "That went well."

"Right." That's all she could manage. The whole scene was frustrating and a bit embarrassing. She felt as if she regressed to a scared little girl every time she spent time with her father. She talked tough and held her own, but their relationship was so unhealthy. So skewed to him demanding and her ignoring.

Wren reached his arm over and balanced it on the side of her seat. "Are you okay?"

"He treats me like I'm still a kid." And sometimes she let him because that was easier, but she had to fight that tendency. It only made things worse in the long run.

"I'm sure that's related to Tiffany's disappearance. Knowing you could have been with her when she disappeared had to exact a toll."

She had a therapist years ago who said the same thing. Her father didn't know how to relate to a child and he had these fears and they made his feelings come out all wrong. *Blah, blah, blah.* "Don't be logical. I want to be irrationally angry right now."

"Seems fair." Wren's fingers slipped through her hair. "The way I see it is you fight him and demand to be heard. That's the important thing. I love that you don't back down. It's impressive."

She rested her head against the seat and stared at him. "Thanks for supporting me."

"You can count on that."

Those eyes. That face. Yeah, she was falling, all right. "I'm starting to."

CHAPTER 25

Later that night they stood on opposite sides of Wren's big bed. They'd watched some mindless television while she tried to unwind from the visit with her father. A dinner and a shower later and it was almost eleven.

The time didn't matter. The lack of sleep didn't bother him. He wanted to crawl under the covers and lose himself in her. Wipe away all the questions of the day and the constant analysis running through his brain about Tiffany and what really happened to her. Mostly, he wanted Emery.

Watching her struggle with her father and not cave in to him impressed Wren. She carried this huge weight almost all alone and didn't break down. He kept waiting for it, but she stayed strong. At times he wondered if she stayed too strong. There was only so much a person could take.

He'd worked his pain out on a shooting range and through the slow destruction of his marriage years ago. Emery didn't have any refuge. Even her work centered on loss. She forced herself to move forward and built a life around the one person she might never see again. That wallowing in so much pain could destroy something deep inside. At least it had in him.

He watched her now. She rubbed some sort of lotion on her hands and up and down her bare legs. A nightly ritual that went along with brushing her teeth and combing her hair.

The bikini underwear and T-shirt covered enough to send his imagination running on a wild journey. If he got a vote she could skip the clothes. He only peeled them off once they got into bed anyway. There, skin touched skin. He didn't want any barriers other than the condom.

But there was a pretty big wall standing between them right now. She'd been distracted all night. Physically there, but her vision stayed clouded and she seemed to be a step behind in every conversation. Not her usual style at all. Hell, he usually had trouble keeping up with her, but he'd spent most of dinner repeating whatever mundane thing he said to burn through time. She hadn't really been paying attention and, instead, spent long periods staring off into space.

He knew one topic that might remove the haze.

"He knows we're sleeping together," Wren said as he pulled back the comforter and caught the pillow he sent tumbling toward the floor.

She snapped the cap back on the bottle and put it on the chest of drawers. "Here's a little hint, Levi. Don't talk about my father when we're standing near the bed and you want to have sex."

Yeah, she looked wide awake now. He was grateful for that, at least. "Noted."

She tilted her head to the side and removed one earring then the other. Just one of the steps she worked through without even thinking about them. He pretty much took off his clothes and brushed his teeth. No big production. He didn't really care how long it took her because he could watch her for hours. But he'd rather touch her.

He slipped behind her and wrapped his arms around her and let them lay on her stomach. Pulling her back, he balanced her weight against his. Smiled in her hair when she brought up her hands to cover his. She didn't fake this part. She was open and affectionate. She knew what she wanted and seemed to enjoy touching him as much as he loved touching her.

"It's late." It seemed chivalrous to mention that. They both needed sleep.

"Not that late."

"You always know the right thing to say." He kissed the side of her head.

She laughed as she turned in his arms. Her face glowed in the room's soft light and those eyes, so big and intelligent, focused on him. No clouds or haze lingered there now.

"Sometimes I know what to do."

He had no idea what she meant, but her sexy smile had him thinking good things. "Oh, really?"

She shoved against his chest. The move normally wouldn't have much impact, but he stepped away because she seemed to want him to. When she pushed a second time, the backs of his knees hit the edge of the bed and he finally got it. He let his body fall until his ass hit the mattress.

He'd barely pushed up on his elbows when she

climbed on top of him. The peek down her shirt as she crawled up his body told him she left the bra in the bathroom. He was about to thank her for that when her head dropped and she began kissing his chest. At first, small nibbles over his shirt then her fingers slid up and under. Her palms flattened on his chest as her legs straddled his hips.

While she shoved his shirt to his neck, her soft hair brushed over his shoulder. Every touch, every kiss, lit his skin on fire. He had to ball his hands into fists to keep from grabbing her, turning her over and plunging inside of her.

But no. She ran this show. The seduction, the speed—all her. Even if it killed him.

Her mouth traveled down his stomach to the top of his boxer briefs. Leaning back, she studied him. Ran her hand over the growing bulge in his shorts. Touched every inch before bending down and fitting her mouth over him through the material.

He almost flew off the bed. The sensation—the rough friction of his underwear and nip of her teeth—had him opening his legs to give her more access. His heart hammered and his breathing sped to heart attack range. When she did it again he drove his shoulders into the mattress and lifted his hips toward her mouth just to get closer.

But she had other ideas. She controlled time.

Her hand replaced the caress of her mouth. She outlined his shape until his erection pressed against the material. Then she peeled the briefs off. Slow and making sure to brush the elastic over his sensitive tip.

"Fuck, Emery."

"Eventually." She took him in her hand. Pumped up and down. "But I'm in charge now."

She sure as hell was. This would haunt his dreams. Her touch. That hot, sweet mouth. When she slid him between her lips he slammed his teeth together to keep from moaning. Closed his eyes and tried to concentrate on the feel of her tongue as she surrounded him.

She licked and sucked and instinct kicked in. He started thrusting into her mouth without any signal from his brain. He tried to hold back, but she set the pace. She held him. Swallowed him.

Looking down, he saw her there, curled over his upper thighs. Her hair fanning out and her eyes closed. Over and over he watched his length disappear into her mouth. Felt her tongue sweep over him.

His control broke.

He tried to warn her, to say something, but his body took over. His hand moved and his fingers slipped into her hair. The tightening inside him exploded and his ass lifted off the bed. He came as his body bucked. Kept moving while she squeezed him in her hand and held him in her mouth.

When he finished he fell back on the bed. Staring at the ceiling, he tried to slow his heartbeat. To get his pulse back within normal range. He concentrated on the white paint and studied the light fixture. Anything to bring his body back under control.

Then her face floated above him. She slid over him and balanced her elbows on either side of his head. "Are you okay there, stud?"

"Pretty fucking perfect." He somehow managed to lift a hand and trail it down to the small of her back. Slip his fingers under the waistband to cup her ass. "So are you, by the way."

"I've been dying to do that."

That wasn't a comment he heard every day. "You should feel free to do *that* anytime. Really, I volunteer. You have an automatic green light."

She smiled and her happiness was enough to light up the room. "I meant to see you lose it."

That wasn't anything new. "I go half-mad every time I push inside you."

"That's so romantic." The amusement was right there in her voice.

God, he loved being with her. Not just the sex, though that was pretty spectacular. Everything. The talking, the joking. Most people considered him humorless. With her, he felt less stiff. More human. A bit like the guy he was before everything changed, only without the irresponsibility part.

"What does Owari mean?" she asked as she traced the outline of his mouth with her fingertip.

He had to force his mind to catch up to the new topic. "Wow, that question came out of nowhere."

She wiggled her eyebrows. "I have so many."

"Really?" As far as he was concerned he'd been a pretty open book. She knew more than even the other Quint Associates guys, and he'd known them for years. Suffered and trained with them.

"Do you know how tempting it is to snoop through your house while you're asleep?" She moved her leg over his. "With everything that's been going on and your tendency to rush me into bed right after dinner, I've seen, maybe, four rooms and know there are many more."

He bent his arm under his head so that he could lift up and see her better. "You can go anywhere."

She snorted. "Right. Because you wouldn't lose your shit if you saw me pawing through your desk."

He hoped she wouldn't feel the need, but he let that go. "Try me."

She pulled up a little and stared down at him. "Are you kidding?"

"Do you want the official house tour?" He squeezed her ass. "I mean, there are other things I'd rather do now that my underwear is almost off."

"Later."

Not the clearest answer she'd ever given him, so he tried again. "The house tour or the underwear thing?"

"We can come back to a discussion of your underwear."

"I was afraid that's what you meant." He groaned as she sat up, using his body for leverage.

She stood and fixed her underwear. Unfortunately, put it back on rather than took it off. "Well?"

"You want to go right now? As in, this second?" Her timing really sucked.

"Were you just telling me what you thought I wanted to hear when you offered?"

She had to know that would get him moving. That pretty much guaranteed it.

"Oh, woman." He shifted his legs over the side of the

bed and stood up. The T-shirt came off, but he pulled the boxer briefs back up. "The end."

"What?"

"Roughly translated, Owari means 'the end' in Japanese." He held out his hand to her.

She came around from her side of the bed and slipped her fingers through his. "I don't get the significance."

The simple touch felt right. Kind of perfect actually. "It signaled the end of my life as it was then."

She made an *ahhh* sound. "A start of a new one."

He knew she'd get it. "Exactly."

It took him about fifteen minutes to take her through the house, and that was only because he stopped to feel her up twice. After studying all the floors and opening every closet door for her to inspect, something she declined to do, they ended up in his study. His favorite room and private sanctuary. It was more of a library, really. Walls lined with bookshelves. He didn't get rid of books, so the paperbacks were stacked two-deep.

She walked around the room, touching the side of this book and taking a few out to page through. "This is an impressive collection."

"Said the professor's daughter."

"Oh, my father would not be happy with your selection. Mysteries, Wren? Don't you know popular fiction ruins the mind?" She pitched her voice lower, mimicking her dad.

He loved the joking. The ease of being with her.

He rested against the edge of his oversized desk. "Then I'm in trouble because that's what I stockpile."

"I know it sounds weird, but I didn't imagine you as a reader."

That didn't sound too great for him. "Is this that *not human* thing again?"

"Oh, trust me. I see you very much as a flesh-and-blood man." She let her gaze wander over him before turning to slide one of the books back into its assigned spot. "No, it's about the time commitment. You strike me as a guy who works fifty hours a day and doesn't leave much extra for play." She glared at him. "And don't correct me. I was going for exaggeration."

"Reading clears my head." When he was younger, it saved him. All those years of his father being a suspect but not arrested. Wren lost himself, escaped his world, in books about heroes vanquishing demons, and slaying dragons and solving mysteries.

She leaned back against one of the bookcases. "I haven't seen you do it since I got here."

"The time I usually spend unwinding with a book I've spent with you."

"Sorry about that." She didn't sound sorry.

Neither was he. "I'm not."

"Sweet talker."

He walked around the desk and slid into his chair. Rubbed his thumb over the worn leather on the armrest. "You can help yourself to anything in here. Anything in the house."

"You're not ready for me to leave so that you can get back to your bachelor days?"

She seemed to forget they were dating. The word

still sounded weird to him, but the idea of having her around didn't. "I want you to stay."

She pushed off from the wall and stalked toward him. "That's a pretty big comment."

"Why do you think I'm sitting down?" He shoved the chair back so there was a bit of space between his legs and the desk. Just enough room for her.

"I'll join you." She didn't wait. With one leg on either side of him, she sank down on his lap. Faced him and didn't look away. "This is nice."

His hands went to her hips to hold her steady. There was a floor between them and the nearest condom, so they needed to be a little careful. "Damn right."

"You asked about my father's whereabouts on the night Tiffany disappeared to tick him off, right?"

Wren whistled. "That is a huge conversation shift."

For a second he wondered if he'd been set up to have the difficult conversation in a fun position. Thought about it and discarded it. She was not the type to play games. She'd been fine to tell him what she wanted, when she wanted it.

She shrugged. "It's been bugging me."

"I'm double-checking everything." That wasn't a lie. He was going through every statement, analyzing every angle. There wasn't much about her father in the police files, and that bugged Wren. So did wasting time talking about the guy now. "Any chance we can focus on something other than your father for the rest of the night?"

"Depends. Do you think this chair will hold us if the dirty talk gets out of hand?" She put her hands on the back and shook it a little.

He righted them before they lost balance. "The condoms are upstairs."

"We can still make out down here. Consider it foreplay."

That sounded like the perfect solution to him. "I love the way you think."

She lowered her mouth until it hovered over his. "Show me."

CHAPTER 26

Wren dragged his exhausted body into the office over the weekend. This wasn't fatigue. No, it was the good kind of loss of sleep, but still. For the first time in his adult life he needed a nap.

He pushed open the conference room door to find Rick Cryer and Garrett already sitting there. Files were piled around them. They both had coffee and there was a pot on the tray in the middle of the table.

Garrett looked up and smiled. "You look tired. Like shit actually."

"Shut up or you're fired." Wren reached over Rick to get to the caffeine. He grabbed a mug and the pot and poured.

"It's only ten." Garrett looked at his watch. "And it's Sunday, which is proof I need a raise."

"I'm willing to fire you off schedule." Wren downed the cup. Black, hot and strong. He wanted an intravenous tube pumping it directly into his veins.

"*Threaten* to fire."

Wren ignored that as he took his seat at the head of the table. "How are you, Rick?"

The detective had driven in and brought some boxes

with him. That was the only explanation for the extra ones piled on the chair next to him. The boxes Wren didn't remember with the handwriting he didn't recognize on the side.

"Working harder in retirement than I did on the job."

"I doubt that." Wren knew better. The man was a bit of a legend. He closed difficult cases. He worked on awful homicides. That's probably why he stuck with Tiffany's case. It was like the one that got away.

Rick stretched. "Getting old."

"Some of us look older by the second," Garrett said with a laugh.

Time to work. Wren looked at both of them. "Where are we?"

"Where's Emery?" Garrett asked.

Wren's mind flashed to an hour ago. She'd grumbled about getting out of bed. There was also some whining about not being able to find a sandal. It had been so long since he lived with a woman that he actually enjoyed the chaos of it all.

She had whipped through his house like a tornado. Not exactly neat and tidy in the way she ran her personal life. There were clothes all over the bedroom. He was pretty sure he saw her car keys on the steps, which made no sense at all. There was a place for those, but when he told her that her only response was "Uh-huh."

Toiletries, bottles of stuff meant to prevent this and fix that, littered the countertop in the bathroom. He had no idea what any of it was. He'd poked around, but only waded in long enough to take the top off her shampoo and smell it. It was the scent he identified with her. And now it lingered in his sheets.

He loved that part. He loved seeing her there, feeling her presence. Smelling her.

"She's at her friend Caroline's house having brunch." He'd been invited but passed. Meeting the boss, who was also a good friend, at the office was one thing. Taking on her entire family, including her psychologist partner, Ruth, and two kids was a bit more than he could handle. Fending off questions from that many people demanded more sleep. He'd almost preferred coming to work to that sort of baptism by fire. "There are two bodyguards there with her, which seemed to be an endless fascination for Caroline's kids."

Garrett made a face, kind of like what he might make in a horror movie. "Sounds festive."

"It's safe and that's all I care about." And Emery was happy, which apparently was a big issue for him these days. She smiled, he smiled. She'd been laughing and running after one of the kids when he drove away. But now they had much more sobering topics to discuss. "What did we find out?"

"We studied the security tapes." Garrett opened the laptop next to him and hit a few buttons. Black-and-white, somewhat blurry video started playing. The clip was clear enough to show Tyler. "Apparently he got into Emery's building by coming through a maintenance door near the garbage shoot."

Tyler didn't exactly walk through an open door. He looked around, seemed nervous. This was a deliberate act. He didn't want to be seen.

The security breach ticked Wren off. He knew about that door and the lock and alarm. He thought his guys could limit their access to hourly checks of that one instead of having a man standing there because the door wasn't exactly general knowledge. Tenants didn't use it. Couldn't because they didn't have access or keys and it was inside a supply closet.

All that raised one very big question. "How exactly did he know it was there and figure out how to use it?"

"Very good question." Garrett closed the lid and cut off the video's sound. "I have a meeting with building staff tomorrow morning."

Wren wanted to know now, but he could pretend to be patient. "And insight as to why he's even in town?"

"I'm waiting to hear back about his job in New York and why he isn't at it."

"His alibi was always a little squishy," Rick said.

"Interesting word." Wren preferred *questionable*, possibly *unbelievable*. The kid had been in love and dumped. Some guys didn't take that well, especially if they'd been raised to think they could have anything.

Some days Wren appreciated having nothing as a kid. Made him work harder now.

"I always suspected him, but it's Sunday. I was trying to use nice words and not to swear," Rick said.

Garrett waved the concern away. "Fuck that."

Now on to the harder question. The one sure to raise eyebrows. The avenue he was exploring more or less behind Emery's back. Wren inhaled and dove in. "Where are we on Michael Finn, Emery's father?"

Rick sat up straighter in his chair. "What?"

"I'm not a fan of the man. Thought I'd go on record on that point before we get much further." Wren poured a second cup of coffee. At this rate he might drink the whole pot in less than an hour.

"That doesn't make him a suspect." Garrett held up both hands. "Technically."

"It puts him on my list. So does his story about being at home when all of this happened." The details were sketchy. Wren had been inside the house. He knew the bedrooms were in the back, away from the doors in and out. Sneaking away would not be that difficult.

Rick searched through his file until he found whatever he was looking for and opened it. "Emery backs that story up."

Yeah, about that. Wren had checked the timeline and read over every detail. The alibi wasn't as clear as everyone said. "No, she says they fought and she was in her room doing some assignment he gave her. He could have used that time and snuck out."

Rick shook his head. "Seems flimsy."

"What, you don't think he stepped out, killed Tiffany and then went back in and watched television?" Garrett asked. "That spur of the moment opportunity is tough to imagine in light of him having a daughter at home, right there."

"I've heard of stranger things." Rick hesitated, as if he were choosing his words. "He was never really on our radar. The piece with Emery made sense, and honestly, she was a mess. I know he's an asshole, but he really did step up back then. Was adamant about protecting her."

They both had good points. Perfectly valid. But Wren had run through it all and something still nagged at him. His mind refused to accept and move on. He'd learned the hard way to listen to that irritating voice in his head. "But Tiffany's disappearance didn't seem to bother him, not outside of the impact it had on Emery."

Garrett looked at his notes. "He was on the search crew for Tiffany. And not just once."

"It would have been odd for him not to be since Tiffany was his niece and Emery was out there looking." Wren had seen the photographs. Scanned every inch, looking for any lost hints. "Then there's his over-the-top interest in the case now. Hell, the man stalked Senator Dayton."

Garrett's eyebrow lifted. "So did Emery."

Rick scoffed. "She didn't hurt Tiffany."

No one was saying that. Wren wanted to be clear about that before Rick lunged over the table at him. "Of course not."

"Now that that's settled." Garrett flipped a few pages on his lined notepad and started writing something down. "What's his motive?"

That part was not as clear for Wren. It was hard to imagine a grown man killing or hiding a young girl except for the most obvious reasons, and he had no idea how the man would have gotten away with that for all these years. There should be more victims . . . something.

He offered the only piece he had. "Niece or not, Michael Finn didn't talk about Tiffany with much affection."

"He also has a thing for younger women," Garrett said. "Though that fact likely doesn't support your point."

Rick frowned. "Twenty-somethings. That's a lot different from underaged girls."

"I agree, but there's something that doesn't feel right. He's triggering an alarm in my head." Which was an understatement. Seeing the mix of frustration and sadness that moved through Emery when she dealt with him made Wren like the older man even less.

"You've met him?" Rick asked.

"Well, now." Garrett refilled his cup then topped off Wren's. "The bigger question: Does he know you're sleeping with his daughter?"

Rick coughed up his swallow of coffee. "Wait, that's happening?"

"When did my private life become part of the case?" Wren didn't agree to that at all.

"Dunno, but you've got to admit it's pretty damn interesting."

Rick pushed his files aside and leaned on the table. Shot Wren a let's-be-serious expression. "Look—"

"Save the lecture." Wren was absolutely not in the mood for another talk from anyone about his relationship with Emery. It was new and a bit fragile. Having third parties step in, well-meaning or not, guaranteed an early death. Sure, with his reclusive tendencies it had to end sometime. He just wasn't ready for that to happen yet. "I'm not fooling around."

"Then I'm confused." Garrett didn't even try to hide his grin. "What exactly are you doing with her?"

Wren decided to answer it as if it were a real question. "I'm not sure yet."

"That sounds promising . . ." Rick frowned. "I think."

"If you ask me, it sounds out of character."

Wren didn't remember asking Garrett to weigh in on his private life either. "Back to the case. We're dealing with someone local or someone who is still here who knows something. The person heard Emery talking about restarting an investigation or is close enough to her to know it's happening."

He hated that she had a target on her. Someone sat out there for a long time, just waiting. Now they'd awoken and she would not be safe until Wren tracked the person down.

"The break-ins are connected and we all know it." Rick nodded. "Now you're thinking we need to rule out Tiffany's dad, Emery's dad or Tyler. Vet them."

That sounded about right to Wren. He'd prioritize the people differently, but the order didn't really matter.

Garrett whistled. "That's a grim list."

Wren didn't like the tone. Garrett sounded serious and concerned. "What do you mean?"

"You tell Emery that any of those three men took Tiffany, men she's close to, and you won't have to worry about what you have with her because it will be over." Garrett's words hung there in the silence.

Wren turned them over and thought about them, but he didn't have a choice. Not this time. "I promised her."

"I'm just being realistic." Garrett shrugged. "Like you are when your head's not up your ass."

Wren got the point, but he had one of his own. "I won't lie to her."

Garrett didn't break eye contact. "I think you should be more worried about losing her."

Wren was. Every damn day.

EMERY WATCHED WREN stab the meat on his plate. Mrs. Hayes had come in and out while they were at work, slogging through a long Monday. Emery never saw her, but the woman did fold and pile up Emery's clothes. Also collected all of her things and put them in a basket in the bedroom. Also left behind a fancy dinner for them to heat up. That made Mrs. Hayes one of Emery's favorite people on the planet. Potatoes and carrots. The entire house smelled like Christmas morning.

But Wren kept stabbing. He moved this piece here and that one over there. She actually felt sorry for the food.

She lowered her fork to the table. "Did the roast offend you?"

His head shot up. "What?"

"You're picking at your dinner." She glanced at the plate and the potato he had mashed into something that looked like oatmeal.

He shoved it to the side and put his elbows on the edge of the table. "I had a late lunch."

A lie. She'd never really caught him in one before and this one seemed stupid. "No, you didn't. I called, remember? You ate a salad at your desk."

His eyes narrowed. "Did I tell you that?"

"Garrett did." The only person who picked up Wren's phone and sounded happy. Wren tended to bark his name over the line in greeting. Not the most pleasant hello.

"Why is he touching my phone?" Wren folded his cloth napkin and put it on the table.

"Even you need to go to the bathroom sometimes." At least that's the excuse Garrett gave her for answering what was supposed to be a private no-one-knows-about-this line. "He also gave me his direct work number and cell number, just in case I needed to find you and couldn't."

Wren hadn't stopped frowning. "I'm not sure I like that."

"It's hard being around other humans, isn't it?"

He pushed his chair back but didn't get up. "Look, we need to talk about something."

Her heart fell. She swore it tore away and took off in free-fall toward her feet. A wave of sadness hit right behind. She had to swallow twice and force lightness into her voice before she could talk. "Is it time?"

"For what?"

He was going to make her say it, the dumbass. She knew some men preferred that. Forced the woman to do the nasty tasks and then they looked like the mean ones. "You want your house back."

"Okay, let's get this subject out of the way." He reached a hand across the table. Didn't quite touch her but came close. "I want you here. In fact, the idea of you leaving makes me want to have your building condemned so you have to stay with me."

The stiffness across the top of her back vanished. So did the need to throw up. "That's not weird or anything."

"The fact that I want you here?"

"The idea that you'd make me homeless to do it." Before he could move away, she put her hand over his. Caressed his fingers with hers. "And please don't. You don't need to do anything drastic because I don't want to leave."

"Then why are we having this conversation?"

"Because you're acting weirder than usual." A low chime sounded a "dong" that sounded more like a gong than anything else. "Is that your doorbell? It's kind of extreme."

He dropped her hand and stood up. "Who the hell can that be?"

She thought about the layers of security. The key, the alarm and the number pad. You had to nail all three or you probably got shocked or shot or something equally awful. She made up the last part, but she wouldn't be surprised.

Following him, she saw him stop to look at the video screen that showed the small landing outside. Saw a very familiar face.

Wren unlocked the massive front door and stared at Garrett. "Why didn't you call first?'

"I did." Garrett took out his cell and shook it in front of Wren. Then he looked at her. "Am I interrupting?"

"Come in." She figured she should say it because Wren didn't seem to be doing much of anything other than standing there.

They walked in silence back to the kitchen. Wren and Emery retook their seats. Garrett picked the one in front of the platter with the roast.

Wren didn't offer him a plate or even a fork. "What's going on?"

"If it's about Tiffany's case, you can say it in front of me." Emery decided to make that clear before anyone tried the embarrassing clear-the-room thing and she had to yell.

Wren nodded. "Go ahead."

"Tyler is on a leave of absence." Garrett took out the folder he had tucked under his arm and put it on the table next to Wren's plate. "He didn't just happen to show up in town. He's been struggling, not going into work. He said he had a family issue and had to come back here for a few weeks."

Wren didn't reach for the file and it killed her not to. She almost dove for it. She settled for asking a question instead. "What's wrong in his family?"

"Nothing. His parents are overseas."

Emery looked from Garrett to Wren. "You two think this is about Tiffany."

"Hard to believe it's not," Wren said in a monotone voice.

Her brain crashed to a halt. All the arguments piled up in there as the anger started to bubble in her stomach. "There's no way."

She knew Tyler. He'd been there. They'd all been friends.

"Did you talk to him about restarting the investigation?" Garrett asked her.

That was the point. There was no restart. Not really. "It never really ended."

"Emery, you know what he means."

She hated when Wren used that tone. It happened less frequently lately, but it still snuck in. Each time she felt more like his employee than the woman he was dating.

"We talked on the phone a few weeks ago and I told him I found a note in Gavin's file."

Garret tapped the closed file. "A few weeks ago is when he started having trouble at work."

When Wren started to talk, she talked over him. "To be clear, I didn't tell him your name, or mention the specifics of the note, but I said I had a new lead. A promising one." She knew she sounded defensive and tried to rein it in. "He had a right to know. He was her friend, too."

Wren kept watching her. "More than a friend."

This wasn't a secret and she refused to act like it was. "Tiffany had a crush. I had a crush. They kissed and Tiffany decided she didn't feel anything. We were kids. It was no big deal."

"Have you ever watched a true crime show?" Wren sighed at her. "That's the basic fact pattern in about fifty percent of them."

She shook her head. She wanted to shake everything. "I don't believe it."

"Okay. Look, this is just information." Wren reached out his hand again. This time he held it palm up until she put her hand in his. "Now we analyze it. Compare it to the facts, talk to him."

He made it all sound so easy. So reasonable. "Tyler kind of hates you."

"That's hard to believe," Garrett said as he popped a carrot in his mouth.

Wren scoffed. "The feeling is mutual."

Which meant trouble. She had enough of that right now. Her life had been turned upside down. Wren stormed in. She was still fighting for equilibrium. "I'll go alone and—"

"No." Wren's tone suggested this issue had been settled.

Wrong. "You don't get to say no."

"But I am."

Garrett grabbed a piece of the roast this time. "You guys are cute together."

"We'll meet him in public, ask a few questions and that's it. Public is better because I'm less likely to strangle him." Wren threw up his hands as if he'd solved every issue and there was no more need to talk. "Done."

She thought about stabbing him with a fork. "Why do I think it won't be that easy?"

"Because you've spent time with Wren," Garrett mumbled under his breath. "He's known for being difficult."

Wren moved the platter away from Garrett. "Anything else?"

"That's it." Garrett looked over the table and to the roast, as if willing it to come back to him. "Unless you want to invite me to dinner."

"Of course," she agreed, and jumped up to find him a plate. She figured that was easier than listening to Wren say no and watching Garrett look sad. She also needed a diversion, a reason not to think about Tyler and what all of this meant. "While we eat you can tell me all about Wren before he was Wren or Brian or whatever other name he went by other than Levi Upton."

"She even knows you changed your name?"

Wren nodded. "And some other stuff."

"But not all, so we should eat." She put a plate in front of Garrett. "That way you can tell me the interesting parts he left out."

"Emery."

She ignored Wren's disapproving tone and smiled at Garrett. "Make sure to chew before you start gossiping."

Garrett smiled. "I like her."

Wren didn't look as thrilled. "I usually do."

"You will again." She shoved the platter in Garrett's general direction. "Now, talk."

"Did Wren tell you he also told Rick his real name?" Garrett asked. "Well, that he was Wren. I can't remember if Rick knows the Levi part."

"You did?" That stunned her. She'd been so careful not to tell anyone. "Why?"

Wren smoothed his napkin but didn't look up. "Because you asked me to."

She almost choked. "What?"

He waved the words away, looking completely uncomfortable while he did it. "You said something about us having a relationship and you not wanting to worry about messing up and divulging it."

She remembered most of that conversation, but that's

not what had her heart melting into a giant puddle of goo. "That's really why? Because of me?"

He looked at her then. "Isn't that good enough?"

"It is." More than that, it was perfect.

Garrett grabbed his fork. "Now, let me tell you some stories."

CHAPTER 27

Wren watched the scene unfold from the counter of The Beanery, standing there among the bags of beans for sale. He'd ordered a cup of coffee and waited off to the side, out of clear view of the table but where he could still see Emery. When Tyler came in, looking disheveled, face drawn, he headed right for her. His laser focus allowed Wren to move in. Step right up behind the guy and listen in.

Tyler flopped down in the chair across from Emery. "I'm not used to being summoned."

"That seems like an overreaction since I asked you to join me for coffee." She slid a cup over to Tyler.

He didn't reach for it. He folded his arms in front of him and slipped down in the chair. "It didn't sound that way."

Looked like Tyler had the angry-young-man vibe down today. He spoke in a clipped tone and his body language suggested he did not want to be there. Wren knew when she called him earlier and asked to meet him that Tyler wanted to come to her house. To talk in private. Wren nearly grabbed the phone from her and threatened the guy, but Emery handled it like she handled everything. With more grace than Wren had at his disposal.

She was in total control of the meeting, too. At eleven on a weekday, the place still buzzed with customers. Most came in, got their coffee and left. A few sat scattered around nearby tables. None within easy earshot.

She cradled her to-go cup in her hands. Rolled it between her palms. The rest of her stayed still, which was not usual for her. Even in a calm situation she was a bundle of nerves and energy. Always moving. Now she waited. Looked Tyler up and down as concern moved into her eyes.

Yeah, that was enough of that.

"We need to talk. All of us." Wren pulled out a chair and joined them. Ignored Emery's scowl because he had warned her he'd be joining them rather than just looming behind them. This should not be a surprise. It wasn't his fault if she thought he meant he'd step in *after* she got some answers from Tyler.

"What the hell is he doing here?" Tyler didn't even look at Wren, but he did raise his voice. Stayed just this side of a yell, but was loud enough to have a few heads turning.

Even though Tyler's demeanor didn't match the furious tone, it didn't matter. Wren was not a fan of yelling. "Keep your voice down."

"Why?"

He leaned in, hoping to make his position perfectly clear. "Because I am looking for any excuse to punch you."

"This is the guy you're dating?" Tyler fell back into a slouch as he stared at Emery. "Your father figured it out, by the way."

She made a face and not a good one. "Why are you and Dad talking?"

"We know each other." Tyler shrugged. "We talk."

Emery looked less concerned and more wary by the second. "What does that mean?"

"Okay." As much as Wren wondered about the connection between Tyler and her dad, this wasn't getting them anywhere on the questions about Tyler. Wren put a hand on the table. "Let's everyone take a breath."

"I'm not really in the mood to listen to you pontificate."

Wren glanced at Emery. "Do I pontificate?"

That wasn't a word he heard every day. It had been well off his radar for years. He ordered and demanded but wasn't really given to long speeches. But if Tyler wanted to hear one, Wren would oblige.

She shot him a crooked smile. "Sometimes, but it's cute."

"Emery, what the fuck?" Tyler's voice didn't rise. His affect had gone flat. "Why him?"

Medication, maybe? Wren wasn't sure, but except for one yell the heated anger from their last meeting seemed muted. The edges were gone. Hell, Tyler could barely sit up straight. Wren waited for him to drift away and slide to the floor.

Emery's finger tightened around her coffee cup. "Why did you take the leave of absence from your job?"

"You're checking up on me now? Yeah, no thanks. I have parents for that." Tyler stood up. More like stumbled to his feet.

Yeah, something wasn't right. Wren had his bodyguards right outside, but he didn't want to call them. Emery didn't need a scene and this kid needed coffee. "Sit down."

Tyler shook his head. "She might jump when you order, but I don't."

That was the worst description of Emery that Wren had ever heard, and that was including her father, which was pretty damn bad. "You don't know her at all, do you?"

"Explain it to me, Tyler. What's going on with you?" Emery asked. "You seemed fine the other night, but now you're a mess."

"Thanks."

"We've been friends most of our lives. I'm sitting right here." Emery's voice didn't change. She didn't plead. She sounded reasonable. Caring yet firm. "I tell you I'm trying to kick-start the investigation and you just show up. You come into my building without using the front door. The behavior is weird." She sighed. "Just talk to me."

Tyler hesitated for a second, but something must have gotten through because he sat down again. This time he played with the cup. Spun it around a few times. Took the lid on and off. Wren was about to grab the thing and hide it when Tyler finally started talking.

"I worried he had men outside." He glanced at Wren. "I didn't want to be jumped again." He leaned in and whispered as he talked to Emery. "But how did you know about me not using the front door?"

No, they were not doing it this way. Wren's head would explode if they just sat there exchanging questions. "Answer her."

"I did."

Not even close, but Wren was happy to move on. The biggest question, the one he really cared because it put Tyler in town, still sat out there. "The leave of absence."

Tyler's fingers clenched around the cup. His eyes looked a little wild now. "It's not your business."

"Is it about Tiffany?" Emery reached her hand across the table and rested it on Tyler's arm.

The touch seemed to calm him down when it looked like he was going to spin out of control. Wren didn't like the frantic feel to the guy all of a sudden. His mood swung from one end of the spectrum to the other. He went from being out of it to looking hunted.

Wren recognized that feeling of being trapped. He'd lived with it for years. "You might feel better if you just say it, Tyler."

"I'm not like you." Tyler's gaze shifted away from Emery. Bounced around the room. "You moved forward but never forgot her."

Emery frowned. "Did you?"

"That's the problem. No." Tyler put his hand over Emery's. "God, you mentioned her name and—bang—I was back there again. Panicking. I can't sleep or eat. All I see . . . I remember the police and all those questions."

"I understand," she said in a soft voice.

Wren did, too. The struggle was right there on Tyler's face. The guilt and the frustration. The feeling of not having mourned enough and of being too happy with his life.

"Everything changed that day. Who I was and what I believed. How my parents looked at me. The way friends and family whispered." Tyler's words trailed off, but the unspoken part about how everyone thought he did something to Tiffany lingered in the silence. "I went to that place in my mind and the bottom fell out. Again."

"Again?" Wren asked.

Tyler wasn't holding back now. His chest heaved as he talked. Every word sounded as if it were being dragged out of him. "The last time I had to go away to get my head straight. I learned these tools to help with what really happened and only own the parts that were my responsibility, like going away to school instead of being here to finish off the investigation. Tools to help me stay focused on the future, but they aren't working this time."

Well, shit. Wren didn't want to get it. He wanted to decide Tyler's culpability and walk away, but that's not really what he was hearing. "It's guilt."

Emery's eyes grew huge as she stared at him. "Hey!"

He rushed to explain. "Survivor's guilt."

Tyler snorted. "What do you know about it?"

"A lot." Everything. Too much. "Your world changed, but your life didn't stop. The reminders were everywhere and you couldn't escape them or ignore them. When you tried you only felt worse."

Tyler nodded but didn't say anything.

Wren kept going, reliving as much as explaining. "You go back and forth between being plowed under with grief and guilt and having good days. Sometimes the good days are worse because, for a short time, you forget about Tiffany and then you hate yourself for that, too."

"Did you know her?" There was no anger or distrust in Tyler's voice now.

"No, but I know loss." Wren glanced at Emery. "So does she. She feels it, too. Anyone who's been in this situation does."

"You don't get it." Tyler's head dropped and he stared at the table. "I upset Tiffany. We kissed and then she cut me off and I called her names. Stupid kid shit, but still. Our last conversation was me calling her a slut, which was so . . ."

"Something dumb a kid would say," Wren said, filling the blank.

Emery's hand squeezed Tyler's arm. "Do you know what happened to her?"

"God, I wish I did. Maybe then all of the shit in my head would stop."

"There are good doctors." Emery didn't break the connection with Tyler. She stayed there, comforting with her words and hand. "I've seen some over the years."

"I've had good doctors." Tyler looked up again. "How does this not kick your ass every day?"

"God, Tyler. Why do you think I'm still searching for her?" The ache in her voice mirrored the pain pulling across her mouth and lurking in her eyes.

He shrugged. "Because you're a better person than the rest of us."

Wren finally found something he agreed with from Tyler. She *was* better.

"Because it's the only way I can get through," she said. "And you will, too."

Wren nodded. "You will."

Damn, he hoped that was true.

EMERY GRABBED ON to the headboard and lifted her body up one last time. Almost separated from Wren but kept the very tip of him inside before plunging back down again. Feeling him fill her. Listening to his labored breathing.

The heat of their bodies and sweat from the lovemaking set her skin on fire. A final thrust of Wren deep inside her, of riding him as she straddled him on that big bed, and she came. Every nerve ending tingled and the pulsing inside her wouldn't stop.

Her hips moved and energy bounced around the room. The electricity between them sparked hotter each time.

She leaned in and kissed him. Put her mouth over his as he gasped from the force of the orgasm hitting him. She breathed him in. Put her hands on his and traveled up and down her sides. She fell against him with her breasts smashed against his chest. Heavy breathing had her turning her head to the side. The frantic beat of his heart echoed in her ear.

Her body still shook from the force of it all. From switching her mind off and surrendering. After a terrible day and more than two hours talking Tyler into getting help and easing off the self-medication, she'd wanted an escape. Wren offered one.

They'd barely made it upstairs when they got home. Stripping their clothes off as they mounted each stair, they'd tripped and fumbled their way down the hall. Once inside with them both naked she'd been out of control.

He took it all. Let her be in charge and set the pace. She loved that about him. The absolute confidence. The self-assurance that came with knowing when she felt free in the sex he would enjoy it even more.

It was about attraction and trust. A mutual respect.

Then there was the part where she was falling for him. Hard and fast, almost stupidly so. He was wrong for her in so many ways and right in so many others. They clicked. And she couldn't deny the need that rolled through her when he touched her, or how much she loved the simple act of looking at him across the breakfast table.

She kissed his bare chest. Ran her hand over the muscles on his arm, savoring the hardness of him in comparison to her softness. "I love that position."

He chuckled and his body vibrated under hers. "You're very good at it."

She knew he meant it. "You do know how to make a woman feel special."

He made her smile. Sometimes he still came up with some sentence that had her reaching for a Wren-to-English dictionary, but he was more relaxed now. More accepting of her putting a stamp on every aspect of his life.

"You are that."

She was so lost in her thinking that she missed what he said. "What?"

"Special." He put his fingers on her throat. Lifted her head so they could see each other. "And I think it's unbelievably sexy how amazing you are in bed."

"You make me feel confident. Pretty and powerful."

He smiled down at her. "You are all of that, too, and more."

She tucked her head under his chin. "Keep that fancy talk up and I'm not going to give you a lot of downtime before the next round."

"You know I was serious, right?" His fingers tangled in her hair.

She lifted her head again because his tone sounded so serious. She also had no idea what he was talking about. "You lost me."

"When I told you the other night that I wanted you to stay here. That wasn't a line or me being chivalrous. It was selfish as hell. I want you here for me. For us to get to know each other better."

This was serious. The kind of serious that usually made her shaky and had her reassessing a relationship as she sprinted to the door. She waited for that panic sensation to whoosh through her and wipe out everything else. For her brain to click on and remind her that she had a vow to Tiffany to uphold and shouldn't find happiness until she did.

She didn't even sense a touch of any of it, which made no sense. They barely knew each other. He lived this reclusive dangerous life, things she did not want.

All good arguments, but for some reason she couldn't say any of them. "For a man who claimed not to get the concept of dating, you seem to be embracing it."

He frowned at her, which was a pretty regular thing with him. "Is that a no?"

"It's surprise." She let the words settle in her brain. Thought about how big a step he was taking. The risk, one she was too scared to commit to.

"What kind of surprise?"

She thought about not being there, in that house she had explored and found comfort in, and realized that sounded just awful. "A happy one. Very happy."

Yes, that felt right. The hollowness had eased. Saying the words, making a commitment to him, made her feel lighter not weighed down.

His frown only deepened. "Okay, so is that a yes?"

The poor thing. "I love when you stumble over people stuff."

His expert fingers kept skimming over her skin. "I know it's annoying," he said.

"It's actually pretty cute." It no longer bothered her. She wasn't sure it ever really did. "I love that you try."

"Did you answer my question about the house?"

She'd ducked it. Brushed past it hoping a half answer was good enough. Maybe it was fear that had her stalling. She wasn't sure since she didn't feel any hesitation on the inside. And he deserved to know that.

"I don't understand how it happened or why it did, but I know that I'm comfortable here. I feel at home and welcome. Bigger than that, I want to be with you. No matter where we are." The words tumbled out of her.

Instead of measuring them and protecting herself from future heartache, she didn't hold back. "So, that's a yes."

Satisfaction flashed across his face. "Good, since I know I'm not really great at dating."

"Wrong." She gave him a small kiss. Then another, this one a bit more lingering and with a slip of tongue.

He pulled back and stared at her. "What?"

"You're very good at it."

"Are we talking about sex?" His hands were more insistent now.

He cupped her breasts and gently massaged them. Brought her body screaming back to life.

"We're talking about everything. The things you said to Tyler today." She couldn't think about that meeting without feeling conflicting emotions. Her heart expanded after listening to Wren. It broke for Tyler.

"He needed to know he wasn't alone."

Wren got it. He totally understood all the insecurities that went along with being in this horrible exclusive club. "You don't think he has anything to do with Tiffany's disappearance, do you?"

"Probably not." Wren put a hand on each of her cheeks. "I think everything that happened messed him up as a kid and he never got past it. Maybe his parents were too busy trying to protect him legally to see that he needed something else."

"You could have been a dick and you weren't. You made a difference." She leaned in and gave him a real kiss. Long and sexy enough to have her squirming on his lap, and when she pulled back he looked as dazed as she felt. "You should see your expression."

"The conversation is jumping all around."

"No, it's not." It totally was, but she didn't care. "We're talking about us and how much I enjoy being with you."

He nodded. "That all sounds good."

"I don't date much either. Haven't had time, but I want to find the time. With you." She waited for him to panic, but he just sat there. "I need you to commit to the same."

"Done." He started speaking almost before she stopped.

He was so clear. So sure. And she believed him. Still, she needed more than a quick one-word answer. Romance dictated that he at least show some excitement. "Really? That's all you have to say?"

He cleared his throat. Also sat up straighter, taking her with him and making them both groan.

"Except for Shauna who already knew it, I've never told another woman my real name. Never set out all the details of my past. Certainly never admitted to almost killing my father. With you, I felt like I could. After only a few days, I opened up and I don't regret it." He caressed her cheek with the backs of his fingers. "I trust you. Weirdly enough, I also really like you."

Other men might have said it prettier and skipped the word *weird*, but he found the perfect words for him. They actually choked her up a little. "Believe it or not, that worked."

He winced. "It did?"

"Honesty is hot."

Interest sparked in his eyes and he started getting hard again. "How hot?"

"Hot enough to start round two."

"We're going to need to buy more condoms." With that he turned them over. When the room stopped spinning she lay under him with his rock-hard body pressing against her, over her.

"How could a woman resist that line?" She couldn't and she was done trying.

CHAPTER 28

Wren barely had been in the office for two days, which never happened. No one said anything because they wouldn't dare. He ran the office with an iron fist. It was not a democracy. His poor personal assistant handed him a stack of messages then scurried away, clearly afraid of his wrath over the pile of work ahead of him.

No one said anything to him about his absence except Garrett. Now he stood on the other side of Wren's desk still talking. "You looked pretty cozy with Emery the other night."

"We were eating." Wren kept on signing the paperwork that needed his attention. Contracts, checks. People deserved to be paid and the work needed to keep moving. He also hoped half ignoring Garrett would make him go away. Not that the option had ever worked before.

"Together. At the table. At home."

With an extra person. That's the part Wren remembered and wanted to forget. "I'm told normal people do eat dinner."

"But you?"

Wren put his pen down and sat back. Garrett clearly wanted his attention. Now he had it.

"I take it you don't like Emery." Which sucked because, despite the back and forth, Garrett was his best friend. Wren never had a brother, but he guessed the bond they shared was about the same.

They'd been through some terrible shit together. They both had histories they wanted to forget. He talked tough, but no one else could take a shot at Garrett. Wren would do anything for him. That was the unspoken promise.

"Oh, I do. A lot. I like her in general and I like her with you." Garrett moved up until his legs almost touched the edge of the desk. "Some of the questions she asked made me laugh. I love how interested she was, how engaged in the topic. Of you, I mean."

That all sounded good, but Wren sensed a change in mood. Something was coming. Either in what Garrett said next or in the file he kept tapping against the side of his leg. "Okay."

Garrett nodded. "So, there you go."

What the hell did that mean? "I'm assuming you're trying to make a point."

"You have it bad for her." Garrett stopped tapping the file and the strange scratching sound in the room ceased.

Wren would have preferred some background noise. Anything to cut through the tension and help with the sudden tightening in his gut. He'd always been so clear—no relationships. Not after he blew the last one so badly. He didn't want any woman to go through what Shauna had to endure with him.

Yeah, he was different now. The anger had subsided, or at least he managed to control it. But he lived in a web of secrecy and danger. The idea of pulling anyone into that mess with him struck him as selfish. No matter how much he wanted to be with Emery, and that feeling kept growing, he couldn't imagine her agreeing to live his life. Even if she did, she'd grow to regret it. He knew that from experience.

He was not a forever guy. No question.

Still, the idea of saying "no" out loud to the question made bile roll in his stomach. It felt like a betrayal of Emery in some way.

"I don't . . ." Jesus, he couldn't even deny it. Garrett stood there, his friend and a person Wren never lied to, and the words sputtered out on Wren.

He did have it bad for her. How had that happened?

Garrett put a hand behind his ear. "Huh?"

"Yeah." Fucking damn. He did not mean to let that out. The plan was to change the subject, throw his boss-weight around. Not to answer and certainly not with such a weak word.

Garrett's eyes widened. "You're admitting you have big-time feelings for her?"

Wren grabbed on to the armrests of his chair then let go. The tiny indents from his death grip stayed behind. He had the sudden urge to walk around, maybe somehow exercise this feeling away, but he didn't.

He opened his mouth then closed it again. Okay, yeah. He felt it now. This huge zoom of unwanted emotions. He wanted to write it all off as attraction, but they went so much deeper. He worried about her. Liked being with her. Felt better when he saw her. Even enjoyed arguing with her.

She challenged him. She made him hard.

God, he was in love with her. Like, right on the verge of losing it over her.

"I moved her into my house." That had been the major step. The one that should have tipped him off since it was a pretty huge clue. It wasn't as if he moved people from other cases into his house. "Even I have enough self-awareness to know that was big."

"I thought that was for her safety."

"That's how I sold it, yes." But he knew better. Not then, but now. It was so clear to him. Hell, he even liked the sound of her voice.

"You really have a problem now." Wren was about to answer when Garrett dropped the file on his desk. "Here."

Wren didn't pick it up. That's how they operated. Garrett gave oral reports with backup documentation. The system had worked from the beginning, and Wren didn't mess with success. "What's this?"

"It's on her father." Garrett glanced at the cover then back to Wren. "Actually, it includes some intel on Tyler, too."

"I thought we agreed he likely wasn't involved." Last thing they needed to do was waste resources on a job where they weren't getting paid. Wren also wanted to give Tyler some space.

"Emery's dad has been poking around, asking about

you. Doing internet searches." Garrett didn't explain how he knew that. Didn't have to because the office had protocols for this. Ways of tracking keystrokes and getting into other people's computers.

Okay, that was annoying but not really a big deal. "Is that really a surprise? I'm sleeping with the man's daughter."

"So you've said."

Funny how easy that was to admit now that he'd admitted the rest. "Even for a mediocre father it's probably natural to want to know who has walked into his daughter's life."

Garrett shook his head. "You're not getting this."

There was nothing light or joking in Garrett's tone. No amusement. None of the usual crap he liked to say to drive Wren to frustration. He didn't even smile.

Wren knew that was really bad. "Explain."

"He's searching for Wren. He's been obsessively trying to track you—the Wren, you—for days."

He got this part. He didn't understand why Garrett kept dwelling. "Right."

"He should only know the name Brian Jacobs." Garrett hesitated for a second then continued. "You told me you didn't give him your name on purpose, yet he knows to investigate the name Wren. He's been looking into it since the night the boxes were stolen out of Emery's apartment."

The words came together in Wren's head. Her father knew more than he should. There were a limited number of ways that could happen and Wren hated them all. "Shit."

"I talked with the senator and the detective. Neither of them gave him your real name. You said no one else knows it except Caroline, who promised not to repeat it." Garrett sighed. "I mean, I guess it's possible but—"

"He got it from the boxes he took from her apartment." He wasn't having the man followed back then, but that was the answer. They could dance around it and try to come up with convoluted explanations or wrongly blame someone, but one answer rang true in Wren's mind. He broke into his daughter's house while he thought she was staying with Caroline and then he took papers about Tiffany's case.

"We know Emery had a piece of paper with your name on it, part of it anyway," Garrett said.

"She would have checked it everywhere. She'd have had files and a paper trail." Because that's what Wren would have done. He had some memory of them talking about this.

Even if she hadn't told him, he'd expected the first thing she'd do with the name was check the name she'd found. The same was true of his birth name. By now she'd looked up every detail of the case against his father.

Garrett cleared his throat. Looked every bit the professional giving a presentation. "There's more."

Wren flipped the cover open, but the words blurred in front of him. He looked up at Garrett again. "Of course there is."

"In the original detective notes from his meeting with Emery she talks about being at home that night. She never mentions her dad being there or hearing him."

Garrett walked around to the other side of Wren's desk and started typing on the computer keyboard. "That piece comes in later and seems to be taken as gospel."

"That doesn't sound like evidence Rick Cryer would get wrong."

"I watched the interrogation tapes. We have them." Garrett cued up a tape and then paused it. "The first time there's talk about her dad being home it's raised by Rick's partner during the questioning. Everyone runs with it from there. Rick watched with me. Neither of us saw it until the fourth or fifth run-through. It looked inadvertent, but it happened."

"Fuck me." Wren didn't need to see the tape. Not yet. If Garrett said that was on there then it was. Part of Wren didn't want to watch. Once he did he wouldn't be able to go back to not being sure.

The break-in. Michael Finn's shaky alibi. The fact he stopped Emery from going out that night and kept her busy. All those years of being angry. His insistence the investigation stop. The tape of the questioning. The timing. It all piled up until Wren was pretty sure he knew at least some of the answers about Tiffany.

Garrett folded his arms in front of him. "What are you going to do?"

"I don't know." Wren really didn't. His mind went blank. The only thing in there was the image of Emery's face. Hearing the accusations from him would destroy her.

"I don't think she's in any real danger."

"But that's not the point, is it?" Wren dropped his head in his hands and tried to think. Tried to reason it all out. But he didn't need much time because the answer was all too simple. He looked up again. "Who am I kidding? There isn't a choice about what I have to do next. Like it or not, I promised her answers."

"Let me ask her questions. Let me be the target," Garrett said. "It's okay if she's angry with me."

It was an easy solution to an impossible problem, but it likely still wouldn't work. It also ignored who Wren was and how he lived his life. "When have you ever known me to duck a hard task?"

"I've never really known you to be in love before, so I don't know what the rules are now." Garrett's eyebrow lifted as he stood there not saying anything. "You're not denying it."

"There's no way I can be after only knowing her a short time." Right? That was the rational answer. It was too soon. They barely knew each other . . . but she did know almost everything about him. Despite that, she hadn't run.

"Yet, you are."

Yes, he was. "And now I have to blow it all up before we can figure out what we have. There's a missing girl out there."

"I think we both know that's not true."

Wren didn't even want to think about that part of the puzzle. The how and why and what really happened out on that street that night. He couldn't even let his mind go there yet. "I never should have gone to that coffee shop that first morning."

"I warned you."

"Remind me of that the next time I try to fire you."

EMERY HEARD WREN come in. He'd called to say he wouldn't be home for dinner. Since it was almost nine, she'd eaten long ago, but she hadn't expected him to be this late.

"Keith played chauffeur today. Not a bad way to come home." She peeked around the corner to welcome Wren. That's when she saw it. The stern expression and clipped walk. "What's wrong?"

His footsteps thudded against the floor. He kept walking until he hit the kitchen and put his briefcase on one of the stools at the breakfast bar. "You're going to hate the next few minutes. If it's any consolation, so am I."

She tried to remember if she'd ever seen him like this. All clenched and bubbling with fury. "What are you talking about?"

"You searched the name Wren once you spotted it in Gavin's file, right?"

"Of course." There was no way that could be a surprise. Any normal person would do the same thing, even him. "God, this is why you look like that? Come on, Levi. You investigated me, too."

"I'm not upset about the search. It was smart. Expected." He took a bottle of water out of the refrigerator then put it back in.

He seemed to be wrapped in a weird haze. Walking around. Doing odd things then turning and walking again. Tension radiated off him. She could feel his anxiety. It pinged around them. And she'd never seen his eyes so lifeless.

Something terrible had happened. She was terrified to ask what. "Then what's the problem?"

"Did you keep a file on that name?"

"Yes." Wait . . . she thought back to the boxes. That only mad her angry, so she tried to block the break-in out again. "Well, I took notes and kept the searches so I wouldn't repeat them and waste time."

He swore under his breath as he closed his eyes. "And all of that information was in the files missing in your boxes."

That was it. Someone figured out who he was. That was the only explanation. She didn't remember writing anything down that would logically trace back to him, but maybe.

Guilt crashed into her from every direction. "Oh, my God, did someone come after you?"

She took a step toward him, thinking to touch him. Give him some sort of support. He backed away. Actually circled around until the entire breakfast bar sat between them. The move sliced into her. Cut right through.

He finally stopped looking around and moving and generally not looking at her, and faced her head-on. "Your dad has been searching the name."

"Wait . . ." She hadn't expected him to say that. For a second the words just sat there in her brain. "What?"

"Wren."

She kept trying to shake the cobwebs out. "He doesn't know that name. He knows Brian Jacobs."

"Exactly."

Dread spilled over her. She felt it wash over her and seep into every muscle. She didn't know what was coming, but she knew it would end with a fiery explosion. "What are you saying?"

"That he has the boxes, your files. He has your research."

The strangling haze refused to lift. "That's not possible."

"We both know it is."

It took her an extra second to snap out of her stupor. When she did, fury screeched through her brain. He was actually blaming her father for . . . that couldn't be. "No. That's ridiculous. My father wouldn't scare me and steal from me. I must have messed up and said it."

"That didn't happen. You wouldn't make that mistake when the stakes are so high."

She'd tried not to. She made a conscious effort to stick to Wren, but she was human. Her father shouldn't be blamed for her mistake.

Something choked her throat. She had to fight to not throw up. Force her body to stay still while she got this out. "Sometimes . . . sometimes I get excited and—"

"Look at me." In two steps he was in front of her with his hands on her forearms.

She shook her head. Tried to push out all the thoughts jamming up inside of her right now. "There's a logical explanation."

"He wasn't in the house that night."

The jump in topics threw her. "What, when Tiffany went missing? Yes, he was. I was there. I saw him."

"No." He squeezed her arms then his hands dropped to his sides. "I've watched the videotape questioning, Emery. That is not what you said. The detective said it."

"Because it happened." She backed up. Ran right into the stove. "It absolutely did."

"Listen—"

"No, I don't get what you're doing." She scrambled out of his path when he started walking toward her. She knocked mail off the counter as she raced to the other side of the bar. Far away from him. "Why are you saying these things?"

Every word cut into her. He hated her father and had this twisted theory. But the accusations couldn't be true. She never expected Wren to strike like this. It wasn't who he was . . . or maybe she didn't know him at all. She'd spent all day thinking about him, trying to believe she was falling in love with him, and he was plotting this.

"You hired me to—"

"No." She held up her hand in a feeble attempt to shove the words away. "I didn't hire you to do anything. I thought you took Tiffany."

"You know I didn't."

"Neither did my father." She waited for all the explanations to start tumbling out. She only came up with one. "Our dads were best friends. We were related. For God's sake, Tiffany is his niece. There was no reason for him to . . . no."

"He hated her."

"He hated the guy at the gas station, but he didn't kill him." She screamed the words at him.

The more even and in control he looked, the more furious she became. She wanted to pound on his chest and make him feel something. Make him apologize.

"Emery." He took another step toward her.

She held out both hands this time. "This is about you."

Her mind raced. She needed to understand how this happened. Everything had been so good this morning. A few hours apart and he was attacking everything she believed in.

"You're twisting this. You want to find an answer, I get that." She tried to think about who he was and how he reasoned things out, but his accusations still didn't make sense.

Pain flashed in his eyes as he shook his head. "You know that's not it. I would never make something up."

"Like your name or your history? God, Levi. You lie every single day by pretending to be someone you're not."

His face went blank. "You're lashing out."

"You're damn right. Just because your father is a killer doesn't mean mine is." Her voice shook as she screamed. "Don't suck me into your reclusive sickness."

For a second nothing moved. The big house went silent. The television was on in the other room, but the mumble of voices faded into the background.

"We, ah, need to back up and think about this." He rubbed his forehead.

No, he didn't get to play the injured party here. "I'm done thinking and talking."

"Tomorrow—"

"Tomorrow I'll be gone at work and then maybe at Caroline's house. You can sit here all alone with your conspiracy nonsense." She couldn't imagine looking across the table at him. Sleeping with him. Her mind recoiled at the idea. "Tonight I'll be in one of the other bedrooms."

She started to walk away, but it took all of her energy to get her legs to move.

"Emery."

She hesitated for a second, looking at him over her shoulder. "I wouldn't want you to sleep with the child of a killer. Of course, I guess you do that all the time."

THE GREEN LIGHT of the alarm clock beamed through the dark room. Wren knew the minute she left the house. There was no way to get out without tripping at least two alarms. Neither of them screeched through the quiet night. His watch buzzed and his cell rang. That was it.

He'd checked on her twice over the last two hours. Knocked on the door, but she wouldn't let him in. He couldn't sleep. Hell, he might never sleep again after that explosive fight. But he'd hoped she'd be there to talk with him in the morning. Maybe they could find some common ground. But no.

A little before four in the morning. That's when she gave up and walked out. Wren didn't even have to sit up in bed to know she'd left only with what she was wearing. The rest of her things were strewn around his room.

He picked up the phone to call Keith, but he'd already texted. The alarm tipped him off and he and Stan were following her. They would check in with her location and status. Wren just had to hope she wouldn't try to lose them.

The phone was right there, so he started to call her then disconnected. She didn't want him. She'd made that pretty clear. Lashing out wasn't a surprise, though the subjects she picked to throw at him weren't ones he'd soon forget. She used every secret he ever told her against him.

He got the anger, but the show of hate was unexpected. It boiled inside of him, too. He could feel the frustration and disappointment rise and churn.

He whipped the phone against the wall. Heard a sharp crack then a thump as it fell against the hardwood floor.

He'd fucking blown it.

CHAPTER 29

Every muscle in Emery's body ached. It hurt to walk. To breathe. She'd been ripped apart and glued back together again, but nothing fit anymore. It was all off. She wondered if she would ever feel whole and human again.

Another day, another shock. She left a message at the office saying she had a family emergency. That didn't even come close to the implosion Wren had set off. Even if her father explained, doubts would always linger. She'd analyze every word now.

Levi. Just thinking his name made her heart ache.

She'd said awful things to him. Unforgivable things. He'd delivered the message and she burned him and it to the ground. Guilt wrapped around her, weighing her down. She shook with the need to apologize. The memory of his face as she yelled at him, as the slicing words popped out and she couldn't grab them back, nearly knocked her over. She'd seen the very moment the pain shot through him. When the betrayal hit.

She deserved to lose him, and she would. She'd turned every moment of trust he shared with her back on him. Whipped him with his own words.

Bile rushed up her throat. She started to heave. Actually turned to the bushes and thought she might topple over. Somehow she bit it back. Got her body back under control, at least for now.

She looked again at the steps to her father's front porch. She had no idea how long she'd been standing there or how many people had walked by. She buried her head in her hands and tried to find the strength to get through the next few minutes. She didn't believe her father was capable of such horror, but she had to know.

"Emery?"

She hadn't heard the door open, but when she looked up her father stood there. He wore his usual dress pants and plain shirt. He had his bag in his hand, which meant she likely caught him on the way to class or office hours. No doubt he'd use that as an excuse to put her off.

"I need to talk to you."

He didn't move. "Now?"

"It has to be now." She might not have the nerve later.

This was the kind of news you buried. Planted it deep and never looked at it. She didn't believe it, couldn't even wrap her mind around it, but she needed him to explain the inconsistencies. Put her mind at ease. Give her something to go back to Wren with right before she begged him to forgive her.

"Come inside." Her father opened the door and gestured for her to go first. "I only have a few minutes."

Her brain messaged her legs to move. Somehow she got up the steps and through the entry. She didn't stop until she stood in the middle of the family room. She'd spent very little time in the space growing up because it was her father's domain. Where he entertained guests. Where he and his wives and girlfriends watched what little television he would allow.

She preferred the quiet of her room. There she could read and dream. Out here she had to deal with him, just like now.

"I'm going to ask you some questions and you need to tell me the truth." When she realized she was shifting her weight from foot to foot, she stopped.

"What's wrong with you?" He looked her up and down and frowned.

He always did that. Made it clear he didn't like what he saw. Reeked of disappointment. He wrapped his arms around his precious bag like it was a fragile baby. The one he always carried and hung on to like a shield. With her, he used his words like a whip.

She tried to figure out things to say. She didn't welcome a game of verbal gymnastics or want to look for him to wiggle his way out of answering. She'd literally trashed her life and destroyed everything she had with Wren—the one man who meant something to her—and there needed to be a payoff. She deserved answers and so did Tiffany.

When she failed to come up with anything clever, she just spit out the question. "Have you been investigating the name Wren?"

His arms fell and he now held the bag by his side. "What's this about? Is your boyfriend territorial and upset someone else is investigating this issue? And yes,

I figured it out. You can do much better than him." Her father waved her off and started to turn. "We'll talk about all of this and whatever has you rattled later."

Just as she feared. But this was too important for her to be ruled by fear. "Now, Dad."

He sighed at her. "Emery, please. I don't have time for nonsense. Today I'm supposed to—"

"I don't care." She took a step closer. The distance gave her comfort, but he used it as a way to hold her off. "How did you know that name?"

"What?"

She refused to back down. Not this time. "Wren."

"This is ridiculous."

The more he hedged, the more the anxiety churned inside her. "Just answer the question."

"You told it to me." Her father took his keys out of his pocket. Signaled that the conversation was over as far as he was concerned.

But she wasn't done. "I didn't, but you knew what to search."

"This is what happens when you don't concentrate. You aren't remembering this correctly."

Right on cue he flipped to condescension. She saw the plotting now. The tools he used to hold her off and minimize her. Wren might phrase things strangely, but he never talked down to her. He respected her, let her battle him.

Regret clogged her throat. The pain of losing him battered her now. Later it would have her curled in a ball and weeping. It had been years since she cried over a guy, and that one hadn't been worth it. Wren was.

But right now she had another demon to battle. One she didn't even understand existed until that morning. "I purposely didn't tell you that name. So, how did you find out?"

All she needed was one reasonable comment. Maybe Uncle Gavin told him. Hell, she'd grab on to anything, but he offered nothing.

"Probably from Tyler, then. He's worried about the influence this man has over you, and frankly, so am I."

Dizziness struck her out of nowhere. She wanted to sit down, but she didn't. She needed to be on her feet and in fighting form right now. Push every other emotion out. "Tyler didn't know it either."

"I'm going to work. You should do the same, though it would not be a tragedy to lose that position." Her father marched up one step to the landing. "I'll walk you out."

"You weren't in the house that night." Saying the words left her feeling hollow.

He spun back around to face her. "What?"

Her knees started to give out. It took all of her energy to stay on her feet. "You know what I'm talking about."

"Actually, no. I don't." He stepped back down and put the bag on the step behind him.

"The night she disappeared."

He didn't hesitate or act surprised. "You're the one who provided my alibi. You saw me and said so."

"That's not what the evidence shows."

For a second he didn't say anything. Then his mouth screwed up in an expression of pure hate. "What are you talking about?"

Without thinking, she stepped back. Her calf hit the coffee table, but she barely felt it. She negotiated around it, thinking for the first time in her life that she might not be safe around him. He hadn't done anything specific, but a feeling of menace fell over the room. He stayed in control, but she didn't know if he could maintain it.

"Are you okay?"

The sound of Wren's voice had her snapping out of her blinding panic. She actually thought she dreamed him. That she wanted to see him so badly that she conjured him up. He stood there, frowning as his gaze flipped from her to her father.

When he moved she let out the breath she was holding. He was there. Right there. Then he was beside her with a hand on her lower back. He looked down, watched her with concern showing in every line of his body.

"How did you get in here?" Her father barked the question.

"The door was open." Wren never broke eye contact with her. "Emery?"

She leaned into him, soaking up some of his strength. "He won't give me any answers."

"You did this. You've sold her on some ridiculous theory." Her father grabbed his bag, but this time he didn't stomp away. He stood only six or seven feet away with his rage festering just beneath the surface.

Wren edged forward and pulled her in tighter. "You mean the theory where you took Tiffany? I think we both know that it's based in fact."

"That's . . ." Her father swore under his breath. "Emery, listen to him. He doesn't even make sense." He looked directly at Wren. "Get out of my house."

"Gladly." Wren's voice had a rough edge. "The next people in here will be the police."

Her father's mouth dropped open. "For what?"

"You broke into my apartment." Then she remembered. Why hadn't she figured it out before? "Of course, you didn't need to break in, which explains why the break-in looked fake. You have a key. My extra."

Her father shook his head. "Nothing you're saying makes sense."

Emery felt her heart crumble. The pain swamping her was so intense, so brutal. "Where is she, Dad?"

Some of the color left his face. "I don't know what you're talking about."

"We're checking cameras on the street. We'll find one that shows you getting into her apartment building and taking the research." Wren shook his head. "It will be one more piece, but we have others."

She grabbed on to Wren's arm for balance and looked at the man who raised her. The same one who she always thought of as too perfect, too focused on details and getting everything right. "God, you really did do it."

"What? No." Some of the punch left her father's voice.

A revving sensation started inside her. "Tell me about Tiffany."

"She ran away."

She wanted to plow him under with rapid-fire questions. Force him to tell her what he knew. "The police don't believe that. Neither did Uncle Gavin. He never bought that story."

"He was too close and too emotional to see the truth," her father said, talking about the man who was supposed to have been his lifelong friend. "Emery, you know how she was. She liked to sneak out. She broke the rules. She mouthed off."

"To you?" Wren asked.

Her father's shoulders stiffened. "I told you to get out."

"Only if Emery comes with me." Wren didn't let go of her. His fingers stayed under her elbow.

"My daughter stays."

He acted as if he owned her. As he talked she felt something inside her whither. "You didn't want me pushing for a renewed investigation because you'd gotten away with it."

"Stop talking."

She was getting through now. He finally understood she wasn't going to just drop the topic and go away. She could see it in the way he stood there, looking around and losing control with each passing second. "When I went to the senator and then told you I hired someone, you must have panicked."

"Stop."

"I told you I was staying at Caroline's house, but that was a lie. I came home that night." She pushed on. "We probably almost caught you."

"I wasn't there."

"You're covering your tracks." She didn't hold back.

She hit him with every bit of disdain in her body. Let it drip from her voice.

"Fucking shut up."

Wren held up his free hand. "Settle down."

"I will not be talked to like this in my home." Her father reached into his bag and grabbed something before letting the bag drop. The handle cracked against the floor, but he kept talking. "I built this life. I groomed you."

The something came into focus. A gun. She knew he'd taken lessons and had one locked in the safe upstairs . . . or that's where it should have been. The idea of him carrying it around made her sick.

"A gun?" Her breath rushed out of her on a panicked gasp.

It shook in his hand. He aimed it at her then at Wren. "She was trash, just like her drunk mother."

Emery's world fell apart in front of her. The commanding man with a lecturing skill everyone talked about, the man she knew, vanished. This one, frenzied and filled with fury, sputtered and listed to one side.

Now she knew why. The last bit of hope for a misunderstanding died inside her. "Oh, my God."

"She wouldn't listen. And you." He was pleading now. Did it right until he pointed the gun at her again.

Wren stepped in front of her. Reached behind him and kept her waist in a bruising hold so she couldn't move.

"No!" She could not lose Wren. Not like this. She clawed at him. Kicked.

"You can shoot me." He held up his free hand as if trying to placate her father.

She grabbed fistfuls of his jacket and tugged. Yanked with all her might. "Levi!"

He didn't budge. "Do it and my men who are right outside will rush in here and kill you. I promise you that."

She dropped her forehead on his back and begged. "You can't do this. Please stop."

"Your house will become a bloodbath, and you will doom Emery to witnessing it. We'll be gone." Wren pointed from him to her father. "That will be your legacy to her. That nightmare."

Wren kept inching closer to her father. She tried to shove him aside. When that didn't work, the desperation to get through to the man who never heard her crushed her. "Dad, listen to him. Please."

"You can make this right, Michael." Wren kept up the placating tone. His soothing voice floated through the strangling tension in the room.

"You don't understand." He father shook his head. "Tiffany . . ." He visibly swallowed as his voice trailed off. "I told her to stay away from you and she laughed at me. That stupid little girl fucking laughed at me. Told me how you wanted to meet Tyler at night and she'd help you break out and away from me."

Wren nodded. "What did you do?"

"Nothing." Her father's eyes were wild. The hand with the gun lowered, but he didn't drop it. A haze seemed to cloud his vision as he stared blankly, as if lost in the memory. "She came at me and I pushed her. That's all."

"But she fell, right?" Wren took another step.

"I shook her and her head whipped back. She barely hit the pavement . . . it didn't make any sense." The gun pointed at the floor now.

The horror of the crime scene photos hit Emery. She'd forced herself to look at them and then could never erase them from her mind. "The blood at the scene."

"What did you do with her, Michael?" Wren reached out, slow and steady, and put his hand on the gun. "Tell me."

She held her breath. When her father didn't fight, she let it out again. A flash, some movement by the door, caught her eye. Then she saw the lights from the police car outside.

The cavalry had arrived. Wren likely brought it with him.

Her father looked smaller now. He curled in on himself. "I threw her away. Took her to the school. There's a furnace with this conveyor belt."

"Okay, Michael." Rick moved up behind her dad. Put his hands on the other man's shoulders and nodded to Wren.

Her father shook his head. "Detective Cryer?"

"He killed her." It was all she could say as she watched Wren slip the gun out of her father's fingers.

She repeated it. The words echoed in her head as the police officers streamed in. She heard their radios and the shouting. People talked and the sound of the police sirens finally registered in her brain. Detective Cryer restrained her father and someone read him his rights.

Wren was there, holding her up. "I won't ask if you're okay."

She said the first thing that came into her head. "I'm never going to be okay again."

AN HOUR PASSED. Law enforcement officials filed in and out but still filled the room. There was a forensic team on-site now and police officers walking around. Some took photos and others searched the house. Emery just sat there on the coffee table and stared at the floor.

Wren ached for her. He was willing to do anything to ease her pain. He'd called in Caroline, thinking Emery needed a friend now. Garrett came over. She didn't acknowledge any of them or any of the people walking around or the news vans collecting on the street outside.

He wanted to go to her. Hold her. Say whatever she needed to hear to wipe the sharpness of the pain away. But he knew it didn't work like that. She'd mourn and fight off bouts of fury that she thought might destroy her. Guilt like she'd never known would cripple her.

He'd been there. He knew the steps and each one brought a new round of doubt and confusion. Why hadn't she known? Why did it take this long? Did she know her father at all? Those were just some of the questions that would bombard her brain, but there would be other issues. Debilitating loneliness. So much pain.

Someone wrapped a blanket around her as she sat there with Rick by her side. He had a hand on her back and was whispering something to her. Something Wren couldn't hear. Likely words of comfort.

Wren thought about leaving, going outside and getting some air. He took one step when Garrett's hand landed on his shoulder.

"You okay?" Gone was his usual amusement and ability to make a joke out of anything. The strain of the moment showed on his face.

Wren figured he wore a similar expression. But the truth was what he felt didn't matter. "No."

"I hear you tried to get yourself shot today."

"Better me than her." He would have taken the bullets and fought off her father. Whatever it took to keep her safe.

Garrett glanced at Emery and exhaled. "Go tell her."

"What the hell do I say?" There wasn't a card for this. No words could make this better. And he was not the one she turned to for comfort. Not after last night.

"That you love her." Garrett shook his head. "Damn, man. You should see your face. You look . . . I don't know, broken, maybe?"

Wren didn't feel anything. "I'm the one who delivered the news about who her father really was. I'm pretty much the enemy."

"He's the one who did this to Tiffany, to Emery. Not you."

It was a logical argument, but Wren knew it wouldn't work. He started to move again. This time he would go outside . . . but his legs didn't listen.

He walked up to Emery and glanced at Rick. "Hey."

Rick winced. "I'm not sure this is a great time. She's—"

"I know." Wren crouched down in front of her and

watched her wring her hands until she rubbed them red. "You should probably go to the hospital. You could be in shock."

She rocked back and forth while those hands kept moving. "I just want to go home and sleep for a week."

"To your house." He didn't ask it as a question because he knew what she meant.

Without warning, she stood up. She reached out for him then dropped her hands. "I can't do this, Wren. Not now."

"I know."

She shuffled her feet, moving only a bit at a time. "It's just . . . everything is different."

"Not you." God, he had to believe that. She was so strong. If anyone could survive this, it would be her.

She looked at him then. The fear was reflected in her eyes and seemed to weigh down her muscles. "Including me."

"I'll get Caroline for you."

She nodded. "Thanks."

Because he couldn't just walk away, he leaned in and kissed her cheek. Inhaled the scent he'd never smell again. "You're going to be fine. It will take time, but you'll get through"

"Will I?" She looked desperate to believe him.

"I promise." Because he loved her.

CHAPTER 30

Eleven days later Emery stood by the desk in the hall outside of Wren's office. At least she assumed that's what waited behind the tall double doors. They were closed and she didn't hear anything coming from inside.

Garrett stood beside her. "Are you sure about this?"

He reminded her of Wren. There was something strong and determined about both of them. They filled the space around them with confidence. Acted like they could handle any disaster that found them.

She used to think of herself as pretty resilient. Not anymore. "Honestly, I don't know anything right now. I've tried not to think too much or make any decisions."

Garrett let out a low noise, kind of like a hum. "Are the journalists leaving you alone?"

"Weirdly enough they're being somewhat respectful." That part didn't make sense to her. At first, she had people camping out on her father's lawn and her cell kept ringing. Caroline had to bring in volunteers to staff the phones at work.

Garrett laughed. "Not so weird."

The truth hit her. She should have known. "Levi?"

"Of course." Garrett glanced at the closed door then back to her. "He has people watching over you. Has called in favors to make sure others leave you alone. He's basically reordered his life to protect you from afar."

Guilt walloped her again. She should be used to the sensation. She'd been called names and more than one news story questioned how much she knew and when. The waves of punishing sadness and pressure of failed responsibility never stopped.

"I pushed him away." And that was the hardest thing to deal with because it was such a mistake. Her biggest.

"He let you do it." Garrett's mood sobered. "He thinks he deserves it."

Every word stabbed at her. Brought more pain. "Does he know I'm here?"

"I didn't tell him you called."

For some reason that made her feel worse. "Is he going to be angry?"

"I'm hoping it's a fucking wake-up call before he works himself to death."

His tone lightened the darkness churning inside her. "Meaning?"

"He hasn't stopped for a second, Emery. He misses you and is trying to work the feeling away."

So much destruction. "Did he say that?"

"He didn't have to. I know him." Garrett went to the door and wrapped his fingers around the handle. "I hope you stick around long enough for me to get to know you, too."

"That depends on him."

Garrett smiled. "Then I'll definitely see you again."

WREN HEARD THE door and tried to ignore it, like he'd ignored everything but work and Emery's safety for the last eleven days. He pushed until he exhausted himself. He went home each night, showered and climbed onto the couch. He didn't have much interest in his bedroom without her there.

He didn't look up. "I said I didn't want to be bothered."

The door clicked shut. "I asked Garrett to make an exception for me."

Wren's head shot up. He looked and blinked and waited for the vision of her to vanish. But she still stood there. "Emery?"

"You look terrible." The sadness in her voice mirrored the sadness in her eyes.

"How are you?" He regretted the words as soon as they were out. "Forget that. I know the answer. I shouldn't have said—"

"Levi, let me talk." She took a step toward his desk then another.

"Okay." And he'd take it. No matter what she launched at him, he'd let it happen.

"The last few days have been a whirlwind, if they have those in hell. My father insists on seeing me, but I'm not ready."

"Of course not." God, it was way too soon. Going there to see that man would be about what *he* needed and right now she had to concentrate on herself. On making plans and getting through.

"I told him I'd consider it if he spared us all the heartache and pled guilty." She let out a long breath.

"He's going to, so long as his attorney can work out some sort of deal."

"That's good news." But he already knew that. Everyone from the senator to the police to Rick to the prosecutor kept calling to fill him in. So much for the idea of being an island. So many people reached out that he worried he'd need a second alarm system at home just to keep his new friends from stopping by.

"It's the least I could do." She rubbed her hands together. "He killed her because of me."

Wren stood up and came around the desk. He was careful not to touch her or get too close. She needed space and he vowed to give it to her. But she couldn't do this. "Don't take that on. It's his sin, not yours."

"That's so easy to say, but . . ."

He understood what she was saying. Maybe better than anyone. "You need time to process it all. You'll take it apart in your head and eventually be able to tuck pieces of it away. To heal in your own way. You'll close the case in your head. Truly mourn Tiffany and the loss of your father. Just not today."

"It's like he's dead." There was no emotion in her voice.

The pain had her rattled and vulnerable. He wished he could ease some, but that's not how it worked. No one could take it all away. For a few minutes at a time, then later for longer spells, she would shake off all the frustrations and doubts pressing down on her. But it was too early for that.

"The loss is unimaginable. No one who hasn't lived through it can understand." He hated that she would now know.

She dropped her hands to her sides and looked up at him. "You do."

He gave in to the urge to touch her. Giving her plenty of time for her to pull away, he put his hands on her arms near her elbows. "I know life is scrambled right now and nothing makes sense, but I promise you there will be a day when the grief eases. When you feel like you can breathe again."

"I can't imagine that."

"Part of what you have to do is let the emotions roll through you. All of them. The guilt, the horror, the anger."

She let her head drop back and she stared at the ceiling. "I get shots of each, every hour."

"All normal." He'd grown to hate that word, but he guessed it fit here. "Which I know sounds terrible coming from me."

She dropped her head again and looked at him. "I'm sorry."

"No, don't do that." She couldn't take that on, too. He wouldn't let her. "What happened was awful, but there was no other way for it to shake out."

"Not that." She lifted her hands and let them rest against his stomach. "I said terrible things to you. I was so afraid you were right and it made me lash out and punish you."

The memories rushed back on him, but he kicked them out of his head. He didn't want to remember those moments when he could hold on to the rest. "The news was shocking. I get that."

"Don't let me off the hook, Levi." She curled her fingers in his shirt.

Every word tore into him. He wanted to wipe it all away for her. Save her this. "The circumstances were extraordinary. If you said those things to me because you thought I squeezed the toothpaste container the wrong way, yeah. That would have sucked. But this. It's understandable."

Stress pulled around her mouth and eyes. "Teach me how to do it."

"What?"

"Survive this."

That's what she was—a survivor. He knew she could make it through. The rest . . . God, it would kill him to be near her and not touch her, but somehow he'd do it. "I'll be here for whatever you need."

"Don't leave me." She stepped in, closing the distance between them. Pleading moved into her voice and showed in her eyes. "I know it's too early and it doesn't make sense. Then the emotions get all wrapped up with my father and what happened—"

"What are you saying?" Hope flickered to life inside him and he rushed to tamp it down. He'd spent days hoping for a call and nights feeling carved out and raw when it didn't come.

"I am the worst catch." She shook her head as her words rushed together. "You should run and keep running, but I'm asking you to give me a chance because I love you."

"You . . ." He couldn't get the words out. Was desperate to believe, but was sure he heard her wrong or misunderstood.

"Crazy, right?" She smiled. It appeared then was

gone. "All I wanted over the last few days was for you to hold me and you weren't there."

That he heard. "I thought you hated me."

"Not even close."

An alarm went off in his head. His chest ached with the need to rush in, but he knew he should hold back. His job stood in the way. They still had baggage. She needed time . . . And he would have talked about all of those, but the way she looked at him and held on, digging her fingers into his skin, had his brain reordering every priority.

He had to say it. Even if it was only once, she needed to know. "I love you, too."

Her mouth dropped open. "You do?"

He almost asked how she didn't know until he remembered how he fought it. Denied that it could be possible. Then he lost her and the nights dragged and his life collapsed in on him.

"Shocked the hell out of me." His hands slipped up then. He played with the strands of hair lying on her shoulder. Used the other one to caress her back. "It was one of the reasons it was so hard to tell you the truth about your father."

She bit her bottom lip. "I didn't make it easy."

Maybe that was the answer. With them it would never be easy. They didn't come from functional lives. Their backgrounds were dark and messy. They knew death and despair. But the point was always about "they"—them together. They didn't have to be alone.

He linked his fingers behind her back and held her. "You happen to be standing in front of the one man who knows exactly how you feel right now. I understand what you're going through, and I will be there for you. Every day. I want that more than anything."

"And I'll be there for you." Her hand skimmed down his cheek. "To bring you out of hiding."

That was the one problem area he wasn't convinced they could overcome. The one piece that kept him from wanting to throw in and commit. His life could put her in peril. The idea of that made him want to rip the walls apart with his bare hands.

"My job—"

She put a finger over his lips. "Is dangerous, just like a lot of other jobs. You use yours as a shield. Let me teach you to drop it."

Hope didn't sneak up on him. It punched him. Smacked right into him. "Sounds like we can learn a lot from each other."

"Well, we are dating." She played with the knot of his tie. "And in love."

"There's that."

"Yeah, there's that."

Then he leaned down and kissed her, because he couldn't stand one minute of not kissing her. The touch of their lips sent a shock of heat racing through him. Like that, they went from disconnected to together. The harsh words fell away, leaving only forgiveness.

They understood each other. They would make this work.

He lifted his head. "Any chance you want some coffee?" It seemed like a good way to get them back on track.

She winked at him. "I'd rather go home."

That sounded even better.

THREE WEEKS HAD passed. Time where she barely left Wren's side. She went with him to work on the days he went in. Lounged in his library on the days he worked from home. Talked with Tyler, who was now in an in-patient treatment center. The news about her father had been the one hit too many. Tyler heard the news then reached out. When his parents balked, Wren found him a program and provided the needed funds so he could break away from his parents' hold.

She thought about him often, but the bulk of her life right now revolved around a few friends. Garrett and Caroline. No work. Not yet. She needed the leave of absence to clear her head. It was hard to argue that she could help solve cases when she'd never been able to see the facts right in front of her in her own life.

But today she'd ventured out. Wren had declared this Wednesday morning coffee day. If it worked, they'd make it a weekly event. Go out, get the drinks to go and leave. That was the plan. He stood at the counter right now waiting to pick up the cups.

Her instincts told her to stay plastered to him. To hold his hand and not let go. But she forced her mind to blank out some of the fear. To fight off her inclination to tuck in and hide. She'd never felt that before, but it hit her hard now. Every day she battled to be who she was before her father was arrested.

"Ready?" Wren stood next to the table with a cup in each hand.

He wore his usual dark suit and a tie that brought out the sparkle in those intense eyes. Today they reflected love and a lightness that made her smile. He'd been stronger and more supportive than she ever thought possible.

When she needed to sit and stare, he let her. When she wanted to talk and scream, he listened. Yesterday she even got him to dance with her. Right there in the family room as the music streamed through his fancy speaker system.

She used her foot to push out the chair across from her. "Sit."

He glanced around, slipping so easily into protector mode. "Are you sure?"

"I want to feel normal. Just for a few minutes."

He slid his chair closer to hers and sat down. His arm balanced on the back of her chair and he leaned in close. Almost surrounding her. "I'm thinking normal is overrated."

She trailed her fingertips over the scruff on his chin. "True because you're so much better than normal."

"Oh, really?"

That smile warmed her from the inside. "You amaze me every day."

"It's because of you." He slipped his hand over hers. "You're pulling me out of the darkness."

She entwined her fingers with his and cuddled closer. "I'm leaning on you so hard. So many men would crumble."

"I'm not any man." He lifted their hands and kissed the back of hers. "And you are a hell of a woman."

"I love you." The words came easier these days. The relationship was still so new, but she didn't have to wait and see. She didn't need time to pass. This was forever love. The type where they grew old together and made each other better.

"And I love you," he said in a husky tone.

She couldn't believe how the phrase rolled out of him. How she could see it in everything he did for her, how he held her. "Don't stop."

"Never."

"I believe you." Her trust was low right now. It was so hard to believe in anything. To keep her balance and not lose who she was. But not when it came to him. He didn't lie to her or make promises he couldn't keep. He put her first and showed her every day that she could depend on him. That he needed her.

His smile grew even wider. "That sounds like a pretty great start to me."

"Take me home." Not because she was anxious or twitchy about being out around people. She wanted to be alone with him. Climb into bed and stay there for hours.

His head dipped until his hair brushed against hers. "Are you feeling a little naughty?"

"I guess we'll have to go home and see."

His eyebrow lifted. "To our home?"

He'd asked her to officially move in. To let her apartment go and stay. She requested time to think, but she no longer needed it. Not after nights with him and days roaming around the house. They worked better together. They would survive the rest of the fallout and the dangers of his job and the pressure of life by leaning on each other. She didn't want to give up one minute with him.

"Yeah, to our home."

He let out a long breath as a look of satisfaction settled on his face. "I've been waiting to hear that."

"I needed some time." Not to figure out her feelings for him, but for everything else.

"I'll give you forever."

She took that deal.

Acknowledgments

After years of writing about fictional undercover operatives—and loving it!—I was ready for a change. That led to the Games People Play series, filled with mysterious men, strong women, and cold cases. It's been a dream to write these books, and I truly hope readers enjoy them, too. Thank you for trying *The Fixer*.

I owe a huge thank you to my amazing editor, May Chen, for being so supportive. When I said I wanted to try something new with less of a body count, you told me to send some paragraphs . . . then you loved the idea. Your enthusiasm and expertise never cease to amaze me. You make my writing life so much easier.

I also want to thank my agent, Laura Bradford, for all the handholding and the "of course you need to write this series!" cheerleading. I'm so happy to have you on my team.

Big kisses and hugs to Jill Shalvis for doing an early read of the first few chapters and telling me to stop worrying and get busy writing. You always say the right thing.

Thank you to everyone on Team Avon for making

the book better, for selling it, for getting the word out there. You guys are the best!

And, as always, love to James.